Also by Whitney Dineen

Romantic Comedies
The Event
Relatively Normal
Relatively Sane
Relatively Happy
The Reinvention of Mimi Finnegan
Mimi Plus Two
Kindred Spirits
She Sins at Midnight
Going Up?

Non-Fiction Humor
Motherhood, Martyrdom & Costco Runs

Middle Reader Fiction
Wilhelmina and the Willamette Wig Factory
Who the Heck is Harvey Stingle?

Children's Books
The Friendship Bench

The Move

Whitney Dineen

Acknowledgments

Once again, I'm flush with gratitude for all the people that help me release a book. They are all rock stars, and I couldn't do it without them. In order of appearance, not importance, here they are:

The voices in my head: Seriously, y'all are nuts, but I'm glad you picked me.

Libby Bohlen: Mothers rock, opinions and all.

Jimmy Dineen: Being married to me hasn't been boring, but buddy, you've been something of a thrill ride yourself. Here's to another thirty years of fun.

Becky Monson: Your cover designs for my last two series are the best. I thank you from the bottom of my heart for listening to the voices in your head and making sure my books are worthy of being judged by their covers.

Jennifer Peel: Lady, thank you for telling me like it is. I know that's not easy for such a nice person as yourself, but you make me a better author and I appreciate you.

Diana Orgain: I love all of our conversations, from plotting to take over the authoring world to gushing about our gorgeous chickens. I'm convinced soul food like this is the key not only to success, but sanity as well.

Sheryl Babin, Tracie Bannister, Melanie Summers, Kate O'Keeffe, Annabelle Costa, Delancey Stewart, and Virginia Grey: Heartfelt appreciation for always being there for a blurb, tweak, or share, and for offering an opinion. You're my foundation.

Celia Kenney: It's such a gift to have an editor who gets me and doesn't let me pull any crap. My hat's off to you, my friend.

Paula Bothwell and Sandy Penny: My eternal thanks for making me appear literate. Not only are you proofreaders extraordinaire, but you're fast and fabulous.

Karan Eleni: Thank you for nudging me along and keeping me on track. You're the best assistant I could hope for.

Sara Steven and Melissa Amster at Chick Lit Central: Thank you for reading and sharing my books and thank you for helping to keep our fabulous genre alive.

Scott Schwimer: Daddy, it's been a wild relationship from our first lunch out at Kate Mantilini to shortbread in the mail. You are an awesome friend, attorney, and all-around big daddy.

My readers: You guys are the ones who make my dream gig possible, and I heart you for being so awesome! I read every single one of your reviews, emails, and posts on Facebook. Thank you for being a part of my journey.

Dedicated to all you adventurers who know there's someplace you're meant to be, even if you don't know where that is yet.

Prologue

I don't believe in voodoo as a rule. I'm not superstitious or particularly gullible, and I sure as heck have never given much credence to people who claim they can predict the future. Why am I telling you this? Because when I was twelve my grandmother Thelma, who I called Mimi, took me to see a fortune-telling friend of hers in Harlem, just down the street from where she lived. The old lady with the Rastafarian braids, nose ring, and skunky-smelling aroma, read my palm and told me the following, "In your thirtieth year of life, right after the dog jumps over you, your whole world will change in the most unexpected ways. Be open to the change or you will always regret it."

Mimi wrote the message down verbatim and gave me the scrap of paper, making me promise to keep it in my little jewelry box with the dancing ballerina. She said, "Baby girl, that old bat might have been higher than a kite, but she's given me priceless words of wisdom during my lifetime. I have no idea what's in store for you, but I know it was important for you to hear that."

I've long since lost the jewelry box, and Mimi died a handful of years later, but I always remembered the message, just like I promised I would. I haven't thought about it in years, but suddenly life has made certain I'm awash with the memory.

Chapter 1

"Incoming!"

I hit the ground as soon as I heard the warning.

One of my all-time favorite pastimes is walking through Central Park in the fall. The air is crisp, and the colors are mind-blowingly gorgeous. Unfortunately, I have to share this miracle of nature with several million people who inhabit that same seven-mile stretch of land.

The sheer volume of all those bodies can be dangerous when large groups congregate in one area. It can also seriously hinder my enjoyment. I'm currently hindered, lying prone in a pile of damp leaves watching as a German shepherd jumps over me. He's chasing the frisbee that had been destined to decapitate me.

I hear the old Jamaican woman's words like she's sitting next to me, "In your thirtieth year of life, after the dog jumps over you, your whole world will change in the most unexpected ways."

A very attractive doggy-daddy runs towards me calling, "Nice catch, Hanzie!" He whizzes right past me to give his buddy a vigorous rub. I eagerly await my turn. Just kidding, I don't really expect Mr. Hotty Pants to rub me down, but offering a hand up would have been nice. Clearly that's not going to happen as I watch him jog away with his furry friend. There's not so much as a backward glance in my direction.

"Loser!" I yell at his departing backside.

Dear New York,

I love you like the native I am, but you gotta quit letting the riffraff move in.

How do I know he's riffraff? He was wearing an "I Heart Akron" sweatshirt. No real New Yorker hearts anywhere other than New York.

An authentic New Yorker would have run over to help me up before apologizing profusely for the near miss. They may have even offered to buy me a hot dog for my troubles. Stereotypes aside, born and bred locals are generally good people. Sure, they give you hell when you deserve it, but when something like this happens they own it.

I lie still for a moment trying to regain my equilibrium after that jolt of adrenaline shot through me. I adore this island with my whole being. It's the only home I've ever known, but the near miss with Mr. Akron's flying disk has me wondering what life is like for the rest of the world. You know, the people who can enjoy the great outdoors with a modicum of elbow room.

I finally get up and buy my own hot dog to snack on while I walk home. Out of the corner of my eye I see a leaf sticking out of one of my ringlets of hair. Pulling at it, I realize I'll be picking out bits of nature for the next couple of days. My corkscrew curly brown tresses have managed to attract and conceal all manner of things: leaves in the fall, flower petals in the spring, and possibly small rodents if I ever let them near my head, which I don't.

As soon as I get to my building, I head down to the basement to get the rest of my cold weather clothes from storage. An Indian summer has been visiting so I haven't been in a rush, but today, the bite of fall is upon us.

After retrieving two boxes marked "Pumpkin Muffin Clothes"—I labeled them in anticipation of the season where I organically increase my carb intake—I head up to my apartment on the fourth floor.

I probably should have brought up one box at a time, but I really didn't want to make two trips. As I stagger down the hallway, I hear Timothy Sanders, my neighbor and all-around stud muffin, ask, "Hey, Lexi, need a hand?"

"Hi, Tim, that would be great." I happily transfer half of my load into his very capable arms and ask, "When did you get back into the city?"

"Last night. Sadly, Fire Island becomes nothing but a fond memory for another year."

He sighs in such a way that I feel an overpowering urge to wrap Fire Island up in a big red bow and gift it to him. Tim is a handsomely preppy brunette who dresses impeccably. Simply put, he would complete me *if* he ever bothered to ask me out. And believe me, I release all my single girl pheromones into the ether when he's around. So far, to no avail.

Tim remains outside the city through September, which is a month longer than most people who vacate the premises to escape the suffocating heat. "Did you come back at all over the summer?" I ask despite knowing the answer is no. I've been scoping out his unit with the dedication of a confirmed busybody.

"Nah, I worked remotely. It's nice being home though. What have you been up to?" he asks.

"Same old, same old. Doing my darndest to turn Silver Spoons into the next Williams Sonoma."

My official job title of growth manager requires that I closely follow trends around the country looking for the next best fit to take our chain of kitchenware boutiques nationwide. I love my job for the most part, but I've grown bored. When Emmie, my good friend and fellow Silver Spoons employee, left several months ago, some of the joy I felt going to work disappeared. Actually, a lot. Her departure started a string of upsets we haven't quite recovered from.

A little lightbulb seems to turn on in Tim's head. He says, "I forgot you worked there. Listen, can I come in and see you sometime next week? Maybe you can show me around, if you're available." Do fish swim? Do Yankee fans flip you the bird if you accidentally cheer for the other team? *I'm always available for the likes of Tim Sanders. Always.*

I develop lockjaw, and I forget to swallow the excess saliva that fills my mouth. *Tim is going to ask me out.* Why else would he want me to show him around my work? Granted, it's a weird kind of build up to courtship, but whatever gets the job done, right? After five long years, my dreams are about to come true. OMG, that fortune-teller was right! I'm thirty, a dog just jumped over me—I always thought that was a metaphor, but I guess I was wrong—and now Tim is finally going to ask me out. My life *is* changing.

I inelegantly choke on my spit as I answer, "For you, anything. What day works best?"

"Don't know yet. Let me call Tiffany and find out when she's available."

"Tiffany?" I ask, hoping she's his sister. Why would he want his sister to tag along?

"Oh, my gosh, that's right, you wouldn't know," he exclaims.

I await explanation as tingles of dread crawl across my scalp like a spider infestation. "Tiff and I got engaged last month. Can you believe it?"

Imagine how you'd feel if the Big Friendly Giant wasn't truly friendly after all, but was more of a Big Savage Giant. Visualize him shoving his meaty fist right through your solar plexus before ripping out your still-beating heart. That's how I feel. All the hope and anticipation that this time of year stirs within me, mixed with the unadulterated joy of seeing Tim again, has evaporated, leaving nothing but emptiness, which will likely prove debilitating once I get into my apartment.

After several silent moments, where I don't even bother to congratulate him, I finally say, "I didn't know you were seeing anyone."

He looks surprised. "Really? That's weird. We've been together for over a year."

A whole year wasted, hungering for the unattainable. Three hundred and sixty-five days of my life I want back with the same yearning I used to feel for Christmas morning when my age was in single digits. I briefly wonder how serious my feelings have been for Tim. Was it him or the idea of having romance in my life that interested me? I store this question away to address later.

For now, I demand, "Strange I haven't seen your fiancée before. Why is that?" I ask this as though he's making her up.

He shrugs, blissfully unaware of my breaking heart. "We decided to get married when I got the notice about the building going condo."

All romantic angst is put on hold. "What building's turning into condos?" It has to be Tiffany's—I think her name like it's Hitler or Satan—because I never received a notice.

"Lexi, didn't you get the letter from the management company alerting us that the owner is giving us the option to buy our apartments? Surely you've heard the rumors over the last few years."

Of course, I'd heard murmurings. My last three apartments were rumored to either be going co-op or condo and none of them ever had. That's par for the course when you live in the Big Apple. "I didn't get the notice," I tell him. "When is it happening?" I silently curse the myopic mailman who keeps putting my mail in the box of the drug dealer whose apartment is upstairs from mine. I briefly wonder what other correspondences have been misrouted.

"Not for six months, but that's going to fly by in the blink of an eye. You're going to buy, aren't you?"

"I don't know." My head is filled with sharp jabbing pains, like an acupuncturist is sticking needles directly into my brain. "How much are our units going for?" I ask, even though I know it will be outside my budget. I've managed to save seventy-two thousand dollars in the last nine years, but that won't be anywhere near the twenty percent down payment I'd need. Even if it were, there will be condo fees on top of a staggering mortgage payment.

"They're offering current residents who have lived here more than three years, a ten percent discount. You should be able to buy in for about four hundred and fifty thousand. Too good an offer to pass up, don't you think?"

He must be high. How in the world can he imagine I'll be able to afford such a hefty sum on my own? He needs to marry *Tiffany* to afford it. And while I'd make decent money if I lived in Tulsa or Des Moines, living in New York City, conscientiously tucking money aside for future home ownership, I barely get by.

My one-bedroom, one-bath apartment (the whole space is just over five hundred square feet, and that includes the closets) on the Upper West Side has a view of Central Park, if you're not afraid to hang out the bathroom window and crane your neck so far to the left you look like you're performing extreme yoga. A view of any kind of park pushes the price point up. It's tiny, but it's my home. The home I can no longer afford to live in.

Defeatedly, I answer, "I don't have enough for the down payment."

"That's too bad," he says sounding genuinely sorry. "You've been a great neighbor."

Neighbor! Clearly, I've been the only one doing any pining in this relationship.

When we arrive at my door, I unlock it and lead the way in. Tim puts my box on the dining room table. "So about next week, I'll let you know when Tiff and I can come in to register for our wedding. I really appreciate you helping us out."

That's why he wanted to come into Silver Spoons? I mean, *obviously*, in light of his engagement, but still, so disappointing. "I don't know anything about the gift registry, but our sales staff will be more than happy to help you and *Tiffany*." Satan.

9

"Oh, sure. Makes sense," he says. "I'm really sorry to be the one to tell you about the building. If I were you, I'd call the management company asap to find out how much time you have before you need to move out. Maybe they'll let you stay longer."

I nod my head and show him to the door. My enthusiasm over Tim being home, the cooler weather arriving, my sweaters being unearthed, and the start of pumpkin muffin season, has disappeared into a soulless abyss.

I'm thirty years old, a dog has recently jumped over me, and if that isn't enough, I now believe the old kook from Harlem that my life is about to change in the most unexpected ways. It already has.

Chapter 2

My mom fills two wine glasses with a hearty Beaujolais. "You can move back home with us. Think about how much money you'll save if you stay here for a couple of years."

I look around my parents' loft, my childhood home, and observe that nothing has changed. While the vast majority of SoHo has been renovated in the last couple of decades, updated with marble and granite, expensive cabinetry, and gleaming fixtures, my parents' place is an homage to the nineties. Not a slab of stone or gleaming fixture in sight, despite my best efforts and considerable discount at Silver Spoons. My dad's art supplies fill the entire living area, with huge canvases resting against walls and furniture. Books and assorted clutter fill every surface. The kitchen? Good grief, the kitchen, it looks like something straight out of a flea market, but not in a chic, designer kind of way— more like a garage sale meets your grandmother's castoffs.

Lambertos Blake, my dad—or Bertie as he's known to his friends and family—is an artist of some repute. He's had fits and bursts of success during his thirty-five-year long career that has cemented his name as one of the longest standing artists of his time. He's currently experiencing a drought though, declaring that the oppressiveness of the world's political climate is interfering with his creative mojo. Historically, these periods have always been followed by explosions of genius that lead to a record-breaking commission. He makes himself and everyone around him miserable while he waits.

"Where would you like me to sleep? Perhaps on the window ledge?" I ask while pointing to one of the best features in the apartment. Giant ten-foot tall windows fill the majority of the east facing wall, making this an ideal artist's lair.

"No one likes a smart ass, dear," my mom says while cutting up a plate of figs.

Regina Cohen, my mom, is a professor of women's studies at NYU. My friends used to wonder why she didn't take my dad's name when they got married, until I informed them that my parents never got married. Regina felt strongly, and still does, that she is queen of her own destiny and that marriage is nothing more than letting our patriarchal forefathers enslave her. Even though she wanted no part of it, she and my dad have been a devoted couple for thirty-five years.

Her fierce belief that women have been screwed over since Eve radiates from her like a furnace. Her mass of curly brown hair, that I inherited, often bounces in righteous indignation that can easily be perceived as hostile to those who don't know her. Though enormously passionate about her beliefs, she's remarkably kind to the majority of people, you just have to hang out with her long enough to get past her intimidating exterior. It's not a challenge everyone is up to.

I answer, "Have you seen the state of my room lately?" My dad has been using it as a storage room for half-finished paintings and supplies. "It smells like turpentine. I'd probably develop a brain tumor if I slept in there."

"Psh," she says. "Bertie would be so happy to have you home that he'd clear it out for you."

"Mom, I love you guys with my whole heart. But two days back here would have me jumping out the nearest window." With a Vanna White-like flourish, I showcase the alarming selection of exits at my disposal.

She rolls her amber wolf eyes at me and declares, "Beggars can't be choosers."

"I'm not a beggar, yet," I inform her. "I'm going to start looking around for something else. Maybe I can find a widow on Fifth Avenue to rent out her maid's quarters to me for a song."

"I'd rather you move into a youth hostel. Those snooty Park Avenue types wouldn't treat you well at all."

"Why do you say that?" I ask, fully aware that I'm poking the bear.

"Because they didn't earn their money, they inherited it. They have no idea what it takes to hold down a job and raise a family with the sweat from their own brow. They're nothing but entitled …"

I interrupt, "Lords and ladies of the manor pulling the strings of the puppet peasantry."

My mom squints her eyes like she's trying to decipher whose side I'm on. She ultimately decides that no offense was meant and continues, "I do not like entitled people."

"I was teasing you, Mom." I thought that was obvious, but apparently she didn't pick up on my tone. Then I add, "Not that I wouldn't rent the maid quarters in one of those penthouses. I would, but I don't realistically expect those folks are looking for tenants."

"You disappoint me, Lexi," she says.

"Why, because I don't have a chip on my shoulder? Because I don't hate rich people on principle?"

She shakes her head. "Don't make light of the struggles that came before you, Alexis. Women who refused to be cast in the shadows of history are the reason we have the degree of equality we have today. Those who hunt out the wealthiest mate they can, to bring forth new generations of privilege, do not have my respect."

I've heard this lecture many times before. "The sisterhood was tough, so I could be soft, huh?" I ask with a hint of attitude before shifting gears. "It's not that I don't appreciate what's been done, Mom, I have a lot of other things on my plate right now. You know, like impending homelessness."

Regina changes the subject as she knows this could explode into something. "Where do you want to order dinner from?" She pulls out a bunch of menus from the kitchen drawer.

"I want kung pao something. Chicken, shrimp, goat, I don't care." My current mood calls for something spicy to help burn through the cloud of frustration that's filling my head.

"Excellent, I'll have the Sichuan beef, and Bertie will have the cashew chicken. We can share."

Apparently, I like to fight with my mom, and because I'm feeling a myriad of aggressive emotions, I say, "I'm not sharing."

She comes around the counter and stands right in front of me. Putting her hands on my shoulders, she says, "Lexi, you're going to be fine. You've moved before, you'll probably move again. You have to trust in your strength, keep your chin up, and plow through. I promise you'll be better off than you are now."

I don't want to believe her, but that's the super annoying thing about my mom, she's usually right. Not that I'll ever say that to her face. "I've been thinking about finally taking my accrued vacation time at work. If I don't use it by the end of December, I'll lose it."

"How much time do you have?" she asks.

"Five weeks. Maybe I need to get out of Dodge for a while to help clear my head."

"You mean, leave New York City? Why don't you stay and do all the things you want to do but never have time for?"

"Like what?" I ask. "I grew up here. I've pretty much done it all."

She releases a bark of laughter. "You haven't even begun. This city is huge and there are a million things you haven't done." She asks, "Have you taken the trapeze class on the East River? Have you gone to the poetry readings in Bryant Park? Have you taken that Brazilian martial arts class in the village or learned how to blow glass from Frank who lives downstairs?" Not getting a response from me, she asks, "Where do you want to go?"

"I want to visit Emmie in Missouri. I miss her and the baby so much, I think spending time with them will be good for me."

My mom nods her head, but she looks concerned. "Missouri, huh? I've never been there. I can't imagine there's much to see." My parents have been all over the world for art shows and lectures, but they know very little about small town America. As a result, I don't either, but it's time for me to find out.

Chapter 3

Jameson Diamante, my boss, calls me into his office as soon as I get to work. He's good looking in the same way a friend's dad was good looking when you were in high school. You know, elegantly graying hair with crinkly laugh lines that hint at unknown adventures. You could appreciate his handsomeness without ever feeling anything remotely like attraction.

Unfortunately, Jameson is oblivious that his appeal doesn't transcend generations, and he spends a copious amount of time flirting with his staff, of which a solid ninety percent are women who are much younger and not at all interested in his overtures.

He stands when I walk through the door and gestures gallantly for me to take a seat next to him on the loveseat situated in a small seating area adjacent to his desk. "Alexis, how are you this fine day?"

"I'm doing well, Jameson. I'm glad you wanted to see me. As you know, I made an appointment to speak with you, as well."

"Me first!" he declares excitedly while clapping his hands together. "I have the happy news of telling you that you're being promoted to the position of East Coast relocation scout." The clueless look on my face prompts him to explain, "You'll be in charge of relocating our existing stores to different addresses, should it be beneficial to do so."

Huh. That doesn't sound like much of a promotion. I point out, "I'm currently in charge of finding new locations nationwide. How is regional relocation scout more prestigious than that?"

Jameson stands up and walks to the door, which I left open when I came in. He closes it. Then he sits next to me and very inappropriately places his hand on my knee. He leans in and says, "Confidentially, we've decided to stop branching out so aggressively."

"Why?" I ask, even though there's only one reason a company ever cuts back on expansion—financial difficulties.

"We feel that it's in the best interest of the brand to slow things down and make sure the existing stores are performing optimally before we continue with our growth plan."

"Is there a raise involved?" I ask. I mean, he did say it was a promotion.

My boss clears his throat and refuses to meet my gaze while he adjusts a pile of magazines sitting on the side table next to him. "Not as such. But the good news is, it's only a slight decrease in salary."

"Decrease?" I demand. "Jameson, my apartment building is going condo. If I'm going to buy in, I need more money, not less." Not that it's even within the realm of possibility that they'll give me the amount I need to stay in my current digs.

"Ah, yes, but the promotion isn't the only good news I have for you." What? Are they going to buy my apartment for me as a signing bonus or something? It's all I can do not to let the sarcasm shoot out of me like a bottle rocket.

"The position is based out of our Atlanta store. Your cost of living will be much lower down there, so even with the decrease in pay, you'll be able to live a lot better than you do here in Manhattan. Isn't that exciting?"

As exciting as a root canal. "You want me to move to Atlanta? When?"

"We realize you'll have a bit of work to do here, so we'll give you to the end of October to wrap things up. This way you can give notice on your apartment and fly down to Georgia to set up your new living situation. We'd like you to begin in Atlanta on November first."

"Jameson, my parents live in New York. I've lived here my whole life. You expect me to pick up and move to the South?"

"People move for work all the time, Alexis." He raises an eyebrow at me like I'm supposed to shrink beneath his superiority. Clearly, he's never met the woman who raised me. Cowering to "the man" is not within my DNA.

"We need to discuss why I made an appointment to talk to you," I tell him. He nods his head imperiously as though I should keep talking, so, I do. "I haven't taken a vacation in the last two years and I currently have five weeks of paid time that I'll lose at the first of the year."

"Ah, yes," he says as though he gives a crap about my vacation. "But you'll accrue vacation in your new position."

"I would expect so, but meanwhile I'd like to take the time I've already banked in my old position."

Confusion furrows his brow as if I'm not speaking plain English. He finally asks, "What would you think if I could get the company to buy out your vacation time at half-pay?"

"I'd think that I'm already getting a fully paid vacation, so I'd most certainly have to pass on your offer to reduce that."

"Lexi." Jamison never uses my nickname. "The company is in financial difficulty at the moment. I could pay you at half rate for your vacation now and then write in a more substantial package for you in your next contract. How does that sound?"

With the company in trouble, I'd have to be an idiot to agree to move to Atlanta with a decreased salary before taking the vacation I've already earned. I tell him, "I think I'll stay with my current contract. I'll tie up my workload and then I'll take my time at the beginning of November." If the company is still alive and kicking, then I'll consider if I'll accept a new position with them in Atlanta.

Jameson is clearly displeased that I'm not going to dance to his tune, but I'm letting him know loud and clear that I'm no pushover. My mother didn't raise a stupid child. I'm prepared to unleash *the full Regina* if he doesn't go for it, but he eventually stands and puts out his hand to shake mine.

"You've got yourself a deal, Alexis. I'll write up a new offer detailing our agreement and let you know when it's ready to be signed."

If I sign it. As I walk back to my desk, I can't help but wonder if Silver Spoons is a house of cards in a windstorm or if they're simply being fiscally responsible by not overextending themselves. There's no way to know. I'll just have to sit back and keep my eyes open. Meanwhile, I need to give some serious consideration to my housing situation. I can't keep my current place if I move to Atlanta, and I sure can't keep it as an unemployed New Yorker, which is what I'll be if I don't take the job in Georgia.

I decide to forgo actual work and walk down the street to the new bakery that recently opened. Even if a pumpkin muffin doesn't help me think more clearly, it will surely offer a degree of comfort, which is one thing I could use in spades right now.

I stir one packet of raw sugar into my latte before turning around to try to find a place to sit. With nowhere available, I walk outside and cross the street to Central Park. I find an empty bench almost immediately. As I sit down, I realize my life is turning into something of a shit show. I've more or less lost my apartment, my job, and the man I'd been crushing on, all within three days. I watch as people buzz around me. Time on my little corner of the bench has totally stopped while the rest of the world has hit fast forward.

I take two bites of my muffin before realizing I can't even taste it. Eventually I pick up my phone and punch in Emmie's number. She answers on the third ring, mid-laugh, "Hey, Lexi, what's up?" So, I tell her. Halfway through Tim's engagement story, I uncharacteristically burst into tears. By the time I relay that my apartment is going condo I'm so stuffed up I'm not sure if she has any idea what I'm saying. I can't even make it through my job debacle. I don't even know who I am in this moment.

Before snot runs uncontrollably down my face, she interrupts me. "Come to Creek Water and see us. Faye and I miss you to the moon and back."

I tell her I've already decided to do that and give her my dates, asking if they work.

"A whole month!" she squeals in my ear. "You're never going to want to leave after you've been here for that amount of time."

I want to remind her that she lives in Missouri, and Missouri is pretty much a nothing location from a New Yorker's perspective. But I don't want to hurt her feelings. Also, I'm starting to wonder if my life in New York is all it's been cracked up to be. Don't tell Regina I said that or she's liable to have a cow.

Chapter 4

I spend all of September and October dismantling my life, only coping by putting myself on autopilot. I deftly remove Silver Spoons from all expansion negotiations. I give notice on my apartment and sell all the furniture I can live without, essentially everything but my bed and a darling little Victorian end table I picked up at the Hell's Kitchen swap meet. My parents let me store what's left of my life at their place until I can decide what I'm going to do. This way I'll be able to bank my rent payment for the next couple of months.

My dad is nearly apoplectic at the thought of me living anywhere but the borough of Manhattan. I once toyed with the idea of moving to Roosevelt Island, and he threatened a stroke if I did any such thing. When I told him about the Georgia promotion, he lost his voice for two whole hours, choosing instead to communicate through eye-rolls, foot stomping, and dish banging.

"People do move, Dad."

"The only intelligent reason to move is to get closer to New York City. No one with an above average IQ ever leaves," he protests.

My mom has other thoughts. "I don't suppose a year or two outside the city will kill you. It might even be beneficial, you know, give you charming little anecdotes about what life is like outside utopia. As long as you don't start blessing people's hearts and drinking sweet tea, you should be fine."

"I'm not visiting her there," my dad interjects petulantly, talking as if I'm not present.

"Of course not, Bertie," Mom declares like such lunacy never entered her mind. "Lexi will be so desperate to come home, I'm sure we will see her more than we do now."

"As you know, before I move to Atlanta, I'm going to use my vacation and see Emmie. Tomorrow. You could come see me there." I would never say such a thing if I thought there was a snowflake's chance in Haiti that they'd do it.

My dad ignores the invitation and asks, "Do you want me to take the subway into the airport with you?"

"Dad, I'm thirty years old. I think I can manage it on my own." The pouty look on his face has me adding, "Unless you feel like you need to."

"You're my only child," he says. "I both need *and* want to." He looks at Mom and adds, "What do you say, Regina? Should we make it a family affair?"

My mom shakes her head. "I'll be in the middle of giving a lecture. You two go and have fun."

My dad smiles like a kid in a candy shop. "Let's go early and have lunch at that crab place I love at the airport."

Bertie Blake is nothing more than a sixty-year-old little boy. His family has lived in New York since getting off the boat from Liverpool and stepping onto Ellis Island three generations ago.

He went from kindergarten through art school here before going to work at an advertising agency. That ended when he met my mom. She bullied him into pursuing his dream. She told him on their second date that she wouldn't consider a relationship with someone who didn't have the intestinal fortitude to be his own man. My dad quit the next day and hasn't held a traditional job since.

I hold my parents in high regard even though I have every expectation that I will marry someday and have a traditional relationship, a traditional family. It'll probably kill my mother and she'll most likely do everything in her power to talk me out of it, but I'm prepared to stand up for what I believe in. Ultimately, Regina will respect our differing needs out of life and will accept it.

My mom asks, "Will you be staying with Emmie the whole time you're in Missouri?" I nod my head, so she continues, "I'll need her address."

"Why do you need her address? Call me on my phone if you need to get ahold of me," I say.

"In case her house blows away in a tornado or something. That sort of thing always happens in places like Missouri. I'll need to know where you are so I can tell the Red Cross where to look for you."

"I don't think tornado season is until the spring. The only bad weather-related incident that could occur is a snowstorm or something."

"Do they get snow in southern Missouri?" she asks.

I don't actually know. If it happens outside the confines of New York state, I'm pretty clueless. Hence, I may not really know when tornados occur in the South. "I'll let you know when I get there," I tell her.

My mom commands, "Watch out for racists." My maternal grandmother was full-blooded African-American, and my maternal grandfather was Jewish. I think part of the reason Regina never leaves New York City for rural environs is that she's pretty sure people will line up to lynch her. I can't say I blame her; I mean, there are some hideous stories on the news, but rightly or wrongly, I have more faith in my fellow man than she does. Also, I'm pretty watered-down in comparison. I have one of those complexions where my ethnicity isn't obvious. I'm what Bertie calls "exotic looking."

After my parents are through warning me against eating food that contains the word "pone" in it, we sit down on the floor and open up the containers of curry that Dad ordered for dinner. It was delivered while we were busy addressing their copious concerns.

"They probably won't have any decent ethnic food there," my mom warns.

My dad adds, "I think they primarily eat fried chicken and crickets or something."

"Oh, my god, you two are ridiculous. I'm not going to some third-world country. Missouri is part of the union, you know. They even have big cities. Ever heard of St. Louis and Kansas City?"

"Isn't Kansas City in Kansas?" Bertie asks.

That's what I had thought too, but I did a quick Google search on the *Show-Me* state when I decided to go there. I knew I'd have this conversation with my parents, and I wanted to study

25

up to prove I wasn't going off to the wilds of Appalachia or something.

"Be careful," my dad says. "I'm pretty sure everyone carries a gun down there."

"Where did you get that idea?" I ask, expecting a ludicrous reply.

He does not disappoint. "Artie Feldman, down at the newsstand, told me. Apparently, his wife's youngest sister married a man from Missouri. She was scared to death to walk the streets for fear of being shot."

"Would you feel better if I wore a pair of brass knuckles?" I joke.

"Funny you should ask," my mom says, standing up to walk across the room. When she comes back, she's holding a brown paper sack. "Bertie and I picked up a few things for you when you mentioned leaving New York to visit Emmie."

I cautiously open the bag and peek inside. Then I reach in a pull out a pair of brass knuckles. "Really?" You think I'm going to have use for knuckledusters in a place called Creek Water?"

"That's not all," my dad says. So, I look back in the bag and pull out a whistle and a small can of mace attached to a keychain. Look out, Missouri; here I come.

Chapter 5

The first leg of my journey is a two hour and thirty-minute flight to O'Hare; it's the perfect amount of time to plug into a movie and relax. I'm half-tempted to nap as a result of the obscene number of crab legs my dad encouraged me to eat. I'm positively stuffed. Bertie's worried about me ingesting seafood in Missouri since "it's so far from the ocean, you might get sick."

I'm not sure he's aware that I'll be on the same timeline that they are and not stuck in the eighteen-hundreds, with seafood being carried unrefrigerated on the backs of pack mules. Bertie would feel much safer having me walk through Times Square stark naked at midnight than visiting our country's heartland.

I pull up *The Wedding Singer* on my laptop, adjust my earbuds, and let myself get carried away by one of my favorite vintage romcom movies. Although not cinematographically brilliant, it proves that there's someone out there for everyone. And while I'm not a wedding waitress and am definitely not looking for a man with a mullet, if those two crazy kids could find each other, surely there's someone out there for me.

I allow myself a moment of sadness over Tim Sanders and what might have been had he not run off and gotten himself engaged to another. I didn't even bother to say goodbye to him when I moved out of my building, even though I stood outside his door several times, tempted to knock.

I fall into a crab-leg-induced coma right around the time Adam Sandler starts singing "Love Stinks." I wake up when we touch down in Chicago. My flight is direct, so I go back to sleep until it's time to take off again for Missouri. I dream my parents are flying next to the plane on futuristic scooters and they're shouting words of caution like, "Be careful!" and "Don't eat any bugs!" and "If they start to play 'Dueling Banjos,' run!"

When we land, it's with no surprise, yet with great relief, that I discover I'm still in the twenty-first century. I let everyone exit before me and send a text to Emmie to let her know I'm here.

Me: I've arrived! I'll meet you at curb pick-up in thirty minutes.

Emmie: Don't be silly. I just parked. I'll meet you in baggage claim.

When everyone is off the plane, I grab my carry-on from the overhead compartment and make my way down the center aisle. The flight attendant says, "Enjoy your stay."

The pilot is standing by the exit. He tips his hat and offers, "Thanks for flying with us."

Already, the stress of my life is slipping away. I have no idea what this trip holds in store, but I sense that it will be exactly what I need.

I stop by the airport bathroom and make quick work of tidying myself up. My hair looks like I've rubbed a balloon across the top of it. Regina claims that I have nothing to complain about as her hair is half-Afro and half-Jewfro. Being that I'm fifty-percent Bertie, my curls are just that, curls—no 'fro.

I wet my travel brush hoping to reactivate my hair mousse to tame it. Then I touch up my face with a little powder and lip-gloss. According to my mother, I look like a porcelain doll from the Victorian era. Aside from her wild mane of hair, I'm pure Blake. Bertie claims I'm the spitting image of his grandmother when she was my age, but due to a building fire during the seventies, there's no longer any proof of that. I take him at his word.

Emmie is right where she said she'd be, standing at baggage claim looking like a ray of sunshine with her blonde halo of hair. While I would know her anywhere, she seems a hundred times more at ease than she ever did in New York. When she spots me, she throws open her arms and starts to run. She meets me halfway.

"Lexi, you're here!" We stand pretty much eye-to-eye and dance around hugging each other for a minute before I realize she's alone.

"Where's Faye?" I ask.

"I left her with Zach's mama. She's complaining she's not getting enough gramma time." Zach is Faye's dad. Emmie had a very uncharacteristic one-night stand while under the influence of tequila. She got pregnant and wound up moving back to Creek Water to raise her daughter. What she didn't realize, thanks to tequila amnesia, was that her one-nighter was with a boy from home that she'd met in a bar. But that's another story … Suffice it say, they are well on their way to cementing their family relationship and according to Emmie, she's never been happier.

"How's the new job?" I ask.

"Wait until you see the place. The uncles have turned that old sewing machine factory into the most darlin' little shopping center you've ever seen. I hope you plan on spending a good amount of time with me there."

"Of course," I tell her. "I'm not going to sit on your couch all day while you go to work."

"It's your vacation, though, so you have to make sure you get good and rested while you're visitin'." My friend is sounding more Southern than I remember. I guess being back home is making her revert to her native speech pattern of dropping the occasional "g." I find it charming.

"Don't worry about me," I tell her. "I plan on relaxing like it's nobody's business."

We continue to catch up as we grab my suitcases and walk to the parking lot where Emmie left her car. I tell her, "I'm still not convinced I'm going to take Silver Spoons up on their job offer in Atlanta."

"I think you'd like it there," she tells me. "Atlanta's certainly a quieter city than New York, but it's got a lot to offer."

"If it's so great, why didn't you move there?"

"Touché, but still you might enjoy the change. Do you want to be like Bertie and Regina, living in Manhattan your whole life?"

"I guess I always thought I would. Until very recently, it's never even occurred to me to move somewhere else. But now that Jameson brought up Atlanta, I'm wondering if I might put my name in with a headhunter and look at other places, as well."

"Really, like where?" she asks.

"I don't know. Maybe Chicago or someplace like that."

"Chicago has the best pizza," she declares.

I raise my eyebrows in such a way as to warn her that you don't mess around telling a New Yorker that their pizza is second rate. Emmie laughs, "It's different from New York pizza. It's like comparing tuna and salmon. They're both technically fish, but worlds apart in flavor."

When we get to Emmie's car, I let out a low whistle. "Nice ride." The vintage red Mustang with black racing stripes is not the kind of car I'd envision my friend in, but it's pretty sleek, nonetheless.

"It was my daddy's car. Mama never got rid of his stuff. It's kind of like she's pretending he's still around, only on an extended vacation."

"But he died when you were a kid, right?" I ask.

"Yes, ma'am. He's been gone for twenty years."

"Has your mom ever dated again?" I question.

"Nope. Being widowed at thirty, you would have thought she'd have found someone else long ago, maybe even had another family, but Mama wasn't interested."

"I'm looking forward to seeing Grace again. She's a way more maternal figure than Regina." Don't get me wrong, I love and respect my mother, but not once, to my knowledge, has she ever baked cookies. She bought them at the bakery. I don't recall her ever cooking, either. She did fry eggs for breakfast and she sometimes made sandwiches for lunch, but dinner was always courtesy of one of the takeout menus she kept stashed in the kitchen drawer.

Regina Cohen was too busy building up the sisterhood to be

caught messing around a kitchen. My dad once asked if she wanted to take a cooking class together and she replied, "Not if we were starving and our lives depended upon it." She amended that to, "You're welcome to take one if you want, but the kitchen is no place for a woman."

Bertie passed on the offer. He was looking for a fun activity for him and Mom to do together. He didn't really want to learn how to cook, either, and was just as happy reaching for the endless supply of take-out menus.

Emmie says, "You want to stop by the sewing machine factory on the way to Mama's?"

"That sounds great," I tell her. "I'm excited to see what you've been up to."

We drive alongside the rolling foothills of the Saint Francois Mountains, and I feel like I'm on another planet. There is an unshakable feeling that beyond a shadow of a doubt I'm exactly where I'm meant to be.

Chapter 6

The old sewing machine factory is everything Emmie said it was. It's located on the banks of the Mississippi River, which is a pretty impressive sight. The Hudson River, while beautiful, mighty, and the subject of much poetry, has an entirely different feel.

When we walk through the glass door entrance to the old building, I'm blown away by the impact of the space. It's a design I could see working in the Meatpacking District in Manhattan. It's very urban feeling with the thirty-plus-foot ceilings. Emmie shows me around, pointing out the "best steak house this side of the Mississippi," a bakery "so good you'll live there," a hair salon, a book shop, and finally her own store, aptly named Emmeline's. She's opened the toned-down version of Silver Spoons.

"I'm impressed," I tell her. "While you described everything in detail, I thought you might be up-selling it a bit. But if anything, you downplayed how amazing it is."

"Wait until you see the second and third floors. Come on, let's head up and I'll get Beau to give us the keys to the model condo. You'll flip your biscuit."

I briefly wonder where my biscuit is located.

Getting into the old service elevator, I say, "This reminds me of the elevator in my parents' loft. You don't see a lot of them around anymore."

"It's part of the charm. The downtown area is mostly inhabited by folks in their twenties and thirties, and while they don't live in a big city, it gives them the feeling like they do."

When we arrive at the second floor, Emmie unlatches the gate and opens it as the external doors lift to let us out. The second floor is pretty standard office space, but it has a young, contemporary vibe. The floors are dark wood instead of carpet, and the walls are painted a cool icy blue bordering on gray. It's very sleek.

Emmie walks through the double glass doors at the end of the hallway with the words "Frothingham Realty" written across the front in a simplistically modern font.

She strolls right past the receptionist with a wave. "Is Beau in?"

"He is," she says, "but you might want to hold up. Shelby's in there with him."

Emmie stops mid-step and I nearly run right into the back of her. She says, "I need the keys to the model condo."

The receptionist opens her desk drawers and pulls out a keychain before tossing it over to her. "Here you go."

Emmie grabs it, waves goodbye, and turns on her heel leading the way back to the elevator. She explains, "Beau and Shelby are in the midst of trying to decide what they mean to each other."

"Are they boyfriend and girlfriend?" I ask.

"They might have been, but Shelby's mama forced her into giving Beau an ultimatum, which he did not like, and he stopped seeing her before any feelings were declared." She continues, "They started to date again after Shelby miscarried their baby, so I don't know how it's looking at the moment. I think there might be trouble in paradise."

"Shelby miscarried Beau's baby after they broke up? Do you live in a telenovela or something?" I ask.

Emmie laughs. "I know it sounds tawdry, what with me and Beau both winding up with a whoops *baby* without the benefit of marriage." She shrugs her shoulders. "I've concluded that Frothinghams are incredibly fertile and perhaps a bit impetuous when it comes to members of the opposite sex."

"It worked out well for you though," I say. "And thank God for that. I was more than a little worried for you."

Emmie gazes off as though momentarily lost in thought. "You know I've never regretted having Faye, but it sure does make things a lot sweeter having her daddy as part of the story."

"I can't believe you didn't know it was Zach the night she was conceived."

"It's always been like that with me and tequila. While I do enjoy it, I have no memory of what happens when I'm under the influence. All I remembered is that I had the only one-night stand of my life with that actor Armand Hammer, 'cause that's who Zach looks like."

"I remember. We Googled Armie Hammer and his whereabouts the night of *the deed*. Remember how disappointed you were to find out he was in France that weekend?"

"Well, now I'm relieved. Could you imagine the horror of having a one-night stand baby with a famous person? The tabloids would have run me through the wringer."

When we get to the third floor, I follow Emmie down another hallway, this time the flooring is dark-gray slate tile. Its industrial aesthetic fits the building to a T.

Walking through the front door of the model packs such a wallop I feel the breath being sucked out of me. The first thing I think is that my dad would love it here. There's a twenty-foot glass wall facing us that looks out on the Mississippi River. The actual Mississippi River. My mind is blown by its vastness, by its history. And then I realize the natural light is phenomenal. The top ten feet of the wall is poured cement. Several large canvases are showcased there. They're up-lit from the windows beneath and indirectly down-lit from skylights. I pull out my camera and start taking pictures.

"Gorgeous, isn't it?" Emmie asks.

"Beyond words. I have to send these pictures to Bertie. He'll go nuts over the amount of lighting and wall space." I snap several pictures of the view as well. My dad is a sucker for a great view.

Emmie laughs, "Can you imagine your dad down here? My word, he wouldn't know how to act around a bunch of small-town folks."

"Bertie would actually do a lot better than my mom. All he'd need is enough decent take-out food to keep him alive. Regina would want to refight the Civil War. Which side was Creek Water on, anyway?" I'm surprised my mom didn't ask me that before I left.

"The southern part of the state sided with the Confederacy, but I'll have you know that we have two houses right here in town that were part of the Underground Railroad. One of them is even for sale. I bet I could get Beau to take us through if you wanted to see it."

"I do!" I declare. "I went to camp one summer at a farm in Pennsylvania Dutch country that was part of the Underground Railroad. It was super cool with the secret room dug out in the stable floor and the false walls in the basement."

Before we walk up the floating staircase to the sleeping loft, the front door opens and Emmie declares, "Speak of the devil, it's Beau."

I turn to give Emmie's cousin a wave of greeting. We haven't met yet, but I've heard so many Beau stories over the years that I feel like I already know him. I'm not at all prepared for the sight that greets me. I imagined Beau would look a lot like Emmie: tall, blond, medium build. What I see instead is a masculine tower of solid, dark, brooding, hunka-hunka burning love. I mean seriously, *WOW*. My mouth hangs open in a most awkward fashion, and I force it shut before I drool on my shoes or something.

Beau glides by in his perfectly faded jeans that fit like they were made for him—every contour deliciously showcased, like the mice from *Cinderella* sewed them especially for him. He's wearing a blue dress shirt rolled up at the sleeves, highlighting forearms that are no stranger to physical work. He must not have seen me—maybe because I've already climbed two steps to the second floor—because he says to Emmie, "That woman is going to be the death of me."

"Shelby?" Emmie asks.

"Who else? I swear to God when Cootie was pregnant with her she must have drunk a gallon of vinegar a day. That gal is as ornery as the day is long."

"Before you tell me what she did, I'd like you to meet my

friend Lexi from New York." Emmie gestures in such a way as to let Beau know that I'm standing behind him.

He turns to say hello, and my jaw drops open at the sheer impact of looking straight into his piercing eyes. I snap my lips shut, realizing my open-mouthed sea bass look might have him wondering if I'm mentally challenged.

Beau's stare is so intense that I hurry to say, "I'll go on upstairs so you two can talk." God knows what personal things he might have said had Emmie not alerted him of my presence. I don't wait for either of them to reply before dashing up to the sleeping loft. Of course, it's an open loft, so I can still hear every word they say, but at least the privacy is implied.

"You know the dance the club has right after Thanksgiving?" I hear Beau ask.

Emmie replies, "The Cornucopia Ball? What of it?"

"Cootie has proposed that this year the club members elect a king and queen of the ball and she wants me and Shelby to campaign for it."

Emmie starts laughing. "No! You know they'll make you wear a cornucopia on your head if you win." She's giggling so hard she can barely catch her breath.

"Can you imagine?" Beau asks. "I'd feel like Henry the Eighth or something. No, sir, I'm not doin' it." A moment later he adds, "Shelby thinks it's because I hate her mother."

"Well you sort of do," Emmie tells him. "We all do."

"I told her, 'Shelby, it's not *just* 'cause I hate your mama, it's because it's the darned stupidest thing I've ever heard of and I won't be a party to it.' I may have also mentioned that I don't even want to go."

"Beauregard Frothingham, you cannot skip the ball! My god, Cootie would never let you live it down."

"Those demented club ladies are not the boss of me, Emmie. I have never danced to their tune, and I'm not gonna start now."

"I'm guessing you mentioned that to Shelby?"

"I did," he says. "It did not go well."

"Ya think? Beau, that dance is the second biggest event the club throws next to the New Years' Eve gala. They nominate the committee who organizes the following year's ball the day after the current event. For a whole year, they're girdle-deep in the trenches, planning it." Then she calls up the stairs, "Come on down, Lex, I want to show you the rest of the first floor."

I quickly descend as I was sitting at the top of the staircase blatantly eavesdropping—while trying to catch the breath that was stolen from me when I saw Beau.

When I appear, Emmie's cousin looks at me and his gorgeous green eyes squint together before he blatantly frowns at me. I come to a quick stop. I'm not sure if it's because I look deranged from traveling or what, but I get the sense he's taken an immediate dislike to me.

I step forward to shake his hand, having forgotten I'm still on the second stair and I wind up falling down like a drunken circus clown. Emmie rushes to my side, "Lexi, are you okay?" She reaches to give me a hand up while her cousin does nothing more than stand there and stare at me.

"I'm fine," I say, hurrying to my feet. "I thought I'd shake Beau's hand and didn't realize I was still on the second stair. I must be tired from my flight." Or, you know, an idiot.

Way to go, Lexi.

"You poor thing," Emmie says. "Why don't you come on over here to the couch and sit down. I'll get you a nice glass of water."

I do as she suggests, wondering how a glass of cold water is going recoup my dignity after making a fool of myself in front of the most gorgeous man I've ever seen. Beau has not moved an inch, either to aid me or greet me. Emmie passes by him as she walks toward the open-concept kitchen. She punches him in the stomach and says, "Don't be such a dolt. Be sociable."

Beau's feet eventually start to move in my direction. Once he reaches the couch, he stops right in front of me, nearly boring holes through me with the intensity of his gaze. He demands, "Who are you again?"

Chapter 7

"I'm Lexi Blake, Emmie's friend from New York." I'm not sure how I manage a full sentence in the presence of the intense Adonis that is my friend's cousin. Beau has nearly rendered me speechless. But the alternative of not saying anything would be the most uncomfortable silence I'd ever be a party to. I don't know what's going on in his head, but he's clearly feeling something strong regarding my existence.

"Emmie's mentioned you," he says.

"She's mentioned you, too," I reply. He keeps staring at me like I'm a Petri dish and he's a microscope. I wish Emmie would hurry up and get back in here.

"I expected you to be different," he offers.

Different, how, I wonder. Like maybe someone who could descend the stairs without falling on her face. Instead of saying that though, I smile like a simpleton and remain mute.

Beau finally moves with panther-like grace and takes a seat in the leather chair across from the couch I'm sitting on. He hasn't taken his eyes off me. After approximately seven hours, or so it seems, he finally asks, "How long are you visitin' for?"

"Five weeks," I reply.

"Five weeks? Why so long?" he asks.

I can't imagine why he cares how long I stay. "I'm between positions at my company, and I need to take my vacation time now, or I'll lose it." I don't go into any of the details of my situation, like homeless or potential joblessness. No sense making myself look worse than I'm apparently already doing.

Silence from the dark, sexy statue in front of me. Seriously, someone might have chiseled this guy out of granite. I begin to get all fidgety and am on the verge of babbling utter nonsense to fill the air and make less space for tension.

Emmie finally comes to my rescue, saving me from humiliation. She hands me a glass of water and asks, "So, what do you think? Isn't this the most beautiful place you've ever seen?"

I dare to let my gaze flicker to Beau as I answer, "It sure is. I can't wait to show Bertie the pictures."

"Who's Bertie?" Beau demands like my dad is toxic waste or something.

Before I can answer, Emmie says, "Lexi's boyfriend. He's an amazing artist."

My boyfriend? What's she playing at? This is the same kind of nonsense her family played on her when they told Zach that she had been engaged before her fiancé was killed in friendly fire. To say it complicated things between them would be a huge understatement.

I open my mouth to set the record straight, but Beau scowls at me like I boiled his pet bunny. I remain mute.

"Is this *Bertie* looking to move to Creek Water, Missouri?" Beau asks.

I shake my head at the same time Emmie says, "You never know. Artists can live anywhere if they're inspired."

When I was a kid, Dad would take me to Grand Central Station to sit and become one with the space. He'd say things like, "Isn't it magnificent?" and "I could live here." He'd jump up excitedly and show me where he'd put his canvases, then he'd fill in the space around us with assorted imaginary furniture. He even designed a circular bathroom right in the center of the huge waiting room, where the information booth stands. I'd kick back and read my book or people watch in between begging him for money to buy snacks.

Beau reaches into his pocket and pulls something out before gliding over to me like he's floating on air. He extends his hand in my direction. "Give this to Bertie if he's interested in seeing the place in person." I take his offering at the same time he thrusts it forward even farther. For a split second it's almost like we're holding hands. The cells in my body respond by doing a jump for joy, like bread popping out of a toaster. I probably look like I'm having a seizure or something.

I quickly take his business card and say, "I will."

Beau leisurely puts his hand back in his pocket and turns to Emmie. "You going to be up here for long?"

"Only long enough to give Lexi a tour. Zach and I are going to meet with the newspaper in a bit to go over the details of our open house later in the month."

He nods his head. "Are you coming to dinner tonight at the club with the rest of the family?"

"You betcha. Mama's been going on about Chef Jarvis' Beef Wellington; tonight is the first night of the season that he serves it. You and Shelby coming?" she asks.

"Yeah, we'll be there," he answers none too enthusiastically. Then he glances at me so quickly I feel like I imagined it. "See you later." He turns and walks out of the condo.

As soon as he's gone, Emmie squeals like a seventh grader who's just bought her first glitter eye shadow. "What was that all about?" she demands.

"What was what all about?" I reply. She clearly picked up on the tension between us, but I don't want to put any ideas into her head.

"Beau likes you," she declares.

"I don't think so, Emmie. He seemed mad that I was here. He was kind of rude, too."

My friend performs a little dance of joy. "That's how I know. He's trying so hard to work things out with Shelby that the last thing he'd want is to be interested in someone else. That would really tick him off."

"I don't see how anger and attraction are the same thing. Also, I'm not looking to get involved with anyone at the moment, especially as I don't know if I'm going to be staying in New York City or moving to Atlanta. Either way, I'm not interested in a long-distance relationship." That's what I tell myself anyway. But there's something about Beau that draws me, almost like recognition of someone I used to know or someone I'm meant to know.

My friend interrupts my thoughts, "You never know what's waiting right around the corner. Your job is in serious flux, you've moved out of the apartment you thought you'd live in forever, and you're standing here in Creek Water, Missouri. If

I'd asked you four months ago if any of those things were in your near future, you would have laughed at me. Right?"

I think of the fortune-teller's words, *your life is going to change in the most unexpected ways* as I answer, "You're right. But at the very minimum, I'm not looking to get involved with a man who's already taken. I don't operate that way."

"Trust me, Beau's not taken. He and Shelby are mourning the loss of their baby. There's no handbook on how to do that."

Yet he still impregnated her, so in my eyes that takes him directly off the market. "Emmie, I'm not going after a man who's sleeping with another woman, regardless of the fact they haven't made a declaration."

Emmie laughs out loud. "Honey, they only slept together once and you can be darn tootin' they're not doing *that* again until they have some kind of understanding. Beau's not interested in becoming a daddy outside of marriage. In fact, I'd put money on him being a born-again virgin."

"Was he mad when he found out about Shelby's pregnancy?" I ask.

Emmie shakes her head. "He didn't find out about it until right before she miscarried, though. He was shocked for sure, but he wasn't mad. He told me he made all kinds of deals with God to let the baby live. When it didn't, I'm pretty sure he felt responsible."

"Why in the world would he have felt responsible?" I ask.

"I think he figured that if he and Shelby had still been together, he would have known sooner, and could have taken a more active role in making sure she took good care of herself. It's all nonsense, but they both seem to feel guilty that the baby died.

I think they're sticking together out of some false sense of loyalty."

"It's sad they miscarried," I comment, at a loss for anything else to say.

"It is, but God works in mysterious ways. If that pregnancy had stuck, Beau would have felt obligated to ask Shelby to marry him. I used to think they might be destined for each other, but after seeing them together these last couple of months, I no longer believe that's the case."

"Why is that?" I ask, hoping I don't sound hopeful.

"They snatch and snipe at each other like a couple of bratty second-graders. Beau will ask Shelby if she's cold and would she like him to fetch her sweater and she snaps back, 'If I was cold, I'd get my own sweater, Beauregard.'"

Before I can stop myself, I muse that I'd let Beau do all sorts of things for me, the least of which would be something as mundane as bringing me a sweater. Heat rushes to my face as some pretty racy thoughts pop into my head. I say, "Regardless, I'm not looking to get involved romantically right now, and certainly not with someone who is otherwise engaged."

Emmie gives me a knowing smile and says, "You tell yourself whatever you need to. But I'm telling you, sometimes you don't get a say."

Yeah, right. I do get a say and no matter how intoxicatingly attractive I find Beau Frothingham, I am not going to let myself stroll through that mine field. You can put money on it.

Chapter 8

Emmie drops me off at her house before she goes back into town to meet with the newspaper. Her mom, Gracie, fusses over me like I'm another daughter. She leads the way into one of the bedrooms and declares, "This is your room for as long as you like. I mean it. You could move right in here with us forever if you want."

"Thank you, Mrs. Frothingham," I say. "That's very nice of you."

"Mrs. Frothingham? Honey, I've told you a million times to call me Gracie. All my friends do." Perhaps not a million times, but every time she visited Emmie in New York she did.

"Thank you, Gracie," I say. My mother never let my friends call her *Mrs. Anything*, and not just because she wasn't married. She felt the use of marriage-related titles supported the idea of legalized slavery. As a result, she told me I should call all adults by their first names.

Even with my limited knowledge of the world, I was smart enough to realize that most people enjoy a modicum of respect from a younger generation. They don't stop to think where the titles originated, to them they represent good manners.

Instead of Mom and Dad, she wanted me to call them Regina and Bertie. She was beyond annoyed when I refused. Needless to say, this is another area where we eventually agreed to disagree.

Gracie opens the closet and says, "If you need any more hangers, let me know. I'm pretty sure they started breedin' in there, so I put all the extras in the basement." Then she adds, "Come on out when you get settled. I made us some cookies."

I take my time putting away my clothes and unpacking my toiletries, enjoying the feeling of settling into the house, before heading to the living room. I've been in precious few houses in my lifetime as most people I've ever known live in apartments. It doesn't matter if they own those apartments or not, the bottom line is that they're generally one of many units in a large building. Houses with lawns are so far outside my wheelhouse I feel like I'm on Mars.

When I join her, I see that Gracie has laid out the promised plate of cookies. Seeing me, she says, "I made coffee. I figure you being from New York and all, you probably drink a lot of coffee."

I smile at her thoughtfulness, uncertain of her reasoning. "Thank you."

"You want cream and sugar?" she asks.

"Black is fine."

Gracie says, "I invited Lee over to join us. I hope that's okay."

I know from Emmie that Lee is Beau's mother and that she lives right next door. "That'll be nice," I say, even though I feel a bit on edge about meeting his mom after our encounter at the loft. While I know nothing can happen between me and Beau, I still excuse myself to reapply my lipstick; I feel like I'm trying to make a good impression on my boyfriend's parent.

I come back into the living room as Lee walks through the front door. She sees me and smiles so big she looks like she's spotted a long-lost friend. "Lexi!" she says before swooping in, throwing her arms around me, and squeezing to the point of pain. Then she steps back at arm's length and says to Gracie, "She's every bit as pretty as you said she was."

"You're gonna give her bruises, Lee," Gracie admonishes.

Beau's mom turns back to me and removes her death grip only to grab my hand and pull me into the living room. "Come on, let's sit down and you can tell me everything."

I'm not sure what *everything* entails. Maybe my shoe size or my astrological sign, or what I had for breakfast, I don't know. Once we're seated, she announces, "I can see why Beau likes you."

Wait, what? I say, "Mrs. Frothingham, I only met your son for a short time this afternoon. I don't think he's formed an opinion one way or another." Even though I know he has, and that opinion is not a favorable one.

Lee pulls out her phone. "First of all, call me Lee. Secondly, lookie here at this text message I got from him."

Beau: Emmie's friend from New York is joining us for dinner at the club.

Lee: So?

Beau: I'm just saying.

Lee: She pretty or something?

Beau: I don't see how that's any of your business.

Lee: Is she?

Beau: Mama, I gotta go. Make sure you call the club, so they give us a big enough table.

"Mrs. Froth … Lee," I say, "I don't see how you could interpret that text as anything other than your son wanting to make sure we're seated at a large enough table. Also, from what I understand, his girlfriend will be joining us."

"Shelby's no more his girlfriend than I am the Queen of England." Her expression switches from indignation to intrigue as she announces, "Beau has never worried about our seating situation for dinner. Ever. It's one of those things he thinks magically takes care of itself. He gets that from his daddy. Secondly, if he wasn't interested, he would have said, 'I suppose she's pretty enough.' But did he say that? No, ma'am. He said that he didn't see how that was *my* concern. You see where I'm going here?"

Unless she's taking the scenic trip to the moon, I have no idea where she's going. "I don't," I confess.

"Beauregard Jacob Frothingham does not like his mama up in his business when he's interested in a girl. Plain and simple, that boy thinks he's above my involvement in his personal life. So, when he says to me, 'I don't see how that's any of *your* business, Mama,' after I asked after your countenance, that tells me he's interested."

Gracie enthusiastically agrees, "She's right. Historically, Beau has never discussed his lady friends with us. I remember when he was in high school, he wouldn't even tell us who he asked to the senior prom. We had to wait until the knowledge went public and then hear it down at the club."

Lee says, "Hannah White. That was one pretty girl. Whatever happened to her?"

Gracie looks surprised and replies, "Don't you remember?

She married her sorority sister and they moved to Los Angeles and started a family."

Lee smacks her hand on her leg. "That's right! That's not something you'd think I'd forget. I better start taking my *ginkgo biloba* again." Then she turns to me and declares, "Now I know you're not planning on moving to Creek Water or anything, but I would be most obliged if you could be as diverting as possible to my son. He and Shelby need to walk away from each other *fast* or they're liable to do something dangerous like get married out of some warped sense of duty. And trust me, neither of them would be better for it."

"I don't know what you think I can do," I say, wishing I were about anywhere other than sandwiched between these well-meaning and highly excitable women.

"Wear a pretty dress and show a little cleavage. Men are simple creatures. It shouldn't take more than that."

"I brought a nice cashmere dress, but it has a high neck, will that do?" I find that I want to look sexy the next time I see Beau and, if I were to be honest, my motive has nothing to do with pleasing his mother.

Lee looks over at Gracie and says, "Are you thinking what I'm thinking?"

Gracie raises her fists in the air like a pillaging villager rallying the troops. At the same moment, the sisters-in-law declare, "Shopping trip!"

And that's how I come to own the sexiest dress I've ever worn. Regina would have a fit if she could see it.

Chapter 9

"Where've y'all been?" Emmie asks when we walk through the front door.

"We went over to Stevenson to do a little shopping," Gracie answers.

"Looks like you did more than a little," she says, pointing to the several shopping bags we haul in.

"Lexi needed a new dress, so Lee and I took her over to Petaline's."

Emmie asks, "Why does Lexi need a new dress?"

"You know, for this and that," Gracie says.

"This and that, what?" my friend wants to know.

Her mom confesses, "Lee thought she might like to wear a new dress to dinner tonight."

"Why?" Emmie looks perplexed.

I explain, "Because your mother and aunt think I should wear a dress with cleavage to draw Beau's attention away from his girlfriend."

I expect my friend to be on my side here, as you know we're kind of our own little sisterhood, but she does no such thing. She claps her hands rapid fire as though she is trying to kill a swarm of gnats that's been released in front of her. "What a great idea! I hope you got one that shows a lot of boob."

"Oh, honey, wait until you see," Gracie replies. "We pulled out the big guns."

"I want to see it right now," Emmie declares. "Go try it on, Lexi."

I have very mixed emotions. First of all, I really enjoyed going shopping with two women who acted like everything I tried on was the prettiest thing they'd ever seen. Not to mention, I love the dress. It's so feminine and sexy that I feel a million kinds of powerful in it.

On the flip side, I don't really like being used as some sort of distraction to help break up two people I don't know. What if Beau and Shelby really are meant to be together? It's not my place to insinuate myself into their dynamic, especially as I have no skin in the game. I'm leaving in five weeks.

Then again, Beau *is* gorgeous, and it would be highly gratifying to see him appreciate my charms. Also, I should be able to wear anything I like without worrying about how my outfit will affect others.

While the angel and devil on my shoulders fight it out to the death, I grab the bag with my new purchase and head off to my room. The dress Lee coerced me into purchasing is sensual and seductive, but not the least bit slutty. As a matter of fact, it's sophisticated and elegant.

It's a form-fitting taupe-colored jersey that's so soft it feels like I'm being hugged by a cloud. The color is part of what makes it so darn seductive. It's only the tiniest bit lighter than my skin tone, lending an almost nude look. It hits just below the knee, where there's a small flutter-hem that adds the perfect touch of whimsy. That's what Lee says anyway, and I'm one hundred percent buying into it. There's been a sorry lack of whimsy in my life.

The top is fitted, as well, and the three-quarter length sleeves have a matching detail to the hem. Every time I move my arm the fabric wisps around gracefully like it's doing interpretive dance. The neckline is rounded and wouldn't show off anything of interest if not for the keyhole cutout right between my girls. It showcases enough hills and valleys that you know what you're looking at, but not so much that it's trashy. On Gracie's recommendation, I bought a new bra that will push my cleavage up and closer together to give a better show.

The shoes are a matching three-inch suede pump. Lee thought I should get the four-inch pair, but unless you want to see me fall on my face—which Beau already witnessed this afternoon, thank you, very much—three was all I could risk.

When I walk into the living room, my audience whistles and hoots like they're at a strip club. I perform a dignified curtsey and Emmie declares, "Ho-leee heck, girl, you look like sex on a toothpick! I want that dress in every color in the rainbow."

I thank my friend for her lavish compliment, wondering if sex on a toothpick is a Southern colloquialism or an Emmie-ism.

Lee says, "Gracie and I bought dresses, too. Why don't you wear one tonight, Emmie, then our whole party will shine bright?"

"I have the perfect thing," my friend says. "Let's hurry and do our hair and makeup. Zach is going to meet us at the club in an hour with Faye, and I want to knock his socks plumb off his feet."

As we bustle around getting ready with the same degree of excitement reserved for a first high school dance, I can't help but feel a little thrill at the thought of what Beau will make of my new outfit. Not that I'm really trying to get him interested in me.

Chapter 10

The Creek Water Country Club positively takes my breath away. It's both gorgeous and garish at the same time, like something out of the Antebellum South. I feel like I've stepped out of Doctor Who's Tardis. As we walk up the path to the imposing structure, Emmie's mom and aunt stop to greet several friends. They introduce me, but there's no chance I'll remember anyone's names. We do not have names like Bobby Jo, Blondene, and Reyanne in New York City—they're all foreign to me.

We meet up with Emmie's uncles once we enter the lobby. When our coats come off, both men show proper appreciation of our efforts, offering slow whistles and lavish compliments.

Lee introduces me to her husband, Jed, who gallantly kisses my hand and says, "New York's loss is our gain. Welcome to Missouri, Lexi."

"Mr. Frothingham, I'm delighted to meet you."

"The only Mr. Frothingham I know is my daddy, honey. You can call me Jed." Then he motions to his brother. "And this here's my little brother, Jesse."

Jesse bows at the waist. "Any friend of Emmie's is a friend of ours. We're pleased to have you here."

The dining room is reminiscent of a two-hundred-year-old gentleman's club. The furnishings are dark wood with leather-covered club chairs. Multiple large crystal chandeliers hang overhead and the draperies on the elongated windows are a deep navy velvet.

The hostess seats us at a table for twelve right in the middle of the room, as if we're on center stage. Beau and Shelby are already there along with Emmie's other two cousins, Amelia and Davis, to whom I am immediately introduced. This family is a slice of white bread right out of the middle of the loaf. They look too perfect to be real.

Emmie's other half, Zach, who I'd met a couple months earlier in New York, jumps up to greet me. "Lexi, we're so happy you're here." After a one-armed hug, he hands me Faye, their daughter, so I can give her a cuddle. Faye is the perfect combination of her parents. Her coloring is all Zach, but her face is a replica of Emmie's. Holding her makes me realize how much I've missed her.

Lee gives me a couple moments to love on the baby before taking her out of my hands. She says, "You can have her back later. Why don't you sit down over there?" She points to a chair kitty-corner from her.

Davis stands up and pulls my chair out for me. He charmingly offers, "It looks like I won the dinner companion lottery."

I smile flirtatiously. "I think I might have the winning ticket as well."

Once seated, I learn that Amelia owns a bead shop and Davis carves artisan furniture. I already know Beau is a realtor, so I focus my attention on Shelby who's sitting across the table from me. Beau's girlfriend looks like her appearance is the last thing on her mind. Her light hair hangs lank with no real style, and her clothes look like something she picked up off the floor. There's a haphazard air about her. "What do you do, Shelby?" I ask, genuinely curious.

She jolts like I've spooked her. "I help my mama," she says after a long pause.

"What does your mother do?" I ask. You'd think I'd belched the way everyone turns to stare at me. For a split second I hope Shelby's mother isn't a madam or something. Given the intensity of their reaction, I have to wonder.

Beau answers for her, "Shelby's mama is president of ladies' affairs here at the country club." He stares at me with such intensity I can't help but wish I hadn't asked.

As this is the first country club I've ever set foot in, I have no idea what that entails. "So, you plan women's affairs," I repeat, sounding like a simpleton.

"Pretty much," Shelby offers with no real enthusiasm.

I can't seem to leave well enough alone and need to know. "What kind of affairs?" What in the world do women in country clubs do that requires a president to oversee it—doily embroidery, tea pouring?

Shelby rolls her eyes and drops her napkin in front of her. "Lexi, is it?" When I nod my head, she continues, "I assure you, my job is as dumb as it sounds. Mama plans dances and fundraisers and nonsense like that and I run around doing whatever she tells me to." The look on her face is nothing short of belligerent.

"Sounds interesting," I say, trying to diffuse the tension.

"If you call that interesting, you need to get out more," she retaliates.

Davis comes to my rescue and says, "I'm guessing Creek Water is nothing like what you're used to."

"No, but I think it's charming," I tell him, all the while thinking it's a good thing Regina's not here. She'd be freaked out.

Emmie says, "Lexi got a promotion at work that's going to have her moving to Atlanta."

"Atlanta's nice," Beau says. I have a feeling he'd think Antarctica would be a lot nicer. As in, the farther away from him, the better. Despite his mother and aunt's hopes, which are only fantasies, I cannot help but feel like I've rubbed him the wrong way.

"Not as nice as Creek Water, though," Lee says. "You should move here, Lexi." Beau looks alarmed at her suggestion.

For once we seem to be in agreement. I feel like I'm smack in the middle of a Tennessee Williams play, and my comfort zone is way more Woody Allen. I can't say that in present company, so I tell them, "I wouldn't know what to do here to make a living."

Shelby says, "You could marry someone and raise babies. That seems to be a popular pastime." I'm pretty sure she is being facetious.

Jed says, "You could come work for us at Emmeline's."

I smile gratefully at their enthusiasm over keeping me around, but reluctantly admit, "I'm more of big city girl, I'm afraid."

"Lucky you," Shelby mumbles at the same time Beau says,

"You can keep New York as far as I'm concerned."

Lee intervenes, "I'm afraid my children are small-town people, just like me and Jed. We like to visit the big cities, but we like coming home to our quiet life even more."

Once we order our dinner, I focus on my wine with the intention of keeping quiet. There are so many undercurrents at this table, it's like walking through a minefield without a map.

Davis, who's sitting at my left leans over and whispers, "You're doing great. We're a lot to take on all at once." Davis is every bit as good-looking as his older brother, but he's got light brown hair instead of dark brown. Also, he's not as intense. He seems like the strong, silent type vs. the blatantly brooding type, which Beau seems to have covered.

"Thanks," I reply. Then I ask, "You live in Creek Water, too, huh?"

"I do. I have a place downtown near the river. It's close enough to see my family, but not so close that I don't get some privacy."

I laugh, "I know what you mean. My parents live in SoHo. I moved to the Upper West Side as soon as I could to put a little distance between us. It was for the best."

"Can't live with 'em, can't live without 'em," he jokes. We continue to chat amiably throughout the salad course.

As the entrée is being served, Lee declares, "Davis, honey, come over here and sit by me. I need to talk to you about something."

Davis leans in and says, "She thinks I'm monopolizing you."

Jed stands up to switch seats with his son, but Lee smacks his arm and orders, "Sit down, Jed. Beau can trade places with Davis."

Beau, who looks like he has no intention of moving, turns to scowl at his mother, but she ignores him, and orders, "You go sit next to Lexi so I can chat with your brother."

Before relocating, Davis says, "Beau's been through a lot lately. His bark is worse than his bite." So, I've heard, but it doesn't make me anymore excited to sit next to him for the rest of my meal. I'd normally enjoy the company of a handsome man, but this particular one does not seem to care for me at all.

Beau sighs in resignation and turns to Shelby. "Do you mind if I move?"

She waves her hand in the air and answers, "I couldn't care less."

Those two appear to be no more of a couple than the waiter and I are.

Chapter 11

Once Beau is seated next to me, I lose all interest in the delicious smelling Beef Wellington on my plate. The nearness of this man is creating a butterfly storm in my stomach that I don't think will mix well with food.

I'm toying with the idea of standing up to get some fresh air when a new duo stops by our table. The woman looks like a drag queen caricature, with her teased-up hair and over-applied makeup. She's got a sneer on her face that could scare an angel. The man with her is sporting a dark tan so fake it looks painted on.

"Cootie, Harold," Lee states by way of greeting. A chill washes over the table the likes of which you could ice skate on.

The woman, Cootie, ignores Lee and stares at me. She demands, "Who are you?"

Emmie stands up and says, "Mrs. Wilcox, this is my dear friend, Lexi. She's visiting from New York City."

"What are you?" the woman demands of me.

I'm not sure what she's asking so I reply, "I'm a New Yorker."

She scoffs inelegantly and clarifies, "I mean, are you some kind of Mexican or something?"

Everyone at the table stops eating and stares at Cootie like they can't believe she asked that. I know I'm in shock. I briefly wonder if I'm going to need those brass knuckles Bertie and Regina bought for me after all.

Shelby unexpectedly stands up and faces the woman. "For the love of God, Mama, what kind of question is that?" *OK, that shocks me further. She is Shelby's mother?*

"It's the kind of question I'm interested in having answered."

Beau angrily interjects, "Mrs. Wilcox, Lexi is a guest of my family. While you've recently done your best to ruin your own reputation, if you try your hardest to use some manners, you might be able to save the precious little you have left."

Shelby's mother gasps at the reprimand and snaps, "Don't you talk to me that way, Beauregard Frothingham. As Shelby's mother, you ought to treat me with more respect."

He sits back down and replies, "I'll get right on that when you learn to show some respect yourself."

Harold, Shelby's dad, looks about as comfortable as me, and suggests, "Come on, Cootie, let's go sit down and order."

She follows him warily, all the while casting dirty looks at our table. After they walk away, Shelby immediately tells me, "I apologize for my mother's rudeness. I don't know what gets into her sometimes."

I smile at Beau's girlfriend. "I'm not going to lie, that was a bit of a shock. But, you don't need to apologize for her."

Emmie's Uncle Jesse says, "Old Cootie's jealous of your exotic good looks."

"I don't know how exotic I am," I reply. "I'm half-black and a half-Jewish on my mom's side, and one hundred percent

English on my dad's. Pretty standard stuff, if you ask me."

Emmie interjects, "Lexi's mama is a college professor. Isn't that exciting?"

"That's a huge accomplishment," Gracie, says. "I never even went to college. I can't imagine how smart you'd have to be to teach it."

Lee asks, "What is she a professor of?"

"Women's studies," I reply.

"You mean like home economics and the like?" Lee wonders.

I choke on my wine. "Nothing like that. Women's studies are about women's achievements and how they have affected sociology, history, and literature."

Gracie says, "I wish your mama taught closer. I think I'd like to sit in on some of her classes."

Emmie's uncle Jesse asks, "What does your daddy do?"

"He's an artist," I answer.

Beau looks at me questioningly. "Just like your boyfriend, huh?"

Before I can tell him the truth about Emmie's invention of a fictitious boyfriend, she declares, "Lexi likes artistic men."

Lee looks disappointed. "How long have you been seeing each other?"

"Only a month, Auntie Lee," Emmie answers for me.

"What does he think about you being down here for so long?" Davis wonders.

"He's in Paris right now," Emmie seems bent on digging this hole even deeper.

I'm going to be hard-pressed to remember all the lies being told. My friend leans in and whispers something to her aunt and

Lee looks over with a big grin on her face. She points at me, then she taps the tip of her nose and winks. I'm guessing Emmie told her the truth. As likeable as Lee is, she seems particularly nosy regarding the lives of her children.

I don't tell my parents when I'm dating someone new unless he's been around for a good three months. No sense in getting them attached if it isn't going to work out. Actually, Regina has never shown signs of getting attached to any of my boyfriends. Bertie's the one who's looking to add some testosterone to the family dynamic.

The rest of the meal feels like it lasts a month of Sundays, as Mimi used to say. Beau barely speaks to me, and Jesse, who's sitting on my other side, spends most of his time talking to Emmie's mom. When our dinner plates are finally cleared, Shelby stands up and announces, "I'm going to head home now. Thanks for dinner y'all."

Beau jumps up and says, "I'll get our coats."

"Please, don't. I want to go and get some sleep. You stay with your family."

Beau doesn't put up a fight. Instead, he offers, "I'll call you tomorrow."

She walks off without commenting one way or the other.

When she's gone, Amelia says, "My god, watching you two is like watching a car wreck."

Beau nods his head and says, "I know it. But Shelby's the one who lost the baby and she's going through a lot. I'm not going to be the one to walk away from her. It wouldn't be right."

Lee says, "Honey, she's always walking away from you. You need to take the hint already."

"When she says she doesn't want me around anymore, I'll hit the bricks. Until then, do y'all think you can mind your own business and leave us alone?"

By unspoken agreement, his family changes the topic of conversation and moves onto whether or not they have room for whiskey bread pudding. I sneak a peek at Beau out of the corner of my eye and find that he's sneaking his own peek at me. I quickly look away and fake interest in the dessert menu. I do not need the distraction of this man and I'm going to have to redouble my efforts to ignore this strange attraction I feel toward him.

Feeling the need for space, I ask Emmie, "Can you point me in the direction of the ladies' room?"

"I'll take you there," she says as she stands up to join me.

Beau beats her to it. "I'll show her."

Well now if that doesn't defeat the purpose of my leaving the table, I don't know what does. I reluctantly let Emmie's cousin lead me across the dining room. I swear I can feel the eyes of the whole Frothingham family following our progress.

As we exit the restaurant into the main lobby of the club, Beau leans down and says, "I'm sorry about what Shelby's mama said. That was totally uncalled for."

I shrug my shoulders like it was no big thing, but the truth is, it really was. Verbal assault is still an attack. "Thank you," I offer. "You have nothing to be sorry for though. You didn't do anything. In fact, you came to my aid by telling her off."

"That woman can be a real she-wolf."

"It's hard to believe she's Shelby's mother," I say.

Beau shrugs his shoulders. He doesn't say anything else until we're standing outside the restrooms. "I'll wait for you here."

"I can find my own way back," I assure him in an almost panicky tone. I don't need any more one-on-one time with this man. Not if I want to keep my composure.

"No ma'am," he says. "I'll be right here when you get out."

My first impression of Beau was that my presence angered him, but now I feel something entirely different. He's being gentlemanly and kind. It's a very appealing combination. It's also evoking sensations that I don't want to be having.

Chapter 12

I hurry up and do my business before taking time to scrutinize my face and reapply my lipstick. When I exit, Beau is exactly where he said he'd be, waiting for me. He scans me from the top of my head all the way down to my shoes. A look of admiration crosses his face. "I like your dress," he finally says.

"Thank you," I reply. I'm not a shy person by nature, but I'm also not in the habit of being so boldly appreciated. "Your mom and Aunt Gracie took me shopping today."

"Watch out for those two," he cautions. "When they get cooking on something, they can create a storm the likes you've never seen before."

I got that impression, but I don't say as much. "I had fun," I tell him. "My mom doesn't like to shop, so it was a new experience for me."

"Just be careful. Mama has a penchant for sticking her nose into things she has no business getting involved in." He's obviously been on the receiving end of his mother's machinations, and he doesn't seem to care for the experience.

Beau puts his hand behind my back as though to guide me to the dining room. His touch is so light I can't be sure when he removes it, but I feel the heat long after I see both of his hands at his side.

While we don't speak, there's an electricity in the air that's probably charging every phone in a ten-foot radius. I feel it and I know Beau feels it, but I remind myself that I'm not interested.

Beau pulls out my chair for me and I take a seat as Lee announces, "I ordered bread pudding all around."

"That sounds delicious," I tell her. Bread pudding is not a dessert I've had more than a handful of times, and truth be told, it's not my favorite. But I want to be polite.

"So, what did y'all talk about?" Lee asks her son.

"On the way to the bathroom?" Beau wants to know.

"Yes, on the way to the bathroom. That's where you went, right?"

"Actually, Mama, we took a moonlit stroll around the veranda." While I detect the sarcasm in his voice, Lee does not.

"Really?" she exclaims excitedly.

"No," I tell. "I really did use the restroom. Beau and I discussed what an enjoyable meal it's been."

Lee admonishes, "Beauregard Frothingham, you'd best watch yourself. I don't appreciate you being a wise apple."

"I wouldn't have to be Mama, if you'd mind your curiosity once in a while."

Lee ignores his comment and addresses me, "So, Lexi, tell us about your boyfriend."

Beau's posture becomes ramrod stiff. I can tell he's purposely not looking at me and I'm about to set the record straight, when Emmie says, "Lexi and her boyfriend are perfect for each other!"

The waitress arrives with our pudding, momentarily taking the spotlight off me. For some reason, I lean into Beau and confess, "Bertie is my dad, not my boyfriend. I'm not seeing anyone right now."

He noticeably relaxes and asks, "Then why did Emmie say you were?"

"I think she has hopes that something might happen between you and me. But clearly that's a pipe dream on her part."

He quirks his eyebrow at me and flirtatiously drawls, "Why's that?"

Tingles of attraction start at the base of my neck and shoot through my extremities like a fuse on a stick of TNT. "Well, there's Shelby to consider."

As soon as the words are out of my mouth, his demeanor shifts back to its prickly past. "Yes, there is." Beau distances himself as surely as if he'd gotten up and moved to another table.

I'm not sure what he's angry about. After all, he's the one with a girlfriend. I spend the rest of the meal talking to Emmie's family about god knows what—my thoughts are clearly elsewhere. Beau goes back to acting like I'm not even there.

After dinner, Jesse pulls my chair out for me, as Beau makes his excuses and nearly sprints out of the restaurant ahead of us. His departure leaves a gaping hole in the atmosphere. What in the heck is going on with that man?

As we walk out of the dining room, we pass the table where Shelby's parents are still dining. I consciously speed up to avoid further contact, and while I make a point not to look at her, I hear her hiss, "Stay away from him, Mexican. He's not for you."

Chapter 13

Emmie and I sit on her bed after we get back to her house. "I'm so sorry about what Cootie asked at dinner. That woman has the manners of a tarantula."

"I'm guessing you don't have a lot of ethnic diversity at the club?" I ask, despite Shelby's dad having darker skin than I do. My coloring is tied to undiluted generations ending with a jazz-singing, fortune-telling enthusiast I used to call Mimi.

"Not so much, no. Let's face it, we're a long way from New York, but we have mostly great people here. Don't let Cootie fool you into thinking she speaks for the masses."

"Where in the world did she get a name like Cootie?" I ask, changing the subject.

Emmie laughs, "Story I heard was that in grade school she was always picking on someone, telling them that they had cooties, and one day the kids started to call her that. It stuck."

"It seems appropriate," I say. "But what's up with Shelby? She doesn't seem to like her mother or her occupation."

Emmie grimaces. "Shelby was totally different before losing the baby. She was always dressed up and lording it over everyone like Cootie does. She hasn't been herself lately."

I suggest, "Do you think she's depressed?"

"I do, but I don't think she knows what to do about it."

"Can't Beau help?" I ask.

My friend shakes her head. "She doesn't listen to him. He's tried suggesting she get some counseling, but she just tells him that he doesn't know what he's talking about."

"What a mess," I say for a lack of anything else. I feel sorry for Shelby. She's clearly in distress, but she's not liable to accept help if she doesn't think she needs it. I have a good deal of respect for Beau for staying close in case he's needed.

Emmie says, "What Shelby needs has to come from within. She and Beau aren't good for each other." A yawn clearly takes her by surprise, so she suggests, "The days are long with a baby and working. You must be tired, too. Let's get some sleep." She adds, "I've got an early start in the morning. You're welcome to drive into town with me, if you'd like."

"That sounds like a plan," I tell her. "I'm looking forward to getting to know my way around."

Emmie gets up and leads the way into the guest room. "I put some fresh towels in your bathroom. Let me know if you need anything else."

I give my friend a hug. "I will. Thanks for being such a great hostess, Emmie. I've missed you more than I can say."

"I've missed you, too. I like the idea of your living here and even though you claim you wouldn't fit, I'm still going to campaign for it." She warns, "If I can't get you to agree to move here, I'll be pushing Atlanta on you. It's way closer to me than the Big Apple."

I think of all of my friends in New York and I realize how

different they are from Emmie. It's like they're always on the go. When Emmie lived there, we used to sit and talk, a lot. It's part of the reason I've missed her so much. Ever since she left, I've lost my ability to feel peaceful. I'm alone a lot of the time, like when I'm at home, but I still feel like I've lost the art of enjoying the quiet moments. If nothing else, I'm going to recharge my battery while I'm in Creek Water.

I open the window in my bedroom and feel the cool breeze float in. Not something I do in Manhattan. I'm always trying to shut out the noise there. But here, I want to enjoy all that comes with rural America. After changing into my pajamas, which are a pair of yoga pants and a hoodie, I crawl under the covers to warm up. The only sound is the tinkling of wind chimes, which is oddly soothing.

I can't recall the last time I heard wind chimes in the wild and not in some gift shop. My bedtime serenade is more along the lines of sirens blaring, horns honking, loud music from my downstairs neighbors, and the bottle that gets smashed somewhere under my window every night at eleven. I've never discovered the source of the breakage, but it's become an expected part of my nightly symphony.

The perpetual pulsing of energy that always flows through me starts to subside, like it's on a slow leak. I close my eyes to welcome unconsciousness, but I can't seem to shut my brain off. Maybe I need someone to break a bottle to signal my sleep cycle.

After a full hour of restlessness, I put on some wool socks and a robe I found in the closet, and throw a blanket over my shoulders before tiptoeing out to the living room. Then I open the sliding door and go out back to sit on the patio. I spot a wooden Adirondack lounger and make short work of settling in.

The only time I sit outside at home is when I'm in the park with thousands of other people. There's something unreal about laying under a zillion stars that really makes you appreciate the magnificence of the universe.

It makes me feel small, but at the same time, incredibly connected to the idea that I'm part of something so much bigger. How have I lived nearly thirty years without doing this?

Suddenly, I recognize that by spending my whole life in the greatest city on earth I've missed out on something fundamental. A premonition fills me like a presence under my skin. Something life-changing really is going to happen while I'm here. I only hope it's a good change. The fortune-teller from my childhood was never clear on that point, and all of the unexpected changes that happened in New York were not good ones.

Chapter 14

I wake to hear Emmie singing "Proud Mary" at the top of her lungs. My friend is no Tina Turner, but what she lacks in talent, she more than makes up for with raw enthusiasm. Once she hits, "rollin' on the river," ten-month-old Faye lets out a squeal of delight. I imagine there's a pretty righteous dance performance that accompanies her serenade.

The screech catapults me into full consciousness. That's when I realize I've slept outside on the patio. I have no memory of falling asleep or dreaming or anything. Pulling my robe tightly around me, I make my way into the house wondering why I conked out so deeply.

Emmie and her mom are both wearing yoga pants, t-shirts, and wickedly high heels. They're getting their Tina on in a way that could win them a fortune on *America's Funniest Videos*. Two of the whitest women ever born imitating the best performer to ever live ... I wish I had my phone on me. Not to be left out, Faye is sitting on the floor in front of them shaking her teddy bear to the beat of the music, releasing an occasional shout of joy.

When they see me, Emmie turns the music down and declares, "You slept outside."

I nod my head. "I couldn't knock off with all the quiet, so I went out to investigate the lack of noise. That's the first time I've slept outdoors in my whole life."

"You never went to sleep-away camp as a girl?" Gracie asks, astonished at my confession.

"I did," I tell her. "But we were in cabins." I only went twice, once in Pennsylvania and once in Poughkeepsie.

I point to their getup and ask, "What's going on here?"

Gracie laughs, "We're getting our exercise on."

"To Tina Turner?" I ask.

"Who else?" Emmie replies. "Have you seen the state of that woman's legs?"

"Eighty never looked so good," I agree. "You have any coffee?" I figure after a cup or two, I might join in and show them how it's really done.

"I'll get you some," Gracie says as she glides into the kitchen like her four-inch stilettos are tennis shoes.

"I'm going to grab a quick shower," my friend says. "Can you be ready to go in thirty minutes? We can get something for breakfast at the new coffee place in the factory."

I agree to be ready and gratefully accept a mug from Gracie when she comes back. She announces, "Lee and I want to take you around a bit while you're here. We'll give you a couple days to settle in, but then we're hoping to kidnap you for a few local adventures."

I assure her that sounds delightful before heading to my bedroom to get ready for the day ahead. My wardrobe at home is mostly comprised of business suits. It'll be nice to dress more casually for a change. After choosing a pair of blue jeans, a dove-gray cashmere V-neck, and a pair of black suede booties, I get busy taming my hair. It's a process that requires a load of moisturizing spray and more patience than I currently have.

I choose a coral color palate for my makeup, and when I'm done, I meet Emmie in the living room with moments to spare. We say goodbye to her mother and the baby and then we hop into her dad's old sports car.

"What was it like growing up here?" I ask, wondering at the differences in our childhoods.

My friend takes a beat to think about her response. "I thought I hated it back then. But now that I'm home, I realize what an ideal upbringing it was. If Cootie hadn't been around to orchestrate trouble, I might have actually loved it."

"That woman *is* a bit of a freak show," I say.

Emmie laughs, "She's been pretty tame since Shelby's miscarriage. You should have seen her before."

I tremble at the thought.

Admiring the wide-open spaces, I ask, "Do you ever have rush hour traffic?"

"This *is* rush hour traffic," she says.

It can take a full hour on the bus to go forty blocks in a New York rush hour, which is why almost everyone takes the subway. Of course, in the subway you're squashed in like cattle, the air conditioning and heat don't always work, and you frequently find yourself stopped dead on the tracks while something in the system is being fixed. Walking is my main mode of transport unless I have to go more than thirty blocks. "Five cars at a stoplight is rush hour?"

"Yes, ma'am. Can't beat it with a stick, can you?"

I have no idea what that saying means, so I simply smile. "What's on your agenda this morning?"

"I have a couple of early meetings, but I should be free after three or so. Depends on how busy it is today."

"Have you been getting a lot of business? You've only been open for a month, right?"

"Just about. And yes, to business. There are a lot of towns smaller than Creek Water nearby, and those folks are as desperate for new shopping outlets as we are."

As soon as we park and make our way to the building, we stop at the Muffin Bar for breakfast. We both order dark chocolate croissants before finding a table to sit at. As soon as we're settled, Beau strides past to order his own breakfast. Then, spotting us, he stops by to say hello. After a perfunctory greeting, he asks, "Em, you got a sec?"

"Sure," she says. "Sit down."

He glances at me and says, "I'd prefer to talk in private." *Ouch.* Gone is the charming man I got a glimpse of last night. I'm not sure if I'm supposed to get up and move or if he wants Emmie to go with him. Either way, I feel as welcome as a cockroach at the dinner table.

My friend starts to get up, but I beat her to it. "I wanted to walk around town for a bit. Why don't I do that now and I'll meet you back here later?"

Emmie asks, "Are you sure? I'm happy to talk to Beau over at the shop."

"I'm sure. See you in a bit, Em." I pick up my coffee and walk away without a word to Beau. That man needs a personality transplant, stat.

Chapter 15

My dad has a fascination with Norman Rockwell paintings, which is kind of odd as his own painting style has always been abstract and modern. He owns a couple of signed limited-edition prints that he stares at like he expects the people in them to jump out of the frame and start talking to him. The one he's particularly enchanted with, "The Runaway," depicts a young boy at the counter of a soda fountain talking to a police officer.

When I asked him why he loved it so much, he told me the story of how he got away from his mom one afternoon while they were shopping in the Village. He walked out of the grocery store and hopped on the uptown bus. When he came to the end of the line, he was in Harlem. Luckily, a lady getting off the bus realized he was alone and took him to a nearby diner to call the police. She bought him a root beer float while they waited.

Bertie didn't know who the woman was until fifty years later while we were celebrating Christmas dinner with my mom's family. My Jewish grandfather was not religious, so Christmas was the observed holiday in their home. It was always my grandmother's favorite.

Over dessert, Dad told the story of his adventure, and Mimi

immediately knocked over her red wine, staining the pristine white tablecloth like a crime scene. "Honey, that woman was me!" she'd declared. "I was rushing home to get supper on the table for Leonard and there you were this little scrap of nothing, all alone. I bought you a root beer float."

Mimi went on to say, "Regina, you need to marry this man, already." My grandparents were legally wed and didn't share their daughter's beliefs against the institution.

My mom had laughed and announced, "Bertie and I are perfectly content the way things are." Then she smiled and said, "Aren't we, Bertie?"

Even though I was only in high school at the time, I could tell the smile on my dad's face was forced. He's never said so, but it's my belief he would have loved to have been married to my mom.

The memories rush over me like a waterfall as I stand on the ribbon of sidewalk that runs against the brick façade of Main Street in Creek Water, Missouri. This town is reminiscent of a Rockwell painting. It feels like a slice of life that time has forgotten. Aside from the people and style of cars, I could easily be standing on a street in the nineteenth century.

I'm not sure which way to go, so I let the spirit move me. I pass stores with the original names painted on the sides of the brick buildings. The paint is faded but still legible—Maggie Lou's Baked Goods, Slinger's Fishmonger, and Wilbert's Farm Supply.

After several blocks, the neighborhood changes to a residential one. A small plaque attached to one of the old-fashioned streetlights reads, "Millionaire's Row." The houses appear to be well over a hundred years old with enormous yards and long paths leading to imposing entryways. I can imagine this street when it was dirt roads instead of concrete and asphalt. It reminds me of the street the family lived on in the old Judy Garland movie, "Meet Me in St. Louis." Mimi and I watched that one at least a dozen times together.

One house catches my eye. It's a three-story Victorian-era red brick home, full-on with a turret. I cross the street to get a better look, when I notice the realtor sign out front. Why would anyone sell such a stately piece of history?

As a little girl, I used to beg my parents to take me for walks in the residential parts of Manhattan where the brownstones are. Those are the closest things we have to actual houses. They share walls with the buildings on either side of them.

I remember seeing houses on television, but I didn't set foot in a real one until college when I went to Connecticut with my roommate. It was a pretty trippy experience, to say the least.

I pull an information flyer out of the plastic pocket attached to the For Sale sign. This house was built in 1861, has seven bedrooms, five and half baths, multiple fireplaces, and is seventy-two hundred square feet. I'm shocked. It's so massive it feels like a museum.

I continue up the sidewalk and climb the eight stairs that lead to the front door. The porch is probably as big as my entire apartment. In my mind's eye, I see it with white wicker furniture and hanging flower baskets. Maybe even a porch swing.

I turn around to appreciate the view from this vantage point and need to sit down on the top stair to regain my equilibrium. I feel punched in the gut by the sensation of being home. It's not exactly déjà vu, but it's pretty darn similar. Instead of feeling like

I've been here before, it's more like I know this is where I'm meant to be. Yet for the life of me I can't imagine I'm meant to live in Creek Water, Missouri. That can't be right.

I look at the flyer in my hand to check the price, expecting it to match the name of the neighborhood, Millionaire's Row. When I find the information I'm looking for, I'm relieved to be sitting down, but not because it's so expensive. This amazing property is only a hundred and sixty-five thousand dollars. *How can that be?*

I pick up the phone to call the realtor to see if there's a mistake. I almost decide against it when I notice that Beau's company has the listing. But my desire to know the information wins out and I place the call.

"Frothingham Realty," a feminine voice on the other end of the line answers.

"Hi there," I say. "I'm looking for some information on the house you have listed on Millionaire's Row."

"Ah yes, the old Frothingham place. What would you like to know?"

The old Frothingham place? Emmie's family used to live here? Why in the world did they ever move? "I'm wondering what the listing price on the house is," I say.

I hear her clicking away on her keyboard, before she answers, "It looks like the price was just reduced to a hundred and forty thousand dollars."

I don't answer for several seconds. *Why is it so cheap? Is it infested with bats? Are the pictures misleading and it's really a demolition zone inside?* But instead of asking any of those questions, I surprise myself by saying, "I'd like to set up an appointment to see it, please."

What am I thinking? There's no way I'm going to buy this house. That would be insane. But crazy or not, I know I need to go inside. So, when the woman on the other line asks when I want to see it, I answer, "Right now, if possible."

She puts me on hold before coming back on the line and announcing, "I can have someone meet you there in twenty minutes."

"Perfect, I'll be here."

Chapter 16

I'm so excited, I don't even consider that Beau will be the one to come. After all, he's the owner of the company. But, of course, he's the one to show up. He parks his SUV at the curb and gets out completely unaware that I'm the person he's meeting. I hide behind one of the brick columns and watch him walk up the sidewalk. He looks like he did when I saw him an hour ago at the coffee shop, only he doesn't seem tense right now. There's a carefree quality about him that makes him even more handsome than I'd previously realized. Crap, that's the last thing I need to be thinking.

I have an overwhelming desire to run away but there's no way I can do so without him seeing me. Plus, I need to see the inside of this house, so I have to suck it up. I take a deep breath, square my shoulders, and step out from my hiding place. Forcing a smile to my lips, I greet, "Hi, Beau."

My friend's cousin falters before stopping dead in his tracks. After several uncomfortable moments of silence, he manages, "I didn't expect you'd be the one I was meeting."

Clearly. "I was walking around town," I explain, "and I wound up here. I couldn't resist wanting to go inside."

"You can't possibly be thinking about buying this place?" he accuses like he's on a fool's errand and I'm wasting his precious time.

And while I'm not really thinking about buying it, I feel the need to terrorize him. "Why couldn't I buy it?"

"Because you're moving to Atlanta," he replies matter of factly.

"I'm contemplating taking a job in Atlanta and I've given up my apartment. I'm open to any possibility as I'm kind of in limbo right now."

"But you're going to move to Atlanta," he emphasizes like he's speaking to a child.

"Again, I've been offered a job there," I tell him. "That doesn't mean I have to take it." Put that in your pipe.

He exhales loudly before joining me on the porch. Pulling out his phone, he in punches a code which results in the lock box popping open. Once the door is open, he stands back to indicate that I should go in first.

I walk into a giant entry hall with a marble floor and an enormous crystal chandelier hanging overhead. Straight ahead is an extra-wide staircase with an intricately carved balustrade. Jolts of excitement shoot through my body like I'm on the receiving end of a cattle prod. When I find my voice, I say, "The lady on the phone said your family used to live here. Why are you selling it?"

"These old houses are money pits. It takes a lot to keep them maintained and running. Most folks don't want to be tied down to that kind of responsibility."

"That's why you're selling?" I ask. Who in the world would

turn their back on this kind of family history out of laziness about maintaining the property?

"My family hasn't owned this house in decades. One of our great-great uncles sold it in the nineteen forties."

I shake my head. I can't imagine such a thing. "Don't any of you want to buy it back?" I ask.

"Why? We all have our own places. Living here would be a full-time job." He's trying to put me off buying it.

That's when the craziest thought hits me and I feel my knees buckle at the very idea. "Someone needs to turn this house into a bed and breakfast," I blurt out. I don't add that person should be me. I don't know anything about running a B&B. Although I did watch a movie once where a girl moved to Ireland to renovate an old inn. She was going to sell it and move back to the US when she was done, but she fell in love with it and stayed.

Beau shrugs his shoulders. "I guess it would be a nice B&B, but in addition to already having homes, we already have jobs. I don't think any of us are looking to change careers."

Thought after thought crashes through my brain like high tide smashing onto a rocky shore. I pull out my phone and open the mortgage app I downloaded when I was trying to figure out a way to afford my apartment on Central Park West. I punch in numbers while Beau stares at me like I'm turning into the Incredible Hulk right before his eyes.

He finally demands, "What are you doing?"

"Math," I answer. "According to my calculations, I could buy this house with forty thousand dollars down and finance the rest over fifteen years at a four-point-five percent interest rate. The result would have me paying less than eight hundred dollars a month in a mortgage payment, which is a nearly a quarter of what I've been paying in rent."

I could use the rest of my savings for repairs and living expenses before I turned a profit. I don't say that out loud, though. I mean, heck, I'm not really going to do this. It's just fun dream material. Who knows if Creek Water needs a B&B? There might not be a demand for that kind of lodging.

"Do you have that much saved?" he demands.

Despite his ungracious tone, he does have a right to know. I smile deviously, "I do."

Beau begrudgingly leads me through the rest of the downstairs, which includes a formal living room, dining room, kitchen, sunroom, and library. There are spots on the ceiling where the plaster is falling down and some of the flooring needs to be refinished. The kitchen is a horror show that was last updated in the nineteen eighties. But the built-in bookshelves, china cabinets, high ceilings, stunning light fixtures, and fireplaces are so extraordinary I hardly even notice the work that needs to be done.

The only time Beau speaks is to tell me what a dump the place is. "The electric is knob and tube and needs to be replaced." I shrug my shoulders in response, so he adds, "The furnace is shot."

Perversely, every negative he mentions makes me want it more. "Aren't you the listing agent on this house?" I ask. "I thought it was your job to sell it, not scare potential buyers away."

He doesn't respond. Instead, he leads the way to the stairs. The second floor transports me to another time. The staircase is wide enough for three people to comfortably ascend side-by-side. There are seventeen stairs to the first landing. I stop to look out the french doors that lead out to a small lookout. The back yard is a mess of overgrowth, but it's positively enchanting. There's a ruin of a decorative fountain, old circular benches that wrap around several trees, and a rose arbor so thick you can barely see the arbor. Even in its neglected state, it's positively gorgeous.

Beau interrupts my thoughts. "As you can see, the property is a disaster area. It'll probably take a crew a month of nonstop work to get it back into a reasonable state. That'll cost a fortune."

I ignore his pessimism. Twelve more stairs get us to the second floor. My mind is buzzing a million miles a minute. A salvage crew could come through this house and resell everything for way more than the hundred and forty thousand dollars asking price. The light fixtures, door hinges, crystal doorknobs, and crown moulding are a few of the treasures that could fetch a handsome price. Not that I'd condone that idea, I'm just saying.

"Who's selling this house and why?" I demand.

"The Benter family has owned the property for the last thirty years. When the parents died, the kids kept the place thinking that one of them might move back to Creek Water, but they never did. They put it on the market five years ago and never got an offer, so they're trying again now." He adds, "It's been vacant for eight years, so there's a ton of deferred maintenance. Probably mold and rats ..."

There are six bedrooms and four bathrooms on the second floor. All of them hideously carpeted. There are probably a dozen layers of wallpaper that need to be stripped away, and the two additional fireplaces are in pretty sad shape, but there's simply too much to recommend this house to dwell on the negatives.

Beau says, "You see what I mean about it being a money pit?"

I've had enough of his lackluster enthusiasm. "Beau, my apartment in New York was barely over five hundred square feet and the asking price is over five hundred thousand dollars."

"What?" He's clearly shocked by this. "Why in the world would anyone pay that?"

"Because that's considered a very reasonable rate for Manhattan." I continue, "Bearing that in mind, can you see why spending less than a third of that on something fifteen times bigger *with* a huge property might seem appealing?"

"Luckily, Atlanta is considered a very affordable city, so you should have no problem finding somewhere nice to live there."

My god, this man is like a dog with a bone, and that bone is named Atlanta.

Chapter 17

"Do you want me to look through the rest of the house by myself?" I ask.

My reluctant realtor rolls his eyes and replies, "Follow me." I trail behind him to the bedroom at the head of the stairs. He walks through the door and crosses the room toward the closet. It can't be bigger than five feet by four feet. "Are you coming?" he grumbles.

While I've never been shown through a vacant house before, I certainly never thought crowding into a closet with your realtor was part of it. Unless of course your realtor was putting the moves on you. A thrill of excitement zips through me at the very thought, even though there's nothing about Beau that would indicate he's anything but irritated with me. Which is fine because I'm pretty annoyed with him and all his negativity.

I join him, curious to see what's going to happen. I'm so close I can smell his bay rum aftershave and I lean in to inhale the heady fragrance. "Turn around and face the wall," he demands. I start to wonder if Beau isn't a little bit kinky, and while I might not be opposed if we were dating, in present circumstances, it feels like an odd request.

"Why?" I ask.

He doesn't answer right away, instead I feel his breath against the side of my neck. I swear that man is smelling my hair. My knees are in jeopardy of buckling and as a result I carelessly allow myself to lean against him, feeling the strength and solidity of his body. Mother. Of. God. I'm in a closet with a man who doesn't appear to even like me, and it's all I can do not to jump into his arms and beg him to do something very wicked.

Beau puts his hand on the empty clothes bar and motions for me to do the same, and I briefly wonder if he's thinking the same thing I am. Then he pushes the bar forward until it moves several inches. I have to catch myself from falling.

I expect him to start grousing about broken clothing rods, but he doesn't say a word as the back wall pops open. *Oh, my god, it's a hidden door!*

I follow him through and discover that we're at the base of another staircase. This one isn't at all impressive. It's very narrow and the steps are super steep. "Where does it lead?" I ask with excitement.

"To a hidden room in the attic."

When we get to the top, Beau flips a switch that illuminates a space no bigger than eight by ten feet. There's nothing special about it and I ask, "Did they use this for storage or something?"

"Our ancestors built the house with several secret rooms and passages," he answers.

"Why?"

"This was one of the first houses in Missouri used in the Underground Railroad," he tells me.

Goosebumps erupt all over my body. This is the house

Emmie told me about. I wonder why she didn't mention that it was her family who built it. "Why in the world doesn't your town buy this property and turned it into a museum?" I demand.

"There was talk of that at one time, but the expense was prohibitive. Creek Water is under fifteen thousand people and most of those people probably wouldn't visit the museum. Even if they did, it would likely be only once. Ultimately, the town council decided it wouldn't make enough to pay for itself."

I can't imagine such a treasure existing without people standing in line to be a part of it. Southern Missouri or not, this is a real piece of American history. Surely some federal historical foundation or something …

Beau continues the tour by showing me the basement. There are two more hidden rooms down here. I ask, "Why two instead of one bigger room?" They're both suffocatingly small, and I feel itchy at the thought of anyone being closed into them.

"In case one of them was discovered," he tells me. Taking in my confused look, he explains, "The reason for multiple rooms in the house is so that if one was discovered, it would hopefully be assumed it was the only one."

"Why would anyone have suspected your family of being involved in hiding slaves?" I ask.

"Because folks with means owned slaves and my family didn't. They paid their servants a wage, but they refused to own them. Even though they founded this town and were pillars of the community, some found their abolitionist beliefs hard to accept."

I have great deal of respect for Beau's ancestors. It couldn't have been easy going against the status quo, especially during such a tumultuous time as the Civil War.

He takes me out to the garage, which used to be the carriage house. There's another secret room under the floor there. It's no more than an earthen basement; the thought of hiding in it makes me panicky, like being buried alive.

After we leave the garage, Beau declares, "The property must be full of ghosts."

"Why would you say that?" I demand, angry that he's trying to scare me off in such a childish manner.

"Why wouldn't I?" he answers. "Can you imagine all the fear and anxiety that's flooded through this place?"

I shake my head. "That's not how I see it," I tell him.

"How do you see it, Lexi?" he looks like he might actually be interested in hearing my response.

"While there had to have been a lot of unrest, I think the predominant feeling is one of hope. Your family represented the promise of freedom, a new life. You can't put a price tag on that kind of goodness."

By the time we walk back to the house, I'm convinced I want to live here. I tell Beau, "I'm just going to stroll around the grounds for a bit. You can go ahead and leave if you want." *Please go, please go, please go,* I chant in my head.

He looks down at me almost tenderly, searching my face for the answer to a question he wants to ask but doesn't. "I'll come along," he says.

"No complaining," I warn. "I don't want to hear about how much work needs to be done or what terrible shape everything is in, okay?"

He nods his head once affirming that he understands the

rules. We walk around the path that leads to the backyard, shuffling through dried leaves that have fallen from the trees. The crunch beneath our feet takes on a hypnotizing cadence as we near a small outbuilding. "This is the icehouse," Beau explains.

I open the door to the small brick building, peek in, and say, "I guess I could use it for a gardening tools or something."

"It would make a great playhouse," he offers. Heat floods my body as though I'm standing too close to a bonfire. Thank goodness for my darker complexion or I'd probably be beet red as unbidden images of Beau and me making those offspring pop into my brain. What is wrong with me? More often than not, Beau seems to barely tolerate my presence. It defies reason that I'm so attracted to him.

"As I don't have any kids yet," I manage, "I guess I'll just keep my rakes here." Instead of going inside the icehouse, I turn around and inadvertently walk right into his arms.

Darn this man and the feelings he arouses in me. Instead of backing away or walking around him, I lean into him and inhale his heat. It feels so good to be standing in the arms of a man, this man.

"Beau," I say his name like a plea.

He runs his hands up and down my back several times like he's trying to memorize the shape of me, before gently pushing me away. He clears his throat and grumbles, "It's probably not even structurally sound anymore."

I know I told him no complaining, but I let it slide because I'm pretty sure he's only doing it to try to break this draw we seem to have toward one another.

Once we're standing a respectable distance apart, Beau

announces, "I better get back to the office. Can I give you a ride?"

I shake my head. "No thanks. The walk will do me good." The truth is that not being with him will do me good. I need to gather my wits and steer clear of Emmie's cousin. I'm just afraid that might be easier said than done.

Chapter 18

My reasons for visiting Missouri were two-fold. One, to see my friend. And two, to unwind and hopefully clear my thinking—I need to figure out where in the heck my life is going next. I never expected to further complicate things by actually considering moving here.

I walk down the path to the sidewalk and turn around to stare at the house that has taken over my imagination. After several long moments, I turn, intent on continuing my investigation of Creek Water. I've been here fewer than twenty-four hours and already New York feels like it was a month ago. It's a very strange sensation.

My phone rings as I pass an old firehouse. I look at the number and see that it's Bertie. "Hey, Dad, what's up? You miss me already?"

He doesn't confirm or deny, instead, he demands, "Where are you right now?"

"I'm in Creek Water, Missouri, Dad," I say, wondering how he could have possibly gone senile since yesterday.

"No, no, no. Not what town are you in, *where* in town are you?"

I look up at the street sign and answer, "I'm standing on the corner of Magnolia Way and Cricket Lane. Why?"

"Don't move!" he demands.

I actually stand still for five minutes before wondering what I'm doing. Why doesn't my dad want me to move? I finally start to walk again, only to barely miss getting hit by a car that comes barreling toward me. It comes to a screeching halt right before contact is made, leaving me breathless and in shock. I regularly dodged oncoming traffic in Manhattan, so that's not new to me, but it wasn't my expectation that I'd be doing that here.

Before my heart rate can slow, the passenger side door opens, and my dad gets out. *What's he doing here?*

I watch as he asks the driver to wait a minute. "Dad?"

He looks around all twitchy and nervous while answering, "I need you to take me to that place you sent me pictures of yesterday."

I wrack my brain trying to remember what pictures I sent him. There was one of the airport, several of the drive to Creek Water to prove that I arrived safely, and then there were the ones of the loft at the old sewing machine factory.

I assume he doesn't mean the airport as he was just there. "You mean the loft?"

He nods excitedly. "Yes. Take me there."

I stare at him, concerned for his sanity. His sandy blond hair is all ruffled and going in multiple directions. His handsome, yet distracted, face is flush with excitement. Essentially, he looks like himself, with the exception of the manic look in his eyes.

"Are you planning to stay for a while? Did you bring a suitcase?" I ask.

"Didn't have time," he answers. "My toolkit is in the trunk, though." His toolkit is where he keeps his paints and brushes.

"I'm sorry, why didn't you have time?" I'm beyond confused as to what's going on.

"When I went online to find a flight, I only had enough time to grab my paints and get on the subway. As it was, I was the last passenger on the plane before they closed the doors."

"Dad, why are you here?" I sound like a broken record. My father's previous attitude about Missouri was one of fear, but now he's standing in front of me, demanding to be shown around. He's hijacking my vacation.

"I need to see that loft. I need to see that lighting in person."

The loft space truly is extraordinary, the way the sun reflects off the river, casting shadows in the corners while illuminating the majority of the space like a biblical epiphany could occur at any moment. I can see how it speaks to my dad. That *is* why I sent him the photos, after all. I never thought he'd be driven to come in person, though.

Bertie is an odd duck to say the least, and while I'm used to his eccentric behavior, I still would have never expected him to leave New York on his own. I get into the Uber with him and ask, "What does Mom think about this?"

He shrugs. "I don't know. I left her a note."

What? "You left her a note? I demand. "What did you say in it?"

"That I'd gone to Missouri and would talk to her later." When my parents leave New York, it's always together and always for somewhere in Europe. My mother is going to freak when she finds out my dad has taken off on his own.

"Why were you in such a hurry to get here?"

He stares at me like I haven't been paying attention and yells, "It's the lighting! Why doesn't anyone ever mention the spectacular lighting in Missouri?"

I take a moment to thank God that my dad got here safely. For such an accomplished man, he can be remarkably simple—like Forest Gump simple. I have flashes of us walking through Central Park together and him stopping in the middle of a path and lying down on it, forcing people to walk around him. He was looking at a cloud formation and had to stare at it for twenty minutes to commit it to memory. Once he stayed on the Staten Island ferry all day, going back and forth, enraptured by the wave patterns that formed on the water.

"You came here for the lighting?" I ask.

"Lexi, I came because I was inspired. There's a new series of paintings bubbling up inside me and I need to let it out. If I can capture the feelings in here," he taps his head and then his heart, "I will create the most magnificent paintings of my life! The lighting is the key."

I have no words. Just when I thought my dad was as bizarre as it was possible for him to be, he raises the weirdness bar. The frenzied look in his eyes is the same I've seen multiple times before and during periods of creativity. But there's something different now; it's more intense, like he's a mad scientist or something.

I have no idea how I'm going to explain his arrival to Emmie, but I don't dwell on it. She's had enough exposure to my family to realize anything goes. So, I close my mouth and look out the window as the driver takes us to our destiny.

Chapter 19

"Bertie, what are you doing here?" Emmie claps her hands in excitement before giving my dad a hug.

"I didn't realize what a beautiful sun you have here in Missouri," he says instead of answering. "Why didn't you ever tell me?"

"Dad," I interrupt. "You do realize you're still on Earth, right? And the sun here is the same one that we have in New York?"

"It filters differently here," he explains. "It may be the same heavenly body, but it might as well not be. I need to see that loft, Emmie," he tells my friend.

Emmie looks positively delighted by his unusual behavior. She tells the girl who works for her that she's going to go upstairs and that she should call her if she needs anything. Then my friend leads the way through the old factory, giving my dad a brief rundown as we go.

Bertie doesn't say anything. He's obviously so amped up to get upstairs he's not paying attention to anything or anyone.

When we get to the second floor to pick up the keys, I wait in the hallway. I'm not prepared to see Beau again so soon. My insides are still doing flips over that moment we shared by the icehouse. Also, I can't imagine what he'll make of my dad.

But when Emmie comes out of Beau's office, he's with her. Drat. He stares at Emmie while he says, "I've come to meet your *boyfriend,* Lexi." He's obviously saying that for his cousin's benefit as I already told him I wasn't seeing anyone.

Emmie intervenes, "Bertie is Lexi's dad, not her boyfriend."

"But you told me," he starts to say, when my friend smacks him on the arm to shut him up.

"Forget about what I told you," she says.

Beau rolls his eyes. Clearly he's back to feeling annoyed. Apparently it's the main emotion he feels in my presence. I'm starting to think it's a defense mechanism as he tries to keep distance between us. I know he wanted me in his arms early today, just as much as I wanted to be there. I'd put money it.

Beau addresses my dad, "Bertie, is it?" Then he puts his hand out to shake his. "It's a pleasure to meet you."

My dad is so excited I'm surprised he can speak. He manages to reply, "Nice to meet you, too."

The last time I saw him anything close to this jittery was when he produced his last major exhibit. One of the paintings is currently hanging in the Museum of Modern Art, on loan from the billionaire who bought it. Bertie is certainly on the verge of something. Happiness is building inside me knowing that his funk is ending and I will get to watch his genius unfold.

Watching my dad walk into the loft on the third floor is as close to performance art as I've ever seen. He crosses the threshold, puts his toolbox down, and then he performs a sort of ballet as he's pulled in one direction, then the other before he virtually leaps toward the window.

Emmie and Beau share glances that make me think they're trying to discern whether or not they should call 911. "Dad," I begin, hoping I can bring him back into reality so he's not quite so freaky to watch.

Alas, my one-word plea is to no avail. He starts to shake his hands like he's wielding invisible castanets and says, "No, no, no, no, no … no talking!" Then he lies down on the floor, as close to the window as he can, and stares up into the sky until the three of us are really uncomfortable. Well, I am. Long moments pass before he finally declares, "This is it. This is where I have to be."

Beau looks at me, clearly concerned for my gene pool, and asks, "Why does he have to be here? And more importantly, how long does he have to be here?"

My dad springs to his feet like a fully wound jack-in-the-box and answers, "I need to be here until I don't need to be here. It could be months, years!"

"Sir," Beau starts to explain, "this is our model condominium. We can't have you inhabiting it while we're trying to sell it."

Bertie starts to look panicky. "But I have to be here!"

"How about if I show you the other units? They have the same light and the same view, but they're not finished yet. Maybe we could rent one of those to you for a while."

My dad doesn't look sold on the idea, but he responds, "Show me now. Show me before the light changes."

As Dad retrieves his toolbox, I hear Beau nervously ask Emmie, "Is he sane?"

She answers, "Not in the least, which is why he's a famous artist. But don't worry, he's totally safe."

Her cousin doesn't look convinced, but he leads the way to the other units anyway. After comparing them, some two and three times over, my dad eventually declares that he'll take the corner one.

Beau gives him a ridiculously low quote to rent the space for three months, and another price if it turns into longer; Bertie insists that he'll need the place for as long as he needs it, leading Beau to give me a look which asks me to interpret my father's response. I can't. I'm too preoccupied wondering what my mom is going to make of this behavior. I guarantee she won't be happy.

Once Beau leaves to draw up a lease agreement, Emmie offers, "Bertie, you're more than welcome to stay at my mom's house with us."

He looks alarmed at the thought. "I have to stay here. I have to be here night and day so when inspiration hits, I can work." He gazes out the window and adds, "Winter on the water, who knew that's what I needed?"

Emmie is aware that my dad keeps some pretty strange hours while he paints. She asks, "Can I help you find a bed and some furniture?"

He shakes his head. "I'll pick up an air mattress and maybe some jars for my brushes." He adds, "I need to know where the nearest art store is, so I can get busy building my canvases."

I'm glad there was an unfinished unit because I know firsthand the mess Bertie is about to make. The weathered face of the fortune-teller pops into my thoughts. My life is changing in the most unexpected ways, and for the first time, I'm a bit worried I might not be able to handle them.

Chapter 20

I decide to rent a car while I'm here. My dad is going to need stuff and he doesn't know how to drive, so someone has to run errands for him. Bertie never paints on small canvases, so I'll probably get an SUV or minivan to haul the supplies he'll need to build his frames.

I tell Emmie that I have no idea when I'll be done but suggest it'll probably be late tonight. We have to rent him a refrigerator and pick up some basic kitchenware, as well as bedding, toiletries, and clothes.

She gives Bertie some names of restaurants in the area where he can get breakfast and lunch but has suggested he eat his evening meal with us. Of course, that will depend solely on where he is in his painting.

He tells her, "Sweet Emmeline, you may not see me often enough to even know I'm in town." It's the truth he speaks. My dad is very hermit-like while he's in the process of creating.

"I'll enjoy every encounter," she promises kindly before going back to work.

As Bertie and I walk to pick up the rental car, I realize I haven't told Emmie about seeing the house today. I've been otherwise occupied by the arrival of my dad, who I currently address, "You know this is crazy, right?"

He nods his head. "I do. I don't know how I'm going to explain this to Regina, but she knows me well enough to understand that I need to be where I say I need to be."

I hope she's as understanding as he thinks she'll be. Historically, my mom makes most of the big decisions in our family and I can't see her taking this one in stride.

Bertie says, "I'm glad you learned how to drive. Your mom and I didn't think you'd ever need to, but it's sure going to come in handy now." He's correct. But being that I haven't driven a car in over five years, we're going to have to stick to streets with lower speed limits. I don't think I'd be comfortable going any faster than thirty miles an hour.

I figure with my dad being so high on Missouri, now's the time to tell him about going through the old Frothingham house. "Beau showed me a house I'm interested in buying," I bravely announce.

Bertie stops dead in his tracks and turns to look at me. "I'm sorry, what did you say? My mind's wandering a bit." So, I repeat myself. My dad tilts his head to the side like he's trying to translate my words. "Do you want to live here because of the light?" he finally asks.

While I feel like this might be the only reason he'd accept, I decide to go for the truth and say, "I fell in love with the house. It was one of the first houses in Missouri used in the Underground Railroad."

"Really?" he exclaims. "That's fabulous! I can't wait to see it." I have no idea who this man is and what he's done with my real father, but I figure we'll both have an easier time of breaking things to my mom if we're a united front, so I hop on board the crazy train with him, grateful he seems open to my newfound goal.

"I'll drive you by after we're done shopping. How does that sound?"

"That's probably the best time," he agrees. "I'll be too busy stretching and treating canvases after that."

While I can tell my dad is a tiny bit nervous about being outside of New York City, he's mostly so excited that he buzzes around various stores like a seven-year-old on a sugar rush. *Man, when he crashes, he's going to go down hard.*

After finding an art supply store and making the necessary purchases for him to build canvases, we hit Goodwill for kitchen items. Bertie thinks it would be a waste to spend money to buy new things as he'll only be here for a finite amount of time. He announces, "I need one of everything. One plate, one glass, one mug, one set of silverware."

"What if I come over?" I ask.

"Fine, we'll get two of everything," he says.

"What if Mom comes down some weekend?" I wonder. But before he can answer, we both start laughing hysterically. There's no way my mom is ever going to visit my dad while he's here. In fact, if they see each other at all, he'll be the one who has to travel. This is untrod territory in the life of Lambertos Blake. Things are bound to get interesting for him.

We eventually get four of everything in case Emmie and her mom happen to stop by, despite Bertie's warnings that he's here to work, not socialize.

We stop at the grocery store to get a few items that don't need refrigeration. Dad's rental refrigerator has been scheduled to be delivered tomorrow, so we'll have to shop again after that. Once we have everything, I drive us over to Millionaire's Row. I pull up in front of the house and Bertie lets himself out of the car and starts to wander the property. He doesn't even look at the house.

He stops and stares at the huge oak trees, lies down under a weeping willow, and then moves to stare up at the sky while sitting in the gazebo. After nearly thirty minutes of this behavior, I call him up onto the porch where I've been waiting. "So, what do you think?" I ask.

"I think it's the most beautiful park I've ever seen," he says in awe.

"Dad, it's not a park, this would be my yard," I explain. His brain must be on overload.

"People live like this?" he asks with such confusion that I have to laugh.

"I think this is a little beyond how most people live, but yes, this is all part of the property I want to buy."

"Did you win the lottery or something?" he wants to know. When I tell him the asking price, he slumps down on the steps next to me with his mouth hanging wide open, seemingly unable to speak.

When he finds his words, he says, "Your mother is going to be so mad at us."

"Yes, she is," I agree. "We have to figure out a way to get her down to visit while you're here."

"I thought about that the whole plane ride here."

"Did you come up with anything?" I ask.

He shrugs his shoulders. "I've got a couple things cooking away in the old hopper. I'll let you know when something comes together. In the meantime, I better turn my phone back on. I'm pretty sure Regina has been trying to call me for the last couple of hours."

This really is a new Bertie. Turning off his phone to avoid talking to Mom is not something he's ever done before, well, that I know of. Once he's powered it up, he shows me his voicemail icon and I see that he has twenty-eight messages. We both know every last one of them is from my mother.

Chapter 21

Dad plays my mom's messages on speaker while we drive back to his new digs. They start out concerned and escalate from there. They begin with her calling from work and extend to twenty minutes ago.

Message one: Hi, Bertie, I'm heading home and thought I'd pick up some Vietnamese for dinner. Let me know what you want.

Message two: I ordered you the *Bánh tằm cà ri* and I got the *Bún ốc*, we can share.

Message three: Bertie, where are you? I just got home and you're not here.

Message four: You're in Missouri?! What in the hell were you thinking? When will you be back?

The messages deteriorate from there into total and complete outrage that my dad isn't returning her calls.

Message twenty-eight: I contacted the airlines and found out that your plane arrived safely, therefore you'd better be in the hospital. That is the ONLY excuse for you not returning my calls I can accept. But if you're not dead and you deign to call me back, you should know that I'm not speaking to you."

Oh boy, this is going to be fun … Not. I ask my dad, "Do you want me to talk to her for you?" Not that I want to do any such thing, but as I've mentioned before, I don't mind fighting with my mom.

He shakes his head. "Want privacy?" I'm not sure I want to witness this.

"I might need you." He waits for me to nod before he hits redial. I start to sweat. As expected, my mom doesn't answer. She lets the call go into voicemail. My dad says, "Honey, it's the lighting. I had to see it for myself. I know it's upsetting that I left like I did, but the spirit moved me, and I had to go. I've rented a place in the building Lexi sent pictures of and I'm going to paint my new series here. I hope you understand. Please call me. I love you."

"Do you think she will?" I ask.

"Not sure. It'll probably be a few days, if she does. This is going to be a lot for her to process."

"And you're okay with that?" I ask.

"I'm not exactly happy about it, but if I ignore my inspiration, I might as well get a job flipping burgers somewhere." He continues, "Creativity is a divine gift. It doesn't make sense and it can't be controlled. As such, my only options are to accept it or not. I decided long ago that I would always accept it."

It takes us the better part of an hour to unload my dad's supplies and get them put away. The sun has already set so he's not distracted by the lighting, but as I predicted, his energy rush is subsiding.

"You want to go out for dinner?" I ask. "We can eat downstairs at Filene's." Emmie said that if we wanted great steaks and were in the mood to spend money, we should try their location on the pier, but if we were in the market for sandwiches and the like, we should try their restaurant downstairs.

Dad tilts his head to the side in his signature thinking pose. "I kind of want Vietnamese now that your mom mentioned it."

I look at the list of restaurants that Emmie left and surprise, surprise, there's no Vietnamese food on it. "We can have Italian, American, diner food, or Chinese. Those are our only options."

My dad sighs. "Okay, let's go downstairs."

Filene's Factory, the name of their restaurant in this building, is the only business still open on the first floor. We're seated at a window booth with a view of the street.

My dad, who's been remarkably quiet for the last several minutes, declares, "I like the vibe of this town." He's quick to add, "Don't get me wrong, I don't feel safe yet, but there's a positive energy here that's hard to ignore."

"I'm glad you think so," I say, "because I'm going to put an offer in on the house I showed you." I've decided that my dad turning up unexpectedly is a positive sign. After all, if this isn't an unexpected event, nothing is.

Before you think I'm a complete rube believing in psychic phenomenon, this is a rather new development. I've never had a dog jump over me before, so when one did at the exact age I was told to expect it, I figure there might be something to the rest of the prediction.

My dad replies, "I was barely starting to wrap my head around you living in Atlanta for a while. I didn't like the idea, but I was adjusting to it."

"What do you think about me moving here instead?" I ask.

He nods his head, "I like it. There's something about it that feels right." Then he grimaces, "Your mom is going to be fit to be tied."

Before I can make a comment one way or the other, Beau and Shelby walk in to the restaurant. My dad spots them and stands up immediately. He flags them down by calling out, "Beau, come join us!"

I pray they won't, but Beau steers Shelby toward our table to say hello. He shakes my dad's hand and asks, "Are you settling in okay, Bertie?"

My dad smiles brightly. "I am. I can hardly wait to see what the morning light is going to be like." He quivers in anticipation.

Beau is being very nice to my dad.. He says, "I'd like you to meet my girl … I mean, my friend … I mean Shelby." He turns to Shelby who so far hasn't said a word. She doesn't look particularly happy to be here.

My dad effuses, "I'm very pleased to meet you." He takes Shelby's hand between both of his and doesn't so much shake it as squeeze it.

She forces a sad smile and says, "Thank you. I'm happy to meet you, as well." Then she turns to me and greets, "Lexi, it's nice to see you again." I don't think she really means it, but she's trying. The poor girl is clearly going through something.

My dad motions toward our table and says, "Please join us. Lexi and I would both like to learn more about Creek Water."

Beau looks surprised by the invitation and seems on the verge of declining it when Shelby sits down next to my dad. I guess she's made the decision for them.

Beau appears paralyzed about what to do next. He can either join us or make a run for it. He seems to be weighing his options closely. He finally scoots in next to me, but settles so far away I'm pretty sure he has one butt cheek hanging off the edge of the seat.

My dad doesn't seem to be aware of the uncomfortable undercurrents going on and starts to chatter like a magpie. The rest of us sit quietly and let him.

Chapter 22

Once Beau answers about a thousand questions, Bertie points between him and Shelby and asks, "So, how long have you two been seeing each other?" He might as well have asked them to strip naked while doing the hokey pokey.

Beau falters slightly before answering, "We've been together on and off for several months."

"We were pregnant and then lost the baby. We weren't together at the time," Shelby adds. *Talk about oversharing.*

You gotta love my dad, though. Social cues aren't something he altogether understands, so while most people would have changed the subject to less emotional ground, he jumps in with both feet and empathizes, "Regina, Lexi's mom, and I had two miscarriages. They were brutal." He continues, "I'm so sorry for your loss."

Tears come to Shelby's eyes and she mumbles, "Thank you. I'm pretty torn up over it."

My dad says, "Losing a pregnancy isn't only hard emotionally, there's a physical toll, as well."

Shelby starts full on bawling now. Bertie pats her hand and asks, "Are you talking to someone about what you're going through? Regina met with a therapist for a while and it really helped her. Her doctor prescribed some supplements."

Shelby shakes her head. "My mama would die of embarrassment if I went to a therapist. Beau and I talk about it some, though."

Beau is sitting so rigidly, he looks like he's got a stick up his backside. This is clearly not a conversation he's comfortable having in front of us. He says, "I didn't find out about the pregnancy until right before it ended, so I didn't have as much time to bond with the idea as Shelby had."

Bertie shakes his head. "Son, society underrates the mourning a man goes through when a baby is lost. I'm glad you and Shelby have each other to lean on." Oh, terrific, my dad is endorsing their relationship, which clearly means that I need to stop feeling this attraction. Beau has run so hot and cold around me I can only assume my reaction to him is chemical. The problem is, I'm not sure how to make that go away.

Shelby asks, "How long did it take your wife to start feeling like herself again?"

"Regina and I aren't married," my dad says matter-of-factly. "We've been together for thirty-five years though, so we're a solid couple."

Shelby looks surprised by this news and Beau full on gawps like he's never heard of such a thing. The silence is deafening. For some reason, Bertie feels the need to add, "Regina thinks marriage is a form of slavery."

"Really?" Beau asks at the same time Shelby declares, "She's right."

Beau turns to Shelby and demands, "What do you mean, she's right?"

"Look at my parents," she replies. "They don't even love each other; they simply co-exist like they're in some kinda business arrangement. Mama tells Daddy what to do and he does it, but then he goes off and cheats on her. It's disgusting."

Bertie intervenes, "In Regina's case, she feels like it's the women who are the slaves." He adds, "Which is clearly nonsense. A good relationship is about equality and partnership. Sometimes one person does more, and sometimes the other one does, but in the end it all balances out."

Shelby says, "It sounds like you want to be married."

"I do," my dad confesses. It's the first time I've ever heard him say that.

"I don't think I want to be," Shelby decides.

"What do mean?" Beau demands. "I thought you were always hoping to get married."

"That's what my mama wants. But I think I want what Bertie and Regina have. I want the person I'm with to be bound to me out of love and devotion and not out of legal duty. I think people have to try harder if their partner doesn't have a lawful obligation." She turns to my dad and asks, "What do you think? Do you try harder because Regina could walk away if she wanted to?"

Bertie looks like he's been hit in the face with a bucket of ice water. "I don't know," he finally answers. "I don't think so. I'm pretty sure I'd be the same person I am now if we were legally wed." I think he's suddenly worried that my mom might consider his coming to Missouri as an act of abandonment. If so, there's no telling what she'd do.

Beau stares at Shelby and demands, "Are you saying that you

want to live with someone and raise a family with them but not be married?"

Shelby seems to be missing the defiance in his tone, and answers, "That's what I'm saying."

"That's unseemly, Shelby," Beau decides. Then belatedly, he looks at my dad and adds, "I don't mean to offend you, Bertie."

"No offense taken, son. Like I said, I'd like to be married to Regina, but she doesn't share my feelings."

I can't stay quiet another minute and ask, "Does Mom know how you feel, Dad?"

"Of course, she knows. We talk about it all the time."

"You do?" I've never heard them say a word in my earshot.

"I ask your mother to marry me every year on the anniversary of our moving in together. Every year she says that we're fine the way we are."

My heart hurts hearing this. I never knew he did that. "Dad, you need to stand up for yourself and not let Mom run you over like this."

"Honey, I love your mother. She's giving all that she thinks she can. Just because I want to be married in the eyes of the law doesn't mean she has to want the same thing. And if we have to continue on like we are in order to be together, then so be it. Regina is worth it."

I can't help but wonder if my mom shares his sentiment.

Chapter 23

The rest of the meal is insanely uncomfortable. Beau keeps peeking at me out of the corner of his eye like I'm some kind of science experiment gone wrong. Finally, over crème brûlée, he says, "I suppose you don't want to get married, either."

"I definitely do," I tell him. "I share my mom's beliefs about equality, but I take after my dad on the marriage front."

"Do you wish your parents had been married?" he asks.

My dad waits for my answer, as though on tenterhooks. "I do," I finally answer. "Aside from believing in the institution, I think it's a comfort for a child to know that their parents love each other enough to commit in that way."

Poor Bertie looks like I've kicked him in the stomach when he asks, "Did you worry your mom and I didn't love each other?"

"No, Dad. I always knew you did. Mom marches to her own tune. And while I respect that, my tune is a little more traditional."

Shelby interrupts, "I've never felt like my parents' marriage meant anything other than they were doing something they were supposed to do."

"My folks are very committed to each other and love each

other deeply. I want what they have and that includes marriage," Beau interjects.

Shelby acts like she couldn't care less. She shrugs her shoulders and says, "Then you should go for it." I have a feeling they have a big conversation in their near future. Clearly, they aren't seeing eye to eye on one of the basic principles of coupledom. I try to push away a feeling of excitement that's creeping in.

Beau asks for the check, but when it comes, I make a grab for it. He pulls it out of my hand. "Dinner is on me," he says.

"Beau, we asked you to join us. This is our treat," I reply. Bertie doesn't so much as twitch, let alone make a move for his wallet. My mom puts the food expenses on her credit card, so he's not in the habit of paying when the bill comes.

"No, ma'am," Beau says. "A gentleman likes to pay."

Shelby grabs the check from Beau's hand and declares, "Oh, for corn sake, no woman needs a man to pay for her. I'm buying."

Beau looks at her like her head is about to spin around *Exorcist*-style. "I thought you liked that I paid," he accuses.

Shelby shrugs, "Maybe I used to, but times and people are changing, Beauregard. I don't have to be the woman I always was. I'm evolving." I'm not sure I'd call what Shelby's doing evolving as much as finally realizing who she is outside of her mother's shadow.

My dad announces, "I'm perfectly delighted to have *any* of you take me out and I'm evolved enough to let you." He turns to Shelby, "Thank you for dinner, young lady." Then he looks at me and Beau and declares, "You can treat me another time."

Beau chuckles. I'm not sure if it's out of appreciation for my dad's sense of humor—although I know he's not joking—or a much-needed tension breaker, but either way, he says, "I'll look forward to sharing another meal with you, Bertie. This one was certainly enlightening."

Beau and Shelby leave after Shelby pays the bill. My dad asks for a coffee refill before declaring, "I'm sorry, honey. I never knew before how you felt about your mom and me."

"I didn't spend every waking moment worrying about it, Dad."

"Even so, if Regina knew it meant that much to you, maybe she would have agreed to get married."

"It doesn't matter anymore," I say. "You made your choices and I'm going to make mine. That's how life goes, right? We're all responsible for our own happiness."

Bertie sighs. "Life feels more complicated than it did before I came here."

I snort rather loudly. "*Your* life is a lot more complicated. I'm not sure Mom is ever going to forgive you."

"Maybe not," he says. "But after all these years together and all the concessions I've made for her, she needs to give me a pass on this one."

I'm not sure what concessions he's talking about, but he seems to have discovered a backbone he's rarely displayed in the past regarding my mother. For both their sakes, I hope she forgives him quickly.

I walk my dad back up to his rental and help him blow up his air mattress. Then I make up his bed for him and even fill his new coffee pot so all he has to do is turn it on in the morning.

Before I go, I say, "I'm really glad you're here, Dad. I love you."

He wraps his arms around me. "I love you too, honey. So, so much."

"I'll stop by tomorrow and see how you're doing. Let me know if we forgot anything that you need me to pick up on the way."

"Will do. But don't worry if you don't hear from me. I don't know what's going to happen tomorrow until I see the morning light. I may be too distracted to call."

I know exactly what he means. My dad is notorious for forgetting to feed himself or even shower during times of great inspiration. My mom always nags him into acting semi-human when he's in the midst of a creative surge. For as much as Regina claims that marriage is slavery, she does a lot for my dad. I can't imagine things would be any different in their day-to-day relationship if the state of New York declared them legal. I'll happily take her place while he's here to ensure his continued existence, because that's what family does for each other.

I know one thing for sure, I'm going to call my mom tomorrow and act as my dad's champion. I'm guessing she might feel a little ganged up on, but it's the right thing to do. I probably won't mention the fact that I'm planning on moving here during that particular call. Better to pace myself and let Regina absorb one bombshell at a time.

Chapter 24

Emmie is still out with Zach when I get back to her house, so I quietly let myself in and go right to bed. I lie there for ages, replaying the day in my head before finally giving up and taking a blanket outside. I'm asleep within seconds.

When I wake up, it's morning and I feel refreshed and full of energy. I can't wait to tell Emmie and her mom that I've decided to move to Creek Water. I grab my blanket and rush inside to find them planking to "What's Love Got to Do With It?"

"Don't get up on my account," I say. "I wanted to let you know that I'm going to put in an offer on your old family home." They both drop to the floor.

"What are you talking about?" Emmie demands. "You mean the house on Millionaire's Row?"

"That's the one," I tell her.

Both Emmie and Gracie are on their feet in seconds. Gracie demands, "You're gonna live here in Creek Water? Honey, that's the next best thing to happen since Emmie came home with the baby!"

I love how excited they are. Emmie looks like she's going to pop right out of her skin. "When did Beau show you the house?

What are you going to do for work? You want to come work for us? I mean, the money would be nothing like you're used to, but it would be something."

I shake my head. "I saw the property yesterday, and no, I don't want to work for you, I'm going to turn the house into a bed and breakfast."

"What a fantastic idea," Gracie declares. "I can't wait to tell Lee." She's got her phone in her hand and she's typing away in no time flat.

By the time I'm pouring my first cup of coffee, Lee is storming through the front door. When she spots me, she screams like I'm a rock star and she's twelve. "Oh. My. GOOOODDDDDDDD!!!" she shouts. "What a fabulous idea. I'm so thrilled I can hardly stand it!" "Wait until you meet the neighbors," she says.

"Are they nice?" I ask, momentarily worried.

All three Frothingham women share a look before Emmie exclaims, "So nice!"

Before I can ask about them, Lee commands, "All y'all go get changed. Let's go see Beau together."

We're dressed and down at the old sewing machine factory in under an hour. We do not arrive in an understated fashion, what with all the chattering and flurry of excitement emanating from our little group.

The receptionist says, "I'll let him know you're here."

But Lee waves her off and shouts, "Beauregard, it's your mama. I'm coming in."

Beau walks out of his office. "What are y'all doing here?" he demands.

"Is that any way to talk to me?" Then she leads the march

into her son's office. Once we're all settled, she announces, "We have some happy news."

"What in the world could that be?" he demands. I swear I witness a grimace, but it happens so fast I couldn't put money on it.

"Lexi here wants to place an offer on the old family home. Isn't that the most exciting thing you've ever heard?"

Beau does not seem to share his mother's enthusiasm. In fact, if this were a cartoon, there would be steam coming out of his ears. "That's not a very good idea," he finally says.

Lee replies, "Why not? I think it's just about the best idea I've ever heard."

"It's a big house for one woman, Mama."

Gracie asks, "Would it be too big for a man?"

Beau replies, "A man would have an easier time taking care of it."

"What?" his mother yelps. "I did a better job raising you than that, young man. Don't you go acting like some kind of male chauvinist."

"I didn't say she couldn't do it, I said it would be a lot of work."

Emmie wants a piece of this. "No, sir, you said it was too much house for one woman. You need to apologize."

"I don't need to do any such thing. I do not think that Lexi should buy this house. There, I said it."

"I don't care what you think, Beau. You sit down and prepare the offer like you're being paid to do," Lee admonishes. He stares at her like she's an alien—an alien who might put him into a time-out if he doesn't behave himself.

"Mama," he starts to say, but she cuts him off.

"Don't you *Mama* me. Sit down and do your job."

Beau looks at me and says, "You're going to need an inspection. And just so you know, the roof probably only has a couple of years left on it. A new one will run you twenty grand, easy."

Lee demands, "What's going on here?" She looks between me and Beau.

I shrug my shoulders. "He's trying to convince me that I shouldn't buy the house by predicting doom and gloom."

"No, ma'am," she says. "There's something more." She looks at her son and adds, "If you don't want me to start speculating, boy, you better get busy and do your job."

Boy jumps to it. It's fun to see the kind of pull Lee has over her son. As tough as he tries to be with me, he apparently knows he doesn't stand a chance against his own mother.

Beau sighs. "How much do you want to offer?"

"Full price," I tell him.

"Traditionally, people put in a lowball offer when the house has been on the market for a while. We should go in low and let them counter," he advises.

"Nope," I tell him. "I think the house is worth a lot more than they're asking, so offer the full hundred and forty, contingent on the inspection passing, of course."

"Do you have a mortgage company lined up?" he asks.

"I'll find one today and get going on it."

Beau changes strategy and tries to be nice. "Lexi, I really don't think this is the right move for you. If you're set on living in Creek Water, why don't you let me find you something a little more manageable."

"Beau," Lee cautions, "you're being condescending, and I demand you stop it right now."

"The reason I want to live here is because of that house," I say.

He apparently knows when he's licked because he stops talking and starts typing on his computer, although he looks none too happy about it.

By the time we leave his office, I'm flying high on life. I can't believe I'm about to become a homeowner.

Emmie asks, "Do you think we can take Mama and Auntie Lee up to meet your daddy while we're here?" Three hopeful faces stare at me.

"I suppose now would be the best time. Once Bertie starts painting, he's not going to want to do any socializing." Although I know he won't be overly enthusiastic to have us all drop by, I don't know how to keep that from happening. We're only one floor away, so there's no point in calling to give him two minutes warning.

I say a little prayer and lead the way, hoping for the best.

Chapter 25

I knock on the door, but there's no answer. So, I knock louder, but still nothing. "Maybe he's in the shower," I say to Emmie and family. Although I'm guessing that's probably not the case as personal hygiene often takes a holiday when my dad is in the throes of creating.

Emmie suggests, "Why don't you go in and check on him, and we can come back another time?"

"That's probably for the best," I tell them.

"Shoot," Gracie says. "I was excited to meet your daddy. Why don't you ask him when he thinks the best time is for us to have him over? We can make our schedule work around his."

I agree before saying goodbye to the Frothingham contingent and using the spare key to open Bertie's door. I'm not prepared for what I find. Dad has already assembled three huge canvases that are lying on the floor. Each must be at least ten feet square. It looks like he's already primed them because the canvas is bright white instead of its natural oatmeal color.

"Dad!" I call out as I walk in. No answer. I start looking around the space, but don't see him anywhere. I climb the stairs to the sleeping loft and call out again. Nothing. When I get to the top stair, I'm greeted by a sight that I've never seen before. My dad is near the far wall standing on his head.

I rush over to him, but he doesn't move. I touch his ankle and find that's it's icy cold. My god, has he died standing on his head? He's so rigid, I start to wonder. When I shake him gently and he doesn't come to, I start to panic. I shout, "DAD! WAKE UP!" Nothing.

I'm about to dial 911, but for some reason, I call my mom first. She answers, "Do you see what you've done, traipsing off to God-knows-where, Missouri?"

"Mom, I don't have time for this conversation. I think Dad might be dead."

"Explain." That's all she says. There isn't so much as a hint of concern in her voice.

"He's standing on his head and he's not answering me when I call his name. Not even when I shake his frozen foot. Seriously, I think he's …" I pause as emotion chokes me, before continuing, "gone."

"Could be," she coldly answers. "But before you call the ambulance, try saying the words, 'Ob-la-di, ob-la-da, life goes on, brah, la-la how their life goes on.'"

"You want me to sing a Beatles song to him now?" What's wrong with this woman?

"You don't have to sing it," she says. "Just say it."

I've never read about this particular brand of first aid, but these *are* my parents, so I try it. I repeat the lyrics and watch as my dad's eyes pop open. *What kind of strange magic is this?*

I demand, "Dad, what are you doing?"

He smiles an upside-down smile because he's on his head.

"Hi, sweetheart. I'm meditating. What are you doing here?"

"I was checking on you. I thought you were dead." I add, "You were so cold."

"What time is it?" he asks.

"Ten thirty. Why?"

"I start to go cold after an hour," he tells me.

"You've been on your head for over an hour? I don't think that's safe, Dad."

He gradually bends his knees and rolls onto his back. While lying on the floor, he answers, "Of course it is. I've built up to it."

"I knew you did yoga, but I didn't know you could stand on your head. Why do you do it for so long?"

He answers, "It's good for nearly every bodily system, but I do it to recharge and tap into my creativity. Standing on my head for two hours is the equivalent of six hours of sleep for me."

"Two hours? How do you know to wake up after that amount of time?"

"My internal clock is in pristine working order. How did you wake me up before my two hours was done?" he asks curiously.

I show him my phone, "Mom." Then I remember Regina is on the phone and put it up to my ear. "Mom, he's not dead," I say with great relief.

"Too bad," she tells me.

I say, "Mother! What kind of thing is that to say?" at the same time my dad reaches his hand out and declares, "Give me the phone."

I do, but when he says, "Hello, Regina?" she doesn't answer him. He repeats, "Regina, honey, hello?" Nothing.

He hands the phone back and says, "She hung up on me."

I have so many questions, I don't know where to begin. I start with, "What if there was an emergency like the building was burning down? Would you have regained consciousness first?"

He gradually sits up. "Pretty sure."

"What do you mean by that? Don't you know?"

"I programmed my mind to only respond to the lyrics from 'Life Goes On,' but I'm guessing a siren would probably wake me up."

My dad is like a child. I demand, "How do you program yourself?"

"I go into a deep meditation and then tell myself what words or sounds to react to. It's really a matter of self-hypnosis."

"I don't want you doing a headstand again until you program the following scenarios: When you hear the word 'Dad,' you wake up. Sirens and alarms will wake you up. Excessively loud knocking on your door will wake you up. Do you understand?" I ask.

He nods his head slowly. "Sure, honey. I got it."

"I'm going to move in with you until I know you've done it."

"Why?" he wants to know.

"Because I don't want you dying any time soon!" I yell.

"Okay, but I just told you I'd do it. I promise, I will."

My dad truly believes what he's telling me right now. But the chances of him actually following through are about fifty-fifty. He doesn't set out to lie. The problem is that he doesn't excel at follow through.

"Are you awake now?" I ask.

"You bet. I'm going to make some coffee and see what the lighting looks like now," he tells me.

"Okay, I'm going to go over to Emmie's and get my things. Then I'm going to buy another air mattress. I'll be back in a couple of hours."

"Can you bring me a sandwich?" he asks.

"Yes, Dad, I'll bring you a sandwich. No mediating until I get back," I warn again.

He smiles before changing his mind. "I think I might take a little nap. A one-hour headstand only equals three hours of sleep. I need a tiny bit more."

I leave his apartment, praying that he'll be all right when I return. I briefly wonder how my mom ever leaves him alone, as I'm pretty sure Bertie might need a keeper.

Chapter 26

I stop in Emmeline's to tell Emmie what I'm up to.

She asks, "Do you want me to check on your daddy while you're gone?"

"I don't think that'll be necessary," I tell her. "But I do think it's for the best if I stay with him for a while."

"I'll miss you. But now that you're going to live in town, I suppose I can allow it," she teases.

"You need me to get anything for you while I'm out?" I ask.

"No, ma'am. I'm good to go. I'll see you in bit," she says.

As I walk out onto the street, I look around with different eyes. This is no longer only Emmie's town, it's mine, too. I feel a sense of hope and excitement and perhaps a tiny dash of nerves. I've never done anything this impetuous in my whole life.

Driving over to Emmie's house to collect my things, I try to play out the worst-case scenario. The most awful thing I can come up with would be that I hate living here, have to sell the house, and no one would want to buy it.

I try to envision that possibility, but I can't. I love that house so much that even if my B&B idea is a bust, I'd do something else that would allow me to keep it. Of course, my B&B is not going to be a flop because who in the world wouldn't want to stay there?

After packing up, and buying an air mattress and bedding, I hit the grocery store to get some things that I need. In the deli area, while ordering sandwiches for Dad's and my lunch, I run into Shelby. She's with her scary mother.

Shelby smiles genuinely and greets, "Hi, Lexi. How are you doing?"

"Good," I tell her. "I'm picking up lunch for my dad."

"I really enjoyed meeting him last night. He's quite a character, isn't he?"

"Very much so," I say while grimacing to indicate she doesn't know the half of it.

Shelby says, "You remember my mama?" Then she introduces us again. Hopefully this time will be more successful than the night at the club. "Mama, this is Lexi Blake from New York. Lexi, this is my mama, Cootie Wilcox."

Goosebumps rise to the surface of my skin like I'm standing in front of the devil herself. I reach out my hand and force myself to say, "It's a pleasure to meet you."

Cootie doesn't take my hand. Instead, she demands, "How long are you stayin' here for?"

For some reason, I don't tell her that I'm hoping to become a permanent resident. Instead, I say, "For about a month."

"Why so long?" she demands.

"I'm between jobs and I miss my friend, so I thought I'd visit for a while."

Shelby intervenes, "You let me know if you need anything, okay?"

I smile, feeling a genuine like for Shelby. Last night's dinner went miles toward making her more relatable. "I will," I tell her. "Bertie wants to have dinner with you again and this time it's on us."

Cootie has since glared at me and walked away toward the seafood display. I say, "I don't think your mom's happy that I'm here."

She waves her hand. "Don't pay her any mind. She's not happy about anything since I told her about losing the baby. She says I'm an embarrassment."

"That's horrible," I gasp.

"It's okay. Whenever she says that, I tell her now she knows how I feel."

I giggle before I can stop myself. "You're going through a tough time," I tell her. "You let me know if you need anything, okay?"

"Thank you, Lexi. That's very nice of you." Her gaze veers off to watch as her mother yells at the man behind the seafood counter about the size of his king crabs. She's claiming they aren't even queen crabs.

Shelby says, "I'd best be going. I'll see you around, okay?"

For the life of me, I can't imagine that she was ever anything like her mother. While she's kind of a tragic character, she also seems pretty grounded and unimpressed by her mom's behavior. I wish I knew what she and Beau were to each other.

After buying groceries, I drive back to Dad's loft. He doesn't answer the door, so I let myself in and discover that he's still sleeping. I take the opportunity to go online and apply for a mortgage. Luckily, I'm still employed by Silver Spoons and only need a small loan. I should have confirmation within a few days that my financing is in order.

I decide to call my mom back and demand what her problem is. Actually, I know what her problem is, so I suppose it would be more accurate to say what I need to do is find out how long she's going to be mad at my dad.

She answers, "What?"

"Hi, Mom," I say in an effort to make this a nicer conversation than our last. "Dad's fine. Thanks for giving me the secret code to bring him back to life."

"Why are you calling?" she demands.

"I thought you might want to know that Dad and I are both doing well. Our flights arrived safely, there haven't been any tornados or visits from the KKK." I can't help it; her attitude is giving me attitude.

"When is your father coming home?" she demands.

"I don't know," I tell her. "He's already built three huge canvases and he rented that loft I sent him pictures of. I'm guessing he'll be here for a while."

"You tell him that if he's gone too long, he might not be welcomed back."

"Mother!" I say. "What's wrong with you? I get that you're upset that Dad left without notice, but it's not like you don't know the man. He's artistic and impulsive. That's just who he is. He's the man you encouraged him to be all those years ago."

"Yes, well that might not be working for me anymore," she declares frostily. "I don't need a partner abandoning me without consulting me first. That's not who your father and I are."

"He's not abandoning you. He's following his creative flow."

I add, "Dad was in the midst of the longest dry spell I've ever known him to have. You should be happy he has his mojo back."

"Let me get right on that," she says sarcastically. Then she asks, "Is your father the only reason you called?"

"No," I tell her. "But you don't seem to be in a very receptive mood right now. Why don't you call me when you think you can be a little nicer?"

"Don't hold your breath," she snaps before hanging up.

My god, what's happening here? While not one to embrace ideas that she wasn't part of conceiving, Regina seems to be taking things to a rather dramatic level. Yes, my dad left without notice. Obviously, that wasn't the best way to deal with my mom, or anyone really. But for heaven's sake, she's known my him for thirty-five years, how big of a surprise could it really be that he's done something off the wall like this?

Chapter 27

Four hours later, my dad still isn't awake. I know that sometimes his sleep patterns are off when he's painting, but he hasn't even put any color on the canvas yet. I binge-watch home decorating shows on my phone while I wait for him to get up.

I'm surprised when the call comes in from the mortgage company saying that I've been approved for more than twice the amount I need. I tell the woman, "That didn't take long."

She replies, "You'd already applied for a much larger loan two months ago, and while we couldn't approve that, this request is well within reason."

I feel sick at the thought of what would have happened had I gotten the mortgage for the larger amount. I would have bought my apartment in New York; I would have never visited Emmie. In fact, I would have probably used my vacation to find some part-time work to bring in a couple of extra bucks to use for my down payment. Of course, then I'd have to find another job, one that paid enough to support my new endeavor. How depressing.

After hanging up, I take the elevator down to the second floor to Beau's office. He's about as happy to see me as I expected him to be. He doesn't even stand up when I walk through his door. Instead, he says, "What now?"

I'm not going to let his grumpiness bug me. I smile brightly and say, "I emailed you confirmation that my financing has come through."

"Already?" he demands.

"Yes." Then I ask, "Have you submitted my offer?"

"I have."

"And?" I demand. "Have you heard back from the seller?"

"They accepted it," he says, none too pleased.

I feel a jolt of excitement burst through me like the business end of a firecracker. "When were you going to tell me?" I demand.

"I was going to call you when I was done printing out the contract."

"Oh," I manage. "Sorry, I thought you were still trying to keep me from buying the house."

Beau stands up and slowly walks over to me. I'm tall at five eight, but he towers over me. My whole body starts sizzling as he approaches, like I'm a strip of bacon and he's an open flame. He stops in front of his desk and sits on it so we're looking directly into each other's eyes. "Why do you want this house so much?" he asks.

"I don't know," I honestly answer. "I guess that sometimes our desires don't make any sense." I continue, "I never thought I'd live anywhere but New York, but then I saw that house and felt like it had to be mine. Do you know what I mean? Have you ever wanted something that much?"

He looks like he's in physical pain as he answers, "Yes, I have."

"What have you wanted as much as I want this house?" I ask. It might make him more relatable to know.

He shakes his head slowly. "I don't think I'm going tell you that right now." His answer sends molten hot waves coursing through me. Somehow, I don't think we're talking about houses anymore.

I change the subject and ask, "How soon can I take ownership?"

"If the property passes inspection and there are no delays, you could be in as early as two weeks. But that's only because you've been pre-approved by your mortgage company."

"Two weeks?" Temporary insanity hits me, and I celebrate by throwing my arms around Beau and dancing around.

He's taken completely off guard by my overt display and lets me nearly tackle him. Instead of pulling back, he shifts his hold so that I'm as close to him as his own breath. I feel all warm and gooey like the cheese off a hot pizza.

I briefly realize that we need to stop this. Beau is somehow involved with Shelby. Even though Emmie's whole family says they aren't a couple, I've never heard that from either of them. Granted, they don't act like a couple, but I'm not going to insinuate myself in the middle of whatever is going on there. They have to figure that out on their own without outside complications.

I put my hands against Beau's chest to keep a tiny distance between us and then I rest my forehead against him. After taking a moment to collect myself, I gather all my willpower and gently push away from him. He lets me go like I'm a scorching hot coal fresh out of the fire.

"I'd like to walk through the house again? Can you can give me the keys?" I ask.

Beau clears his throat and inhales slowly like he's also trying to pull himself together. "You can't go in by yourself until closing, but I can take you in about ten minutes, if you don't mind waiting."

"That'll be fine," I manage. "I'll be out in reception." As I leave his office, I once again realize how right it feels to be in Beau's arms. I'm also sure that nothing can happen between us until I know what's going on between him and Shelby. But I don't know how I'm going to have the self-discipline not to throw myself at him again.

Chapter 28

My new address is 30 Dogwood Lane. I might be stretching things, but my grandmother's fortuneteller pops into my head, again. I was *thirty* the year the *dog* jumped over me. Could this all really be preordained? If my love of *Doctor Who* has taught me anything, it's to be open to the possibility that time is circular, not linear. Not that I'm sure I buy that, but it's certainly something that gives me pause.

Beau is all business when we arrive at the house. He says, "Let's do a walk-through. The inspector will be very thorough, but I want us to make a list of concerns that we want him to pay special attention to." What he wants to do is find a problem that's so big I'll walk away. If that's his plan, he's plain out of luck. I'd want this house even if it were infested with vermin.

I watch as he jumps on each and every step leading up to the front door to insure they're solidly made and there are no loose bricks. He seems almost disappointed when he doesn't fall through.

Once we walk into the house, I half expect him to pull out a magnifying glass like Sherlock Holmes. He turns every light switch on and off, checks the water lines in all the bathrooms, and even lies down to look under the kitchen sink. "The kitchen is going to cost you a fortune to update."

"I'm not going to put in some fancy chef's kitchen," I tell him. "I'll probably just strip the cabinets down and then stain them if the wood is in good enough shape. If not, I'll paint them." I'm also planning to buy a lot of accessories wholesale from Silver Spoons before they learn I'm not taking their job offer in Atlanta.

While that may seem a little underhanded—and I do feel bad for a split-second—these are the people who wanted me to work through my vacation at half pay before having me relocate to another state at a lower wage than I am currently earning. I don't feel as loyal as I once might have.

I pull a pad of paper out of my purse and start to catalog the things I want to buy in the next few weeks. As I scribble notes for myself, Beau excitedly says, "Looks like you're coming up with quite a list for the inspector."

"Nope," I tell him. "I'm writing down things to buy while I still have a discount at my old job."

He shakes his head. "I should have known." Then he asks, "Did you see the cracks in the kitchen floor?"

"It looks like cracked tile to me. I doubt it's a structural issue." I hope it's not anyway. I don't know the first thing about inspecting a house for safety, but Beau is seriously starting to piss me off.

"There's a broken window over here." I follow him into the breakfast nook to check it out. Sure enough, one of the bay windows is cracked. "Those are old, so they'll have to be special ordered. That won't be cheap," he warns.

"Beau," I demand, "make your list quietly. I don't want to hear one more negative thing out of you. Do you understand? Besides, you're making a commission. Be happy."

He tilts his head to the side as he shrugs his shoulders. "I understand what you're saying, but right now, I'm doing my job. I suppose I could withdraw your offer, and you could find yourself another realtor if you'd like."

I want to shake him until his teeth rattle. I'm sure he'd be happy to have me back out as it would buy him enough time to torch the place so there wasn't a house here for me to purchase. I decide to ignore him and go off on my own.

The floors are dark wood and some of them look like they could stand to be sanded down and re-stained. Although, upon closer inspection, I could probably lay down some area rugs and put that off for a year or two until some of the other more obvious work is done.

The ornamental plaster mouldings on the ceilings are works of art. My dad is going to go nuts for them. One of the many things that I love about this house is the fact that there are two staircases. The grand staircase in the entry is the one I'm sure the homeowners used. But there's another staircase off the kitchen that's much less impressive. It was probably the one the servants used. Although the passage is so narrow, I don't know how they ever managed to carry up and down trays of food and the like. I love them anyway.

I hear Beau's phone ring somewhere in the house. I'm currently heading up the family stairway to the third floor, which is really no more than a large attic. Happily, it's finished and even has an antique sewing machine that's still here. I'm going to have to ask Beau if it comes with the house.

There's a large wall of built-in closets that juts out off to the side of the room, fashioning a space that allows for a separate work area next to the sewing machine. I'm pretty sure the closets were put here to camouflage the secret room. I walk around them and notice there are doors on both sides. Most people would probably never suspect there was missing space, especially if the closets were full.

I walk inside one of the doors to try to find a hidden panel that would let me into the hiding place, but one doesn't seem to exist. I push and pull on clothing rods, bang on shelves, but nothing happens.

I don't know how long I'm up here, but it must be a good while. I finally walk over to inspect the sewing machine and see that it was made at the old factory here in town. What a cool find. I really hope I can talk the current owners into leaving it. I don't sew, but it looks like it belongs here.

I peek out one of the attic windows to scrutinize the view from so high up and spot Beau. He's standing next to Shelby, of all people. I wonder when she got here. I can't see their faces; from my angle, I mostly see the tops of their heads. They're standing very close together and I suddenly feel like I'm spying on a scene I'm not meant to witness. Which of course means I keep looking, I just scoot off to the side so if they look up they won't see me.

Beau brushes the hair off Shelby's face, and she takes his hand and gently kisses it before rubbing it against her cheek. Damn. So much for everyone saying they aren't a real couple. Moments later, they're in each other's arms hugging like they haven't seen each other in years. My heart falls into the gnawing pit that's developed in my stomach.

As much as I wish I'd never witnessed this, it's a good thing I did. Beau Frothingham is not for me. I need to push any thoughts of a romance with him out of my head for good. While I'm not pleased by this, I find it doesn't deter my desire for this house one bit.

Chapter 29

Beau's mom is standing in my soon-to-be kitchen talking to her son when I finally come back downstairs. Man, this house is becoming Grand Central Station. Lee beams at me like she's got halogen headlights behind her eyes. "Lexi, I came as soon as I heard they accepted the offer. I can't believe you're really buying our old family home. I'm so excited I can barely stand it!"

I return her smile and ask, "How come your family never bought the house back?" I know Beau said they all had their own places, but I still can't imagine they've never considered it.

Lee shrugs her shoulders. "None of us grew up visiting here or anything, so I guess we never connected with it enough. Beau and Emmie's grandmother Selia would have been a different story. She would have moved her family here in a heartbeat if it had gone on the market. She was something of the family historian."

Selfishly, I'm glad that didn't happen. While I feel strongly that a property like this should have stayed in the Frothingham family, I feel even stronger that I'm the one who gets to call it home.

Lee asks, "Would you mind if I looked around for a bit?"

"Not at all," I tell her. "I'd love to get your ideas on what restorations you think I should tackle first."

"Honey, I'm nothing if not full of ideas," she declares enthusiastically.

Beau says, "It sounds like y'all might be here for a while." He hands me the keys and says, "Drop them off at my office when you're through." Sounds like he's changed his tune about me being here alone before I'm the official owner.

When I reach for the keychain, he doesn't release it right away, instead, he takes my hand in his. He looks into my eyes in a way that I can only describe as smoldering, and my insides respond in kind. Then, he gently squeezes my fingers. What in the heck was that all about?

I make a grab for the keys and slide my hand out of his, posthaste. My heartbeat has increased like a war drum marching into battle. It so loud it's reverberating in my ears.

Lee calls after her son, "Don't forget dinner tonight." Beau waves in response. Then she says to me, "We hope you and your daddy can join us, as well. Our house at six."

"I'd love to come," I say, "but I don't know about Dad. I'll ask him as soon as I have a chance." I wonder if Shelby will be there too, and briefly rethink my acceptance. Of course, Shelby being there is probably better than her not being there. It'll be a solid reminder that Beau is off the market.

"Oh, honey, you don't have to let me know ahead of time. Just make sure you let your daddy know that we'd love it if he could come."

I promise I will, and we start to look through the house together. In the living room, I ask, "Do you have any antique stores in town that might carry some furnishings and decorative pieces that would fit in this house?"

"Do we!" Lee declares enthusiastically. "Gracie and I will take you shopping as soon as you say the word." Then she says, "Beau says you're thinking of opening a bed and breakfast."

"That's right," I tell her. "I can't imagine there are any employment opportunities for my skillset outside of a big city, but an inn would definitely pay for itself. I plan on advertising on all the big property rental sites."

"Not to poop on your parade, honey, but how many people do you think would want to come to Creek Water? Don't get me wrong, I think everyone should come for a visit, but I'm not sure they'd agree."

"Given that this house was one of the first in the state to be part of the Underground Railroad, I'm sure I'll get a lot of interest. If I can get enough period furniture, I'd like to open it up to schools, organizations, and anyone else who's interested in the Civil War." Just because the town didn't jump on the idea of a museum, doesn't mean that I can't do tours and share the information from that time. I'm not sure if that part of my business venture will be a moneymaker, but there are some things that simply need to be shared out of historical significance. This house is one of them.

Lee shakes her fists in the air like she's waving around pompoms and cheering the home team on to victory. "Let's get in touch with the historical society and see about getting this house on the National Registry. I bet you could apply for a restoration grant. Even if you don't get it, you'll still get some nice tax breaks."

"That's a great idea," I tell her. Thoughts start running through my head like an old-fashioned ticker tape at the stock market. I need to hurry up and tell Regina about everything. She's only going to be angrier if she thinks I've been planning this for a long time and didn't bring her into the loop sooner, especially in light of her feeling so abandoned by Bertie.

Lee pulls out her phone and gets busy looking something up while I try to envision this room as the grand parlor it surely was when the house was first built. Images of Victorian settees and Directoire-style armchairs fill my brain, along with intricately carved side-tables and marble-topped center tables displaying exquisite flower arrangements. Gilded mirrors and old portraits need to be everywhere between the cupid lighting fixtures adorning nearly every room. Grand floral draperies with velvet swags and valances would be the perfect touch on the windows and might even hide some of the detail work that I can't get to right away.

The first things I need to concern myself with are structural issues. Once those are taken care of, I'll be able to put my resources toward decorative fixes, if there's anything left. I realize my thirty-two thousand dollars might not go very far, especially if I want to decorate with period pieces.

Lee breaks into my thoughts by shouting, "I've got it."

"What do you have?" I ask.

"Oh, just a little thing called the Harriet Beecher Stowe Underground Railroad Grant."

"Which is?" I prompt.

"It's a fund that offers to match dollar for dollar investment with the homeowner to restore and maintain homes that were used to hide slaves in pursuit of freedom." She continues, "It says here"—she points to her phone—"that there are no restrictions on the house needing to be a public building, although homes that are open to the public at least two days a month, will be more likely to receive the grant."

I make a grab for Lee's phone and she hands it right over. I announce, "I have thirty-two thousand dollars. If I can get this, I'd have over sixty thousand to work with. Holy crap, Lee, this is exciting!"

"I know it. We have a couple of friends on the city council. Let me talk to them and see about getting some more information on the house, so we can make your application as compelling as possible."

Sixty-five thousand dollars would fix the electric, plumbing, furnace, and still (hopefully) leave a bit to put toward paint and the like. Of course, I have no real idea what those things cost. My only knowledge on the subject comes from home improvement shows, which is a pretty recent thing in my world.

I can hardly wait to see what other services might be available. I briefly try to imagine what it would be like to raise a family here, and for the first time, a small flicker of doubt creeps in. Living in a small town in southern Missouri will definitely decrease my odds of finding a husband. Although, to be fair, my record hasn't been that stellar while living on an island with seven million other people, so there's no sense in getting maudlin about it.

I try to table my concerns and go back to feeling unbridled enthusiasm. After all, if I could find and afford this house so easily, maybe the universe has a man lined up, too. *Too bad it won't be Beau Frothingham.*

Chapter 30

Lee and I spend two hours at the house together, and we only leave because she needs to go to the store to pick up a few things for dinner tonight.

When I get back to the factory, I check in with Emmie and tell her about my afternoon. She squeals, hitting a pitch previously reserved for kindergartners being sprayed by a firehose after eating their body weight in cotton candy. "You know this was all meant to be, don't you?"

I never told my friend about the fortune-teller from my childhood, so I'm curious how she decided this was serendipitous. "How do you figure?"

"Look at the chain of events leading up to it. If Silver Spoons hadn't been in trouble, they would have never tried to move you to Atlanta. That happening at the same time your apartment goes condo ..." she lets the thought hang in the air for a moment. "What are the chances you'd be homeless and out of work at the same time?"

With a look of horror on my face, I answer, "I guess when you put it like that." It's true though. Both of those life altering events happened right after Emmie moved home—and she swore she'd never live in Creek Water again. Then I come visit and happen to run into the house of my dreams—the one I never realized I'd been dreaming about. I mean, of all the places I saw myself living someday, they were all in New York City and none of them looked like a three-story Victorian mansion.

I tell her, "I'll see you at your aunt's house for dinner tonight. I need to run upstairs and check on Bertie." On my way to the second floor, I stop to pick up a couple of muffins at the coffee shop to tide us over. I figure now that I don't live in New York City anymore, I need to find a place as good as Sarabeth's Kitchen for my muffin fix. I'd best get researching that.

I stop on the second floor and return the keys to the receptionist of Frothingham Realty. I beat it out of there. My nervous system cannot handle seeing Emmie's cousin right now. It needs a break to prepare for dinner tonight. Luckily, the whole family will be there, so I don't have to be alone with him. I only have to watch him with Shelby. Good times.

I can tell my dad's awake even before I open the door to his loft. He's blasting Roberta Flack. "First Time Ever I Saw His Face" fills the air like the hauntingly tender ballad that it is. I walk in, and as expected, Bertie is performing his opening ballet that he likes to execute when he starts a new series.

He's wearing cargo pants and nothing else. He has a paintbrush in his mouth as though it's a rose, and he is doing the tango. There's another in his right hand and he's swaying side to side. He'll graduate to the Jethro Tull album *Songs from the Wood* when he starts painting and then move on to the Grateful Dead once he's about a quarter of the way through. For as unpredictable as Bertie can be, his musical routine is one that hasn't altered in years.

Standing in front of a giant canvas that's propped up against the wall, he stares at it like he's gazing at the completed picture. He's so caught up in whatever is going on in his head he doesn't even know I'm here yet.

I drop my bag of muffins on the counter and take a bite of the pumpkin one. While I like it, it's not quite as good as Sarabeth's. However, the blueberry muffin is probably the most delicious thing I've ever put in my mouth and I eat the whole thing while considering running downstairs for another.

"Killing Me Softly with His Song" comes on next. Bertie closes his eyes and starts running his hands across the blank canvas. How I turned out as normal as I am is anyone's guess.

Once this song ends, my dad spins around and finally notices me. "Lexi!" he exclaims. His eyes are full of feverish excitement. "I'm starting to *feel* the painting. It's really going to happen."

"Do you know what it's going to be yet?" I ask even though I never think my dad's paintings look anything like their titles. For instance, the one he calls *Moonlight Over the Hudson*, looks more like something I'd call *Punk Rock Mayhem*, but that's the beauty of art. It's subjective.

Before he answers, I tell him, "We've been invited to dinner at Emmie's aunt and uncle's house tonight. You know, Beau's parents?"

I fully expect him to tell me there's no way he can leave at such a critical time in his process, but he surprises me by saying, "I should shower then. When do we need to be there?"

"Six." Not only is he coming, but he's showering first? "I thought you'd need to stay here and visualize or something."

"I normally would, but Missouri feels different. It's going to be a very unique process creating here. Also, now that you're going to be living here, I really ought to meet your friends, don't you think?"

Um, okay. I ask, "Have you tried calling Mom yet?"

"Fourteen times," he says. "But that was before I turned on Roberta. I'll try her again when I get out of the shower."

While my dad gets ready, I pick up my phone and call Regina. Maybe I can soften her up a little, although I'm not holding my breath. Her voicemail comes on, and she's changed her message to: *This is Regina. I may or may not be on my way to Europe or Japan or the moon. If I get a chance, I'll call you back. If I'm currently mad at you, don't hold your breath.* Beep.

I say, "Hi, Mom. I hope you have a safe flight wherever you're going. I wanted to remind you that there's no reason to be mad at me. I have some very exciting news that I'd like to share with you, but I'm not going to keep calling only to have you ignore me. So please, call me back soon." I don't add, "Quit being such a baby," but I'm certainly tempted to.

Chapter 31

My dad comes out of the bathroom looking quite respectable. He's showered, shaved, and has on a nice pair of slacks and a sweater. "You look very handsome."

"Don't sound so surprised."

"Well," I try to defend my previous tone, "that's not something I've ever said to you while you're in the midst of a creative surge. You normally look a little homeless."

Bertie laughs, "Don't try to pigeonhole me, young lady. I'm evolving or metamorphosing. Something big is happening to me here."

"How do you figure that?" I ask.

"First of all, I've painted all my works in the same loft in SoHo. I've never wanted to paint anywhere else. Secondly, I left New York on a whim, for a place called Creek Water, of all things," he shudders dramatically. "And finally, I'm completely on board with you moving here. I've never thought you should live any farther away from us than uptown, but I've decided that you belong here. What do you make of that?"

"I'd say, there's definitely something going on with you. I'd normally guess a Vitamin D deficiency or something like that, but all your changes do seem to be for the better. Like you're becoming open-minded."

He claps so loudly I'm glad I don't have a full bladder, or I may have peed my pants. "That's why I can't wait to get started on this painting. I know it's going to be something completely different from anything I've done before. I just don't know what yet."

I'm happy for my dad. As an artist with a matching temperament, he's prone to wildly vacillating emotions. Lately, he's been downright depressed. This new upbeat, almost manic version of him, while a bit disconcerting, is also kind of exciting.

We stop off at a liquor store to pick up a couple of nice bottles of wine. Lee said she was making Beef Bourguignon, so we get cabernet. It only takes us ten minutes to get to their house once we get back to the car. I like how it feels driving through the countryside with my dad. We're quiet and pensive as we go.

There are several other vehicles in the driveway when we arrive. Beau's dad answers the door and I introduce, "Jed, this is my dad, Bertie."

Jed shakes my dad's hand enthusiastically. "Come on in. Imagine how excited we were to learn that Lexi's going to be living here in town. And knowing her daddy's going to be here for the next little while makes it all the nicer, dontcha think?"

My dad says, "I think we're both very happy to be here."

"Can I get y'all a beer or a cocktail or something?"

I raise my grocery bag in the air. "I brought wine."

"Well, darlin'," Jed says, "you go right on in and take that to Lee"—he points the way—"I'll show your daddy around."

My dad goes willingly as I head in the opposite direction. Jed and Lee's house is quite stunning. It's a large two-story brick home that's probably twice the size of Emmie and Gracie's house. But of course, twice the number of people used to live here.

The furnishings are classic and comfortable looking. There's a positively huge sofa upholstered in a butter-colored whale bone corduroy that makes me want to curl up on it. The colors are primarily neutral with pops of burgundy and teal blue. It's warm and welcoming and I love it.

When I turn down the hall leading into the kitchen, I run smack into Beau who's coming from the other direction. He's texting and not watching where he's going so I have to jump out of his way to avoid getting run over. "Whoa, hey there," he says when he notices me. "I didn't see you, sorry."

"No worries. I was on the way into the kitchen to see your mom."

There's something crackling in the air that feels remarkably similar to when he handed me the keys at my house—I'm already thinking of it as mine, even though I don't have the title yet.

Beau is staring at me in *that* way again. I try to break the intensity of the mood and ask, "Is Shelby here yet?"

He shakes his head, "No, ma'am. She's not joining us tonight."

"That's too bad," I say, really meaning it. If I hadn't witnessed that snug little scene between the two of them earlier today I might not feel that way. But they're clearly a couple, so the less I see of Beau without Shelby, the better.

"Why is that too bad?" he asks.

"Because I like her." And while that's true it has nothing to do with my wishing she was here.

"She's a nice girl," he says, not really selling it. "Can I get you something to drink?" he asks.

"I was taking the wine to your mom. I thought I might get a glass."

He reaches out and says, "Let me take that for you." I'm left to follow him like a puppy.

Lee and Gracie are in the kitchen mashing potatoes and tossing a salad. They're so excited to see me you'd think I was Tina Turner or something. Gracie drops her salad tongs and throws her arms around me. "You've got a house! Lee's been filling me in on everything the two of you are working on; I want to help."

I laugh at her excitement. "I need as much help as I can get."

Gracie picks up a file folder sitting on the counter and says, "Good. I picked these up at the library today. They're copies, so they're all yours."

"What are they?" I ask.

"Most houses that operated as part of the Underground Railroad never kept any documentation. The Frothinghams were different. They kept records."

"Wouldn't that have endangered them or the slaves they helped?" I ask.

"It would have if they'd ever been found. But they kept them in the family mausoleum."

"In the cemetery?"

"Course, honey, that's where mausoleums generally are."

"I'm missing something, Gracie. If they kept records there, how did you get them from the library?"

"Some Frothingham way back turned them over to the city to preserve. They were getting kind of messed up being stored in that musty old family crypt."

I open the folder and there must be two hundred pages of diary entries and names. "Who wrote these?" I ask.

Lee answers, "Regina Frothingham. She was the wife of Jedidiah. They were the ones who built the house."

"Regina?" I ask, thinking this is yet another sign that I'm supposed to be in this house. "Regina is my mom's name."

Lee laughs in surprise. "Really?" Then she demands, "When are you going to get your mama down here to see your new place?"

"Soon, I hope." I don't want to get into the whole angry-mother story. I'm not sure what these Southern ladies would make of my intense Northern mom.

Beau hands me a glass of wine and says, "May I escort you to the dining room?"

"No, thanks, I'd like to help with dinner," I reply, eager not to be alone with him.

"Nonsense," Lee says. "You kids go on and have some fun. Gracie and I won't be but a few more minutes."

When we get into the dining room, we're the only ones there. I ask, "Where are Emmie and Zach?"

Beau sits right next to me and answers, "Faye was feeling poorly so they decided to stay in tonight."

I try to stand up as I say, "That's silly. I'll go stay with the baby and they can come on over and eat," but Beau reaches out to pull me back onto my chair.

"No, ma'am, Emmie told me to make sure you stayed here."

Then he adds, "I think they're looking for a little alone time."

Crap. Well, now I can't go over there. How in the heck am I going to get through dinner sitting next to Beau?

Chapter 32

Dinner is both delightful and excruciating. Amelia didn't come either, so it's me and my dad; Beau, his brother Davis, and their parents; and Emmie's mom and her Uncle Jesse.

I'm seated between Beau and Davis. Davis happily talks about my new house. "You know I'm a woodworker, right?"

"I do. Emmie says you make the most beautiful furniture she's ever seen."

"Well, I'm at your beck and call if you need my services with your renovation."

I like Davis a lot. He's a world easier to talk to than his brother, probably because I'm not attracted to him. "I will most assuredly hire you before anyone else," I tell him.

"No, ma'am," he says. "You misunderstand. You're buying my family's original home, so as a Frothingham and as a friend, I'm offering my services free of charge."

"Davis, you can't mean that." Although I really hope he does.

"I do mean it. You can have all my free time until you're up and running."

Beau is eavesdropping and doesn't appear to be very happy about what he's hearing. "Davis, you don't have enough time to build me that set of bookshelves I asked you for. Don't get Lexi's hopes up."

Davis chides, "She's a lot prettier than you are, brother. I can find as much time for her as she needs."

Even though Davis says that flirtatiously, I think he's only doing it to tease Beau. If I thought for one minute that he was interested in me romantically, I'd never take him up on his offer.

Meanwhile, my dad seems to be having the time of his life. He's telling stories about growing up in New York that have his audience enthralled. When he starts in on the tale of how he won a David Hockney painting from the artist himself after besting him in a dance-off at Studio 54, every Frothingham at the table is staring at him like he's some kind of exotic bird.

Lee asks, "Did you keep the painting?"

"I wish. The truth is I was young and in need of money to fund my own art, so I sold it for a hefty sum and got busy creating my own works."

"What does Lexi's mom do?" Jed asks.

Bertie proudly replies, "She's a professor of Women's Studies at NYU."

Jesse says, "We sure hope we get a chance to meet her while you're here."

That would be nice—maybe even possible—if my mom wasn't currently livid with my father. I reply, "Mom is very busy right now."

"Surely she gets Thanksgiving and Christmas vacation," Gracie suggests.

My dad decides to take a vacation from reality and says, "I'm sure she'll be down to visit both times." *Keep dreaming, Dad.*

Dinner is delicious and while I studiously try to ignore Beau, I find that it's easier said than done. He keeps accidentally brushing his hand against mine whenever one of us passes something around the table. He's been attentively refilling my wine glass, and by the time I notice that it never seems to empty I'm feeling a little tipsy.

Over dessert, I announce, "It's too bad Shelby's not here."

Lee looks up startled. "Why?"

I know she isn't excited about the relationship between her son and Shelby, so I probably shouldn't have said anything, but I feel the need to remind Beau of her existence. His foot has started to migrate under the table. "I like her," I reply.

My comment is met with awkward grunts that could either be agreement or not. My dad says, "She's a very nice young lady. Where is your girlfriend tonight, Beau?"

Beau corrects, "She's my *friend.*" Not by the looks of what I witnessed this afternoon, but I don't mention it as spying on them doesn't cast me in a good light.

I can tell Bertie wants to say something else as he looks between me and Beau. But before he has a chance, Gracie says, "Why don't we take our drinks into the living room so we can enjoy the fire?"

The Frothingham men immediately stand to pull the chairs out for the ladies. Beau and Davis both make a grab for mine, but Beau manages to get right behind me and bodily shove his brother out of the way.

In the living room, I sink into the sofa I was admiring when I arrived. I'm overcome by a desire to sleep. Beau seems to read my mind and hands me the softest throw in the world. Then he sits down next to me. In my pleasantly buzzed state, it's all I can do not to crawl into his lap and curl up like a kitten.

The sudden warmth and comfort that permeate my extremities make it impossible for me to participate in the conversation. Instead, I lean back and listen to the voices around me as they get lower and lower until I can't hear them at all.

Chapter 33

The next time I open my eyes, it's morning. I'm more than a little confused as I look around the living room. I vaguely remember seeing it before, but even so, I'm not quite sure where I am. I get distracted while trying to put together the chain of events that led me to being here. Beau is sleeping on the couch adjacent to me. He's wrapped in a blanket similar to the one I'm still cocooned in.

That's when it starts to come back to me. I had dinner with his family last night. I'm at Lee and Jed's house. The morning light has just started to make its climb into the sky, and the house feels very still. It appears I'm the first one up.

I've never in my life fallen asleep at a dinner party. I know I drank more than normal, thanks to Beau's attentiveness, but I didn't think I drank enough to pass out. I wonder how my dad got back to his apartment.

After a thorough yawn and stretch, I make my way to the powder room off the entryway. I'm startled by my reflection. My eye makeup has run to the point of entering raccoon territory, my curly hair is reminiscent of a psychotic clown, and my clothes are rumpled like I slept in them, which of course, I did.

Lee left a note on the vanity for me along with a small bag labeled "Guests." I look inside and find a brand-new toothbrush and various other toiletries to help perk me up. Her note says that if I want to shower I should use the bathroom down the hall. I decide not to because once I'm clean I'm not going to want to put on last night's clothes. I'll shower when I get back to Bertie's.

When I go into the kitchen to retrieve my purse and the file that Gracie brought for me about the history of my house, I find Beau standing next to the coffee pot looking so incredibly sexy I nearly let out a groan.

Like me, he's wearing his clothes from last night. His shirt is untucked and unbuttoned rewarding me with a very enticing glimpse at what lies underneath. My knees weaken as butterflies zip through my midriff. His beard is scruffy and his hair mussed from sleep. I nearly walk over so I can run my hands through it.

"Mornin' sleepy head," he says by way of greeting.

"Good morning," I manage. "Why didn't anyone wake me up last night?"

He laughs, "We tried to, but you mumbled something about the couch being your new home and you went right back to sleep."

"How did my dad get back to the loft?"

"I drove him," he says.

"Then why are you here? Why didn't you go back to your own place?" I don't even know where Beau lives, but I assume it's not here or he wouldn't have been sleeping in the living room wearing last night's clothes.

He shrugs. "I thought it'd be nice to have breakfast with you this morning."

What in the world is going on here? Up until last night, Beau's acted like he couldn't wait to get away from me, but now he's going out of his way to spend more time with me. Something doesn't add up.

"Do you want pancakes or eggs?" he asks.

"Pancakes," I answer as I gratefully accept the cup of coffee he hands to me.

"Bacon or sausage?"

"Sausage," I say. "But you don't have to cook for me. I can pick something up in town."

"Nonsense. You sit on down and keep me company. Once my daddy knew I was gonna to stay over, he placed his order. While my mama makes the best suppers, I'm the one in the family known for breakfast."

I sit at a counter stool and watch as he cracks eggs and whips up pancake batter from scratch. He's like poetry in motion. My stomach growls loudly which makes him smile. "Pour yourself some orange juice," he says.

"Where do you live?" I suddenly want to know.

"Not too far from your new house," he answers.

"Where?"

"Next door."

Why am I only now finding out that Beau is my neighbor? This information must be the source the *look* Emmie and the older Frothingham ladies shared yesterday. I wonder why they didn't just tell me then. "Which next door?" I demand. "The brick colonial or the one with the window boxes?"

"Colonial," he answers.

"Why do you need such a big house?" I ask, although I

belatedly consider that he may have bought it for his future family. So, I add, "I mean it'll be a nice home for you to raise your kids in some day." Crap, I don't want to be his neighbor.

"I bought the house ages ago, long before thinking about a family."

"Why?" I demand.

"Why are you buying your house?" he asks.

"Because I love it," I answer, realizing that's why most people choose the houses they do. So, I ask, "How long have you lived there?"

"Five years. I've been working on it ever since. It was in pretty rough shape."

"But you said my house was for sale five years ago. Why didn't you buy that one instead?" You'd think if he wanted something so big he'd have gone for his family home.

"Because I like the colonial better."

"If you love it so much, why are you trying to talk me out of buying my house?" Being that he's fallen in love with a house, you'd think he'd understand my motivation. The man is a puzzle.

He doesn't answer right away. Instead, he pauses for a good long beat before answering, "I know firsthand how much work it can be and how expensive it can be. I wasn't sure you knew what you were getting into."

I don't believe him. Not only has he been trying to talk me out of buying my house, he's been pushing Atlanta on me, as well. Why is he changing his tune?"

Our breakfast is ready before Jed and Lee come down, so Beau and I sit side-by-side at the counter and eat. I roll a pancake around a sausage link, pigs in a blanket style, before pouring warm maple syrup over it. After taking a bite, I unconsciously let out a pornographic sounding moan. Trying to regain my composure, I ask, "Why are they so good?"

He smiles, clearly enjoying my appreciation of his efforts. "I use extra eggs to give the pancakes a crepe-like flavor, then I grind some fresh nutmeg into the batter."

"They're delicious," I unconsciously release another satisfied sound.

"Wait until you try my barbecue," he says. "I'll have you over for dinner once summer comes and I fire up the grill."

While it sounds like a tempting offer, the thought of having dinner at his house with him fills me with dread. How could everything seem so destined to be, only to have a wrench of this size thrown into my happiness. I'm not at all pleased, but there's no way I'm going to give up the opportunity to own my house, even if it means having to suffer through living next door to Beau Frothingham. And believe me, I foresee it being a real chore, especially if he isn't living there alone.

Chapter 34

Once I get back to my dad's apartment and take a shower, I head downstairs to see Emmie. I've barely talked to her since putting in an offer on the house. She's behind the counter when I get there, looking as lovely as always. "We missed you last night," I say by way of greeting.

"I'm sorry we weren't there," my friend says. "Faye had a little fever. She's got some new teeth comin' in and was pretty miserable, so we decided to hang out at home."

"I just found out that your cousin is my new neighbor," I tell her.

"That'll be nice, won't it?" she asks faking an innocent tone.

"Why didn't you tell me before now?" I ask

"I've barely seen you since you first laid eyes on it," she says. And while she's got a point, she knows very well she should have told me yesterday. I don't push the issue though. Truth be told, it wouldn't have made any difference in my wanting the house.

"I'm surprised a single man purchased a place like that on his own."

"Why?" she asks. "You bought your house on your own."

"Yeah, but you don't normally think of men as being so

domestic." After the words are out of my mouth, I realize that I'm pandering to a stereotype, something I try very hard not to do.

"Beau will be a great neighbor," she tells me.

"Shelby, too, I guess," I don't realize how forlorn those words sound until they're out of my mouth.

She raises an eyebrow at me in interest. I've not told Emmie that I'm drawn to her cousin. There's no sense making that information known when there's nothing to be done about it. She says, "Shelby and Beau are not a done deal. I told you, I think he's hanging in until she cuts him loose."

My friend doesn't seem to be aware that Shelby has no intention of letting him go. While neither she nor Beau have ever seemed particularly happy when I've seen them together, the moment they shared yesterday tells a different story.

I change the subject. "Your aunt said there were some antique stores in Creek Water. Which do you think I should go to?"

Her eyes pop open and her mouth forms a perfect letter O before she asks, "Are you looking for furniture for your house?"

"I am. I want period pieces, but I'd rather not buy them in perfectly restored shape. I'd like to save some money and do whatever work I can by myself."

"I haven't been home long enough to know where to send you," she says. "Why don't you walk over to the Creeky Button Factory where Davis has his workshop and ask him. That seems like something he'd know about. Or call Mama and Auntie Lee," she suggests.

I'm afraid if I call Emmie's mom and aunt I'd get so caught up in their excitement that I'd spend more than I intended. If dress shopping with them was any indication, I'm out of my league with those two.

I get directions to the button factory, wish my friend a happy day, and take off for the front door, peeking into the day-spa on my way out of the building. I normally wouldn't think twice about treating myself to a facial or massage, but those two things are no longer on my priority list. Especially until I get the report from the building inspector and find out exactly how much work needs to be done on my new place.

Beau walks into the building as I'm exiting. He's freshly showered and shaved and looks very tempting. He asks, "Where are you off to?"

"I'm going to visit Davis and see if he has any recommendations for antique stores in the area."

A myriad of emotions fly across his face. "Why didn't you ask me?"

"I don't know. I guess I figured with Davis being in the business, he'd have a better idea."

Beau doesn't respond. Instead, he pulls his phone out of his pocket and makes a call. "Hi, Sadie. Do I have any appointments today?" He listens to her response before adding, "In that case, I won't be coming in. I'll be on my mobile. Call me when you hear back from Homer."

He disconnects and focuses his attention on me. "Lucky for you, I know the ins and outs of the antique stores in the area. I've been a regular customer since buying my house."

I'm not sure I call that fortuitous. Something has changed in Beau since yesterday. Up until then, he'd been avoiding me, but now he seems to be going out of his way to spend time with me.

"Lucky me," I say. "My car is parked out front."

He takes my arm in such a way that I feel like we're an old-fashioned couple out for a stroll. Even though it's a totally foreign maneuver to me, it feels gallant and respectful, so I let him. "I'll drive," he says. "That way you can look around and take in your new town without worrying where you're going."

My new town. I like the sound of that. I realize I've been so caught up in the whirlwind of excitement that I haven't even thought about what it's going to be like not to be living in New York City. I don't really own anything there anymore. The few things I have will have to be shipped. Of course, talking my mom into doing that might be a problem. I really do need to contact her, although I don't know how to manage that if she won't return my calls.

Beau is driving a different car than I've previously seen him in. This one is a two-seater vintage Mercedes. It's super cute and makes me feel like an old-time movie star getting into it. "Nice wheels," I say.

He replies, "I bought it in high school and restored it with my daddy. It doesn't work for real estate though, as I can't get more than one customer in it with me, but I like to drive it around town."

He pulls out onto the brick streets and I find myself noticing him as much as I notice the town. He fits here.

He asks, "Which rooms do you want to furnish first?"

"I guess the basics. I'll need some living room furniture and a table to eat at. I should probably look at some bed frames." Suddenly, I'm so overwhelmed by how much I'll have to buy in order to open an inn, I'm not sure I'll be able to do it.

Beau says, "I know the perfect place," as he turns the car around and heads out of town.

Chapter 35

I'm enchanted by all the wide-open space as Beau and I drive through the countryside. "Did you like growing up here?" I ask.

"It was pretty great. I mean, I never moved away."

"Did you ever want to live anywhere else?" I ask.

"No, ma'am. Creek Water's my home. Don't get me wrong, I love to travel and see the world, but I haven't found one place yet that speaks to me like this town. What was it like growing up in New York City?"

"Good," I answer. "I mean, it's the only life I've ever known, so I don't have anything to compare it to, but I always enjoyed it."

"That doesn't sound like a winning endorsement," he says.

"I do love it, but it's crowded and noisy. I think at my core, I've been craving quiet and never realized it until I came here. Does that make sense?"

"I think that we're hardwired for a certain kind of life," he says, "and it doesn't matter how we grow up. When we find what we're lookin' for, we just know it."

"My mom isn't going to be happy when she finds out that I bought a house here."

"You haven't told her yet?" he asks.

I decide to come clean and say, "Regina isn't currently speaking to me or my dad." I explain, "Bertie up and left without telling her he was going."

"I can see how she might not have appreciated that," he says.

"And then he rented the loft without discussing it with her," I add.

"Has he ever done anything like that before?"

I shake my head. "Never. My dad is happy to let my mom call most of the shots in their relationship. As long as he has a space to paint, he's good. Mom has gotten used to their dynamic and I'm sure this is throwing her off balance."

"I bet she'll love it here when she sees it," he says.

I shake my head. "I don't think so. Regina is a New Yorker through and through. She's told me many times that she wouldn't be caught dead south of the Mason-Dixon line."

"Are there any slaves in your ancestry?" he asks.

"On my grandmother's side," I tell him. "But Mimi considered herself a New Yorker and didn't talk much about family history. So, all I know is that her great-great-great-grandparents were owned," I emphasize the last word to indicate the ridiculousness of the concept, "by a family in Mississippi before escaping to some place farther north."

"Your mama should love that you're buying a house that was used in the Underground Railroad then," he says.

"That's probably the only part she'll approve of. I'm afraid she considers all states that were part of the Confederacy undesirable and unsafe."

"You can't really blame her," he says. "When you've had

blood relations treated no better than animals, that has to unsettle your whole view of the world."

"It hasn't unsettled mine," I tell him.

"You're lucky, then. All I'm sayin' is that your mama has a right to be cautious. While the Civil War is long over, it's not quite ancient history."

How in the world is Beau more sensitive to these feelings than I am? I think Regina would like him if she ever got to know him.

We continue to drive quietly for several minutes, each of us lost in our thoughts, when Beau turns into a gravel driveway. "Where are we?" I ask. There are no signs to indicate a store ahead.

"This here's the old Peabody farm. Clovis and Myrah have lived here for as long as I can remember. They have a huge barn full of old stuff that they collect."

"Do they sell it?" I ask.

"To the right people, they do. Otherwise, they hang on to it to make sure that it's preserved and doesn't end up in a junk yard."

"Are they big fans of the era?"

He smiles secretively. "You could say that." He doesn't offer anything else.

As we pull up to an old two-story farmhouse, Beau honks the horn three times. Two giant German shepherds come running up to the car, barking their heads off. "Don't get out yet," he warns. "They're sweet dogs when they know you, but they might tear your arm off if they don't."

Well, that's a comfort. A man with skin so dark I can barely discern his features comes hobbling out. He hollers, "Git over here, dogs!" They sit down as though awaiting further instruction, their barking subsiding into low growling.

Beau gets out of the car and greets, "Clovis, my friend, I've brought you a special customer."

"Who you got with you, boy?" It's hard to tell how old Clovis Peabody is, but my guess is he's eighty if he's a day.

"This is my friend, Lexi. She's buying our old family home on Dogwood Lane."

Clovis's smile is blindingly white as he comes over to the passenger side of the car to let me out. He opens my door and extends his hand. "Come on outta there, young lady, and let me get a look atcha."

I get out of the car and say, "I'm very happy to meet you, Mr. Peabody.

"Psh," he says, "Mr. Peabody nothin'. You call me Clovis." This man has a contagiously happy energy about him.

"I'm very happy to meet you, Clovis," I offer.

He inspects me and says, "Looks like that old house is going to be owned by a lady with some color in 'er. I'm darn glad to see that happen. Where's your brown come from, girl?"

"My mother's side of the family is African-American, sir. My paternal grandfather was a German Jew and my dad's family are English."

He nods his head. "Peabody's an English name too, but I got no English in me," he declares joyfully.

"Then how did you wind up with an English surname, if you don't mind me asking?"

"Don't mind a'tall. My daddy's people going way back was owned by a family named Peabody. He took their name the day they gave him his freedom. They was good to him and he needed to pick hi'self a name, so that's how it came to be."

It's another world entirely down here. People talk about slavery like it's still part of their lives. He continues, "You gotta come on in and meet my Myrah. She's gonna be plumb tickled to make your acquaintance."

I'm not sure why unless it's because I've got color in me, as her husband says. I'm surprised that Clovis could even tell. In New York City, my ethnicity is ambiguous enough that a lot of people think I'm part Hispanic or Italian. Even Shelby's mom thought I was Mexican.

We follow Clovis up his drive to the house. I might be being fanciful, but somehow, I feel like I've walked this path before.

Chapter 36

Myrah welcomes Beau with a hug and says, "We've missed you, son. It's been a couple weeks since you been by. Everthin' okay with your family?"

"Yes, ma'am," he says. "I brought a special customer to meet you."

Myrah turns to me with bright eyes. "I'm Myrah, young lady." She extends her hand to me.

There's an almost regal quality about Clovis's wife. She has a much lighter complexion than her husband. Her coloring is closer to my mom's than mine. She's petite, and she holds her head high. There's a grace to her motions that makes me think she might have been a dancer at some time in her life. I take her hand and say, "I'm Lexi Blake. I'm here visiting Beau's cousin, Emmie."

"We do love our Emmeline," Myrah says. "We were so pleased when she came home." Then she looks down at my hand and gets very still. She closes her eyes for a moment before turning to her husband. "What aren't you tellin' me?" she demands.

Clovis laughs, "Why don't we give you a moment to figure that out fer yourself." Then to me, he says, "Myrah comes from people with *the sight*. They know things in a way that don't make sense for them to know."

Wondering about Beau's thoughts on the subject, I tell them, "My grandmother used to take me to a fortune-teller in Harlem where she lived."

Myrah stares at me so deeply, it's almost like she loses focus and I'm not sure what she's looking at. "She told you somethin' about a dog, din't she?"

"Yes, she did," I say, full of surprise. Maybe there is something to this nonsense Mimi trusted so much. Although to be fair, I haven't really thought of it as nonsense since the day in Central Park when the dog jumped over me and my whole New York life started to fall apart.

"She's buyin' the old Frothingham place," Clovis says.

Myrah stares thoughtfully at her husband, then happily at Beau, and finally eagerly at me, before whispering, "Honey, I have somethin' fer you."

"You do?" I ask, wondering what that could possibly be. She turns and walks across the room to open a drawer in her dish cabinet. She pulls out an envelope so old it's yellowing. Then she hands it to me.

"What is this?" I ask.

She shakes her head. "I don't know. Alls I know is this here letter has been passed down in my family for generations. It's been waitin' for you.'"

"Why do you think I'm the one you're supposed to give it to?" I ask, as chills shoot through me so intensely I wish I were wearing a heavier coat.

"The only thing ever told was that someday a young woman

would buy the old Frothingham place and when that gal showed up, whichever one of us met her, we was to give her this. That's you, honey."

"Really?" I ask, curious and more than a little creeped out.

"You're the first young gal who fits the bill," she replies.

"And you don't know what the letter says?"

"I don't. But I have instructions that go along with this here letter."

"What instructions?" This whole thing is getting seriously bizarre.

"I got some furniture for ya."

"I'm actually here hoping to buy some pieces for the house. I want to turn it into an historic inn." I add, "I hope to give tours to schools and the like."

"Well that makes sense."

"What makes sense?" I ask.

"Clovis and I have a barn full of old stuff, but we have special items up in the hay loft that we don't show folks."

"Why not?" I ask.

"Like I said, honey," she says, "they're yours. They belonged to Beau's people who built the house."

Beau finally speaks. "Why do you have them?"

"They were given to my people when the house was sold out of your family." Then she looks to me and explains, "My people were servants to Beau's people before, during, and after the big war."

"They helped hide the slaves?" I ask.

"Yes, ma'am. When my people came out of the Deep South, they was taken in by the Frothinghams. After that, they led parties to rescue others."

"But how did you wind up with the furniture?" Beau doesn't seem angry that his family doesn't have it, just surprised.

"The lady of the house at the time was given a letter from my grandma that came from the first Mrs. Frothingham. All I know is that my grandma was given the care of some things and told to keep them until it was time."

"Time for what?" I ask.

"Time for you, honey," she says.

I have no idea what's going on, but I do know I need to see what's in this envelope. I suddenly believe beyond a shadow of a doubt that it's somehow going to be tied to what that old lady in Harlem told me all those years ago.

Chapter 37

I pull a piece of parchment out of the ancient envelope and unfold it carefully. When I see the feathery script, I read out loud:

December 12, 1864

Dearest Lady,

I cannot imagine how the future unfolds that a woman will one day be allowed to purchase a house by herself. It must surely mean the world is destined to be a more beautiful place. While I lack the imagination to understand how such a thing will come to pass, my devoted friend and housemaid, Elsie, assures me it will. She has accurately foretold many fates for my family, so my trust in her is complete.

Elsie tells me that you will be her great-granddaughter five times over. She foresaw that someone along her line will name her daughter after me. It will be this lady's child, you, that will call my home her own.

My heart is so full of joy at such a thing that I can barely contain myself. To think, that not only a woman will be in such a position, but a woman of color, it humbles me at the goodness of what is to come. For truth, I live in dark times, where one man is allowed to own another. It is a travesty against God.

Elsie has expressed that you will doubt my words, of which I can hardly blame you. I cannot imagine a time when prophecies such as these will be openly welcomed or trusted, even though it was most certainly so during the time of Our Lord.

I am leaving instructions through my family that whomever sells my home, because it is certain that it must be sold for it to be available for your purchase, must hand over certain items to Elsie's family for safe keeping. Those items, my dear, are yours. They belong in our home, yours and mine.

I reach my hand across time to you and celebrate your family's return. I rejoice that we will win this fight for human decency. Though I know evil will always exist, it calms my soul to know that goodness shall reign.

You and I, dear lady, are a testament that if a person has the strength to fight for what is just, justice will prevail. Welcome home, my dear.

Your humble servant,
Regina Frothingham

My voice trails off as I finish reading, I am one hundred percent at a loss for words, but not frightened or disbelieving. This really is straight out of *Doctor Who*. How can the past know of the future in such detail?

Beau is the first to speak. "Our families have been entwined for over one hundred and fifty years. It took Emmie moving to New York City to bring you back to your roots."

Myrah asks, "Child, how is it that you didn't know of your people's time here?"

I shake my head. "All I was told was that my great-great-grandmother moved to New York as a young woman. She never shared much of her early life, so none of those stories made their way into family history."

Clovis slaps his hands on his overall-clad legs and says, "Well, I don't know about you, but I'm darned excited to take you out to the old barn."

Beau agrees, "Me too, Let's go." I follow along, still trying to process the magnitude of what I've learned.

Myrah takes my hand in hers. "The world is a mystery. While I think folks have freewill, I also believe we are born with many certainties we worked out with our Lord before ever comin' here."

I don't know what to say. I've never really thought about such things before, so I remain quiet while she continues, "I don't believe greatness is random. Do you know our first president, George Washington, used to be visited by angels while he and his men were starvin' and freezin' during their fight for our freedom from the English?"

"I didn't know that," I tell her. "What did they say to him?"

"They said, 'You, sir, are the emissary of the heavens and you have our support. You will be triumphant in your fight.' During the moments when he was so low he lost his fire, his friends from above reappeared to offer encouragement."

"Myrah," I say, "this is all a pretty new way of thinking for me and I'm afraid it's going to take me some time to absorb it. But aside from receiving this beautiful letter and furniture, there's a bigger gift here than both of those things combined."

She squeezes my hand firmly. "You got that right, honey. We been given the gift of kinfolk reunitin'. That there is something even I didn't 'spect."

While we continue out to the barn, still walking hand in hand, I'm positively overwhelmed with emotion. I'm physically present, but my mind is reeling. Whatever led me here, while seemingly random, hasn't been random at all. I didn't even know my family had a history in Creek Water. The chain of events that culminate in my taking a job and meeting Emmie is staggering. Emmie, who left her hometown and never even wanted to live here again, until she *did*. All of that happened before the dog jumped over me in Central Park. Now, I stand with my I-don't-know-how-many-times-great-aunt, buying the very house I'm meant to buy. The only thing missing is Regina.

If this isn't enough to get her to come out here, nothing is.

Chapter 38

The furniture in the Peabodys' barn has been meticulously cared for. I used to watch that television show about junk pickers touring the country digging through people's collections. Their goal was to buy at a low price so they could resell their finds in their antique store. Ninety percent of the time, the barns and outbuildings where they discovered those treasures stored, were in total and complete chaos. That's not the case here.

Bed frames are carefully line up in one area, covered with clear plastic sheeting to keep moisture away. There are dining tables, end tables, and china cabinets, sofas, and armoires. "Why in the world do you have so many things?" I ask, unable to suppress my curiosity.

Myrah laughs, "We jus' gradually started collectin'. Clovis and I been married for near on sixty years now. We always liked goin' to garage sales and auctions. When we could afford it, we'd buy somethin'. After a while people would start to pick up things for us or drop off stuff they didn't want no more. Then others would come and look through what we have and buy from us."

Clovis adds, "Myrah and I think the past is important, and by preservin' it, we're keeping it alive for others to appreciate and learn from."

Myrah says, "It's surprisin' how many people only want new. We picked up most of this stuff for a song." She leads the way through her treasures to a staircase in the back of the barn. "All your things are up yonder. Clovis and I haven't been up there in years, but you and Beau head on up. It's all yours, honey."

Beau and I climb the stairs one at a time. They're steep and a bit rickety, more ladder-like than stairs. When we reach our destination, we stop and look around, mouths slack in awe at the bounty before us. It's like all of my birthdays and Christmases wrapped together for fifty years.

I whisper, "What in the heck is going on here?"

"I couldn't say for sure, but clearly whatever it is was meant to be," he replies while shaking his head.

"It's a good thing you didn't succeed when you tried to talk me out of buying the house," I semi-tease.

"I think all of this," he responds while waving his hands around the loft, "proves that you would have never wavered."

I shout down the stairs, "Myrah, this can't all be for me."

"'Tis, honey!" she yells back before adding, "Clovis and I are gonna head on in now. It's too cold out here fer our old bones."

I watch as Beau reverently picks up an ornately carved cigar box. I ask, "Is your family going to be mad?"

"Why would they be?" he wants to know.

"Because I'm getting all of these things that rightfully belong to them."

He shakes his head. "No, ma'am. Near as I understood, these things belong to you. No one in my family is going to give you any trouble over it."

I don't know where to start looking. I begin by gently pulling back furniture covers. The fabrics on the chairs and settees appear to be original. There are a few moth holes and some fading, but otherwise everything seems to be in remarkable condition.

There are gilded mirrors and paintings, beds, armoires, and side tables. There's a dining room table with twelve chairs and a matching sideboard. If you put everything together, there must be enough here to fill over half of my house.

Beau picks up a framed tintype photograph of two women who I'm guessing are in their early thirties. They're standing side-by-side each with an arm wrapped around the other in a very sisterly fashion. But they can't be sisters for one obvious reason, one of them is white and the other black.

The white lady is very finely dressed. Beau says, "That's Regina. We have other photographs of her."

The other lady is wearing a very simple outfit by comparison, although it appears to have been well made. I say, "That must be Elsie." I look at my relative and I see my grandmother in her as clear as day. I'm so full of emotion that tears of disbelief and excitement start to pool in my eyes.

Beau stands so close to me, I can feel the heat radiate off of him. "What an astonishing day," he says, the timbre of his voice reflecting his words.

I look up at him and try to process how intertwined our histories are. He's not only my friend's cousin, or my realtor, or even my neighbor. His ancestors and mine once meant a great deal to each other. Beau stares down at me and ever so slowly starts to close the gap between our faces. It feels like everything that happened in the past was meant to lead to this very moment.

While I want more than anything to give in to the draw of him, I tentatively put my hands against his chest to halt further intimacy. "How in the world am I ever going to get all of this down those stairs?"

He takes a moment to collect himself before stepping back and answering, "Davis and I can do it. We might need to assemble a lift for the bigger things."

"When is the inspection?" I ask.

"It's all set it up for tomorrow afternoon."

"How did you get one so soon?" Things in Creek Water seem to move quicker than I would have expected. Either that, or it's another indication that my moving here was more than serendipity.

Beau shrugs his shoulders. "Homer had a cancellation. The original appointment was for later in the month. If everything looks good, this is on track to be the fastest closing I've ever been a party to."

While I could spend days up here taking time to appreciate this bounty, I'd rather go inside and spend time with Myrah and Clovis. So that's exactly what Beau and I do.

Once we're back in the house with cups of hot coffee and a plate of fresh cookies in front of us, Myrah sits down and says, "I got a world of stories for you, honey. Where do you want me to start?"

"At the beginning," I tell her. "Start at the beginning."

Chapter 39

When the Frothinghams sold the house in the nineteen forties, my family stopped working for them. The Frothinghams helped them buy the farm that Myrah and Clovis still live on.

The families have stayed in touch over the years and made sure that each generation got to know one another. While they genuinely cared for each other, it was also a tribute to our ancestors' friendship and what Regina and Elsie were able to achieve by working together.

All told, we spend over six hours with Myrah and Clovis. Beau and I don't leave until the late afternoon. Even if I have to fly to New York and drag my mother down here on my own, I'm going to do it. She's needs to feel this connection to our family and the past as much as I do, especially with Mimi and Pops no longer alive.

Beau and I drive back to the sewing machine factory in near silence. Today was a lot for both of us to process. When we pull into Beau's parking space, he asks, "You want to grab some supper?"

I don't know if he considers this a friendly dinner or something more, but either way I want to go.

"I need to check on my dad first."

"I'll come with you," he says. "Bertie's more than welcome to join us. In fact, I believe I owe him a meal."

"How do you figure that?"

"Shelby paid the other night, instead of me," he replies.

"But your parents had us over for dinner last night," I tell him.

"My parents aren't me. Plus, now that you live here, don't think we aren't all expecting to be invited to your house when you're up and running.'"

"That will happen, for sure," I promise. A fanciful image of our ancestors joining us in a ghostly fashion pops into my mind. All of us celebrating the future they believed would one day come to pass.

Beau and I walk through the factory. A part of me wants to run over to Emmie's shop and tell her everything that happened today, but even though I came here to see her, and have done precious little of that due to unforeseen events, I need to sit with all of this for a while, to let it soak in. Being that Beau experienced it with me, he is the only person I can imagine being with right now. I guess it's a case of, "you had to be there."

There is a much-appreciated relief from the intimacy that was cooking between me and Beau while we spent time with Clovis and Myrah. I have a lot to do and need to keep focused on the next step. This is not a time I can allow myself to get lost in a fantasy world—like I did with my old neighbor Tim, whom I haven't thought about once since leaving New York. That was obviously nothing more than a passing fancy.

I unlock the door to my dad's apartment and let me just say

that while I've seen Bertie in all stages of weird while he's painting, this is one takes the cake. He's once again wearing cargo pants and nothing else. Queen's "Can't Stop Me Now" is blasting through the room and he's dancing like nobody's watching. Except we are, and if I videoed this and posted it on YouTube it would definitely go viral.

Beau laughs in what I assume is a combination of shock and amusement. We're ten feet from my insane parent, but he doesn't even notice us. When the song finally ends, he turns before leaping over like he's channeling Mikhail Baryshnikov with multiple groin pulls. Then he throws open his arms dramatically, looking for a hug.

He tells us, "This series is going to be epic; I may be dancing longer than normal before I start painting." Over the years I've met many artists through my dad, and I've come to learn that they all have a process, no matter how mad it may seem.

"How about going out to dinner with us?" I ask, my eyes pleading for a parental chaperone.

But Dad shakes his head as he yells out, "Alexa, play 'Freebird,' the extended version!" Then he says to me, "Maybe you could bring me something soft with a side of something crunchy." As if my dad needs to be any more different than he already is, when he's painting, he craves textures not flavors. I could bring him soft serve frozen yogurt and potato chips or mashed potatoes and peanuts. He would be thrilled either way because both would deliver the textures he needs.

Beau shoots me a questioning look, but I'll explain it to him later. I tell my dad, "You got it. I'll be back with soft and crunchy in a couple of hours. Will you be okay until then?"

He's already begun his "Freebird" waltz, which will last the near fourteen minutes of the song. Then he'll either lie on the floor and regroup for an hour, or he'll power through with a little Meatloaf, "Bat Out of Hell." It's anyone's guess.

I quickly stop in the bathroom, ostensibly to use it, but I don't need to. Instead, I brush my teeth, reapply my lipstick, and try to tame my crazy curls. I opt to pull them back into a low chignon to keep them out of my face.

Beau smiles admiringly when I return. I hope he doesn't think I was getting fixed up for him, but of course I was.

I try to convince myself that he's just my realtor, but I'm not doing a very good job of it.

Chapter 40

"You feel up to a short walk?" Beau asks as we leave my dad's loft.

"Sounds good." I figure the cold air will be good for me and keep me from getting overheated by his close proximity. "What do you have in mind?"

"There's a great fish place down by the river that I love. It's not fancy, but it's the best fish around."

It takes us twenty-three minutes to get there; yes, I'm counting. While the air is chilly and I even wear a scarf with my coat for extra warmth, I could probably be in a tank top and shorts and be fine.

Beau is walking very close to me. So close that when I try to gain some space, I lose my footing on a grassy embankment leading to the riverwalk. He takes my arm to help steady me, but he doesn't let go once we hit firm ground.

I free myself under the guise of checking my purse for something, but once I stop fiddling around with it, he takes my arm again. I'm so relieved when we get to the restaurant I could cheer.

Beau's right, Shuckie's is not fancy. In fact, while it appears clean, it also looks like it hasn't received a face lift in that last several decades. We sit at the booth next to the window, thankfully on opposite sides, or so I initially think. Sitting across from him allows me to watch him studying me in a way that I find very disconcerting.

I pick up a laminated menu on the table and discover my only choices are beer-battered walleye, sauger, bluegill or catfish. They all come with hushpuppies and coleslaw. "Not a very extensive menu, huh?" I ask.

"Doesn't need to be, when you've got the freshest and the best of what you're offering." A hefty African-American gentleman in a white t-shirt and apron hollers from behind the counter, "Whatchoo havin' tonight, Beau?"

"Hey, Shuckie. Can you start us out with two of whatever beer you have on draft and then bring us a sampler?"

"I'm on it," the proprietor replies.

Beau says, "I hope you don't mind me ordering for you, but being that you're gonna live here, you really should try everything so you can decide for yourself what you like."

"Out of the four, I've only ever had catfish. I'm looking forward to trying the others," I tell him.

Shuckie comes over and drops two beers on the table. "I got Float Trip ale tonight." Then he looks at Beau and asks, "Who's this pretty gal you got with you, son?"

He says, "This is Lexi Blake. She's moving here all the way from New York City. She's buying my family's old house on Millionaire's Row." Then to me he says, "Lexi, this is Shuckie. He's a local legend and fish-frying genius."

Shuckie takes my hand and offers, "I'm mighty pleased to

meet you. Welcome to town. You let me know which of the fish you like best."

"I'll do that," I tell him. Once he goes, it's just me and Beau while we wait for our food.

He's staring at me like I'm a Greek dictionary and he's trying to decipher the words. I don't know where to look as his scrutiny is so intense I dare not share it. Finally, I gaze around the restaurant. "I like it here. It doesn't seem too busy tonight, though."

"Business tapers off in the cooler months, which is why Shuckie doesn't have any servers to help him. In the summer, this place is so packed there's a two-hour wait for dinner. Folks take their food out and sit on the dock to eat, but even so, the fryer is so backed up that Shuckie often stays open until midnight."

"It's hard to believe I'm really going to live here," I tell him. "I'm not having second thoughts or anything, but it's all happened so fast."

"You need to get your mama down here," he says.

"I've been thinking the same thing, but that's easier said than done. Regina is not the most flexible person. Also, she's mad at my dad and I think she'd see coming down here as an act of forgiveness."

"She sounds like one tough cookie," he accurately states. "You gotta tell her about Myrah."

"I will. I can't imagine her not wanting to meet her family."

Then Beau does the most unexpected thing. He reaches across the table and takes my hands. I try to pull away, but he holds onto them tighter and says, "Settle down." Then he turns my palms up and studies them. He points to the line between my thumb and forefinger and says, "This here's your lifeline. You see here how it's broken in two?"

I nod my head and ask, "You read palms?"

"Myrah's taught me a couple of things over the years." He adds, "When a lifeline is broken, she says it can mean a major illness or a move. It's always something that irrevocably changes us and puts us on a different path."

"So, you're saying that my move was destined to be?"

"I don't know," he says. "Our ancestors sure thought it was. So maybe it was."

"I don't have a hard time conceptualizing predestination," I tell him, "it's just that I can't quite assimilate it to real life."

"Even after today?" he wonders. "Maybe our problem with it is that we're tryin' to make sense of it in terms of the past and future bein' on a timeline. But what if time isn't linear and it's circular instead?"

I've recently thought the same thing. "So, it's all happening at the same time?" I ask. Before he answers, I tell him, "I'm a big *Doctor Who* fan, so it's not that I have a hard time imagining such a thing, it's just that I have a hard time accepting it as reality."

"And yet Elsie knew that one of her descendants was gonna to buy Regina's house."

I shake my head. "It's a conundrum for sure."

He points to a line running down the middle of my palm. "This here's your fate line. It has to do with your career."

He touches the tip of his finger to the base of the line and says, "Myrah says it starts when you're about five years old. She says that's the age a person is fully grounded in this life and no longer standing with one foot in heaven." He gently traces the line up into the center of my palm. Goosebumps form all over my body as primal currents run through me.

"Right here is about the age you are now, thirty." Being that he points a third of the way up the line, I guess he's assuming I'll live to be ninety. I'll have to ask Myrah about this.

"It's broken like my lifeline," I say. "What does that mean?"

"It means a major career change. Your move here makes a lot of sense with both your life and fate line broken at the same place." Then he moves on and lightly caresses a horizontal line under my pinky finger.

"What line is that?" I ask.

He clears his throat before saying, "This is your love line." His voice is low and rough and causes my insides to drop like I'm being turned upside down on a rollercoaster. I don't ask what he's reading in my love line because truthfully I don't think I'm ready for the answer. But whatever it is, Beau can't stop staring at it.

Chapter 41

Our dinner is so delicious, I could eat here every night of the week. I'd be hard-pressed to pick a favorite fish though, and decide I'll probably order the sampler every time I come. The beer batter on the fish is so crisp the "crunch" can likely be heard across the county. "Is it this good every time?" I ask.

"Yes, ma'am. That's why Shuckie is considered the best. His food is never greasy. It's always cooked to perfection."

We thoroughly enjoy our meal and I eat more than my fair share. When our platter is nearly licked clean, Shuckie hollers across the restaurant, "Beau, Lexi, you want the banana puddin'?"

Beau shouts back, "You know it." Then to me he says, "Everyone down here makes banana pudding, but no one makes it like him."

"What does he do that makes his so special?" I ask.

"Rum. I swear Mama has tried to replicate it, but she doesn't get the proportions right." Beaus builds the culinary tension by adding, "Shuckie blends fresh banana so it's creamy and not chunky." The man himself brings over two half-pint-sized Mason jars filled to the brim. He places them on the table and says, "I got extra if you need it." Then he goes back to the kitchen.

As near as I can tell, banana pudding is nothing more than pudding layered with vanilla wafers, topped with whipped cream and more vanilla wafers. Beau is nearly half-way done with his by the time I finish inspecting mine and take my first bite. I groan at the sheer pleasure. In a word, this dessert is heavenly. The rum is significant, but it doesn't overshadow the banana flavor at all.

"It's soft and crunchy," I announce, knowing that this is exactly what my dad needs to eat in order to fulfill tonight's texture requirements.

As soon as I finish, Beau asks, "You want another?"

"I want six more, but I'd better not. I do want to take a couple of these for my dad, though."

Beau signals Shuckie and orders Bertie the same dinner we had as well as two puddings. He explains, "Your daddy will need some protein, too."

After Beau pays the check and we collect our to-go order, we start the walk home. He asks, "Is it okay if I tell my family about how you're related to Elsie, or do you prefer to do the telling?"

While I'd like to sit with this information and absorb it all for a few days before sharing it with anyone, I want Myrah and Clovis to feel free to talk about what we've all just discovered. I know they're as excited about it as I am. For this reason, and because I can't imagine doing more than sharing the story with my own parents right now, I answer, "I'd be happy if you'd pass on the news." Now all I have to do is force my mother to listen to me.

"Course you know, my family is gonna be over-the-moon excited and will probably drive you crazy with wanting to be a part of it all," he says.

"I don't think it's possible for them to drive me crazy," I tell him. "Knowing how our families have been entwined over the years makes me feel like this is supposed to be a joint effort."

Beau stops walking and turns to look into my eyes. "I'm happy that you're buying the house."

"Why?" I ask. "What's changed?" But instead of waiting for his answer, I speed up my pace so that he's nearly running next to me.

"Lexi, slow down. What's the rush?" he asks.

"I need to get Bertie's dinner to him before he starves," I say. *Liar, liar, pants on fire.*

When we get back to the factory, Beau unlocks the door for us to go inside and announces, "I'll see you up."

"There's no need," I tell him firmly. But he follows me across the lobby anyway. When the elevator comes, I try again. "Thank you for this unique and lovely day, and for dinner." I stick my hand out to shake his, but he doesn't take it. Instead, he nudges me into the elevator and gets on after me.

"What's goin' on with you? You're acting as jumpy as a bullfrog during hunting season." I have to stop and think about that one. I'm not sure why a bullfrog would be jumpy during hunting season unless you were hunting bullfrogs. Oh, my god, do they eat frogs down here? I involuntarily shudder at the thought.

I ignore his question. When we reach the third floor, I say again, "No need to walk me to the door."

He ignores me now and trails after me. Once we get to Bertie's door, I thank Beau for what I hope is the final time. "Goodnight, and thanks again." I sound more annoyed than grateful.

He still doesn't seem to be ready to walk away. Instead, he turns me so I'm facing him. What I see in his eyes makes my knees go so weak I almost keel over. He pulls me closer, and as his mouth hovers a mere whisper above mine, he tells me in a low voice, "I had a wonderful day, Lexi. Thank you very much."

Then, hand to God, the man leans down and kisses me so tenderly, so heart-meltingly, I forget to be outraged and pull away, or smack him for his impertinence. Instead, I lean into him and encourage him. It is the best, most tantalizing kiss I've ever been party to in my whole life, and it's all I can do not to jump into his arms and devour him whole.

The encounter lasts for a very long time. It begins as a peck, turns the corner on a respectable first date smooch, and quickly enters territory that I'm sure is full of signs that read Danger! Violators Will be Towed! and Trespassers Will be Shot! On and on it goes and I do nothing to stop it. In fact, it's Beau who finally pulls away.

When he does, we're leaning on each other with both of us panting for more. He finally manages to say, "Come down to the office at nine in the morning and we'll drive over to the house together for the inspection."

I make this sort of grunting, growling sound that's meant to mean, "okay," but I'm not sure it's successful. Beau takes the keys out of my hands and opens the door for me. Then he kisses me again, quicker this time, before turning to walk back down the hall.

I have no idea what just happened. Well, I mean, I know what happened, but I don't know why I allowed it to happen. I don't believe in fooling around with someone who's already taken, so I need to make sure whatever it was, there isn't a repeat performance.

If Regina's taught me one thing, it's that women are a sisterhood, and we owe it to one another to have each other's backs, no matter what kind of temptation Beau Frothingham is. And while I know this in my bones, my imagination takes flight, and it only occurs to me later that I am not angry at Beau one little bit. What does that mean? More destiny at play in the universe or just my fantasies taking flight?

Chapter 42

Bertie is lying on the ground under his canvas with the lights off when I walk into his apartment. He's using the flashlight app on his phone to gaze at it from a new angle. It's still free of any actual paint.

"Hi, Dad; I'm home," I announce. "Can I turn on the light?"

"Sure, honey." As soon as I do, he sits up and says, "I still don't know what it's going to be. Inspiration is building."

"Maybe something soft and crunchy will help," I suggest.

He enthusiastically bounds to his feet and asks, "Did you have a nice time?"

"I did." Because that's the truth. Even though the evening was fraught with mixed signals, had it been a date, it would have been the best one I've ever been on.

"Your friend Emmie has a nice family," he says. "Now what did you bring me?"

I unpack his meal for him, then drag over my air mattress closer to his canvas for him to sit on. "I have huge news." While I am excited about telling him the story, I'm a little worried he's going to think the whole town, including me, has lost their marbles.

"Shoot."

"Mom's family used to work for the original Frothingham family who founded Creek Water."

My dad stops opening his food. "Did Emmie or Beau tell you that?"

"They didn't know. Beau and I just found out today while we were out looking for furniture for the new house. He took me to a farm out in the country, and I met an old woman who is my direct relation." Nervously, I tell him about the old fortune-teller Mimi took me to in Harlem when I was a girl. Then I hand him the letter from Regina Frothingham.

Bertie doesn't eat one bite while I talk. After he reads what the first Regina wrote to me, he sits in silence for a while, absorbing all of this. He finally tells me, "Your grandmother used to take your mom to the same lady. She hated it."

"Mom went?" My mother is too logical and grounded to ever buy into something like that.

"She didn't want to go," my dad replies. "But Mimi loved it, and your mom loved Mimi, so she went."

"Did she have her fortune read?" I ask.

"Several times, but she'd never tell me what it was. She's said it was all a load of nonsense and there was no point in talking about it, so we didn't."

"I have to get Mom down here," I tell him. "But I'm not sure how. I don't know how to make her listen."

"Why don't you start by telling her the truth?" he asks.

"I would, but it's so bizarre," I say.

"That it is. Let's think on it, I'm sure the perfect plan will present itself." As he says this, I realize once again how different my parents are.

I'm pretty sure my mom is too pragmatic to ever consider that the letter could be real. But, then I think about her relationship with my dad and how that doesn't make a lot of sense given their differences, and I wonder if she might try.

While I'm contemplating this, Bertie eats his meal, making all of the yummy sounds I did. "This is the best fish I've ever eaten," he declares.

"It's fresh from the river," I tell him. "Not from the ocean, so you're perfectly safe." I'm teasing him about his fear of me eating fish while outside of New York.

"I had a preconceived idea of what the rest of the country was like, and I'm happy to say that in the case of Creek Water, Missouri, I was totally wrong."

"So, after you're done painting your series, you think you'll come visit me down here?"

"I might move in with you for half the year. I've never been quite this inspired before."

I laugh. "Even though you don't know what you're painting yet, huh?" Then I say, "I'm going to meet Beau downstairs at nine tomorrow morning to go over to the house for the inspection. You want to come?"

I don't really expect him to break away from his canvas, so I'm shocked when he answers, "I do! I need to see the inside of this house of yours with my own eyes."

Bertie devours every last bit of his food, humming while he consumes the pudding. "Exactly what I needed." After lying down on the floor to stare at his canvas again, he announces, "You know, I always felt like I lived a big life."

"Because you were an artist in New York City?" I ask.

"Exactly. Your mom and I were living our dream in the best city in the world. We were always open to new experiences, and man, did we do some cool stuff."

"You did," I agree. My parents were always off to an art opening or a jazz club or a lecture of some kind. They used to call themselves *Urbanistas.*

"But now that I'm here," he says. "I realize how small that life really was."

"Small? How do you figure?"

"Because we discounted so much of the world. Unless it was a big shiny place with big shiny ideas, we weren't interested. It turns out that Creek Water and small towns like it are the places that paved the way for big change. Without them, Regina and I would have never had the life that we've had together. It's a humbling realization."

I think about Regina Frothingham's letter and how thrilled she was by the idea that a woman would ever be able to buy her home, a woman of color no less. I wonder what she'd make of my parents' relationship. A black/Jewish woman partnering with an eccentric white guy, never getting married, but nonetheless creating a family together. I'm pretty sure it would have blown her mind.

After my dad heads upstairs to his bed, I take a turn and lie on my air mattress and stare at his blank canvas. It's the perfect metaphor for life. We can create anything we want on our canvas, and if we don't like what we make, we can start over until we design the work of art we're happy with. It's an exhilarating thought.

This has been the most eventful and wonderful day of my

life. Never in a million years could I have imagined anything like it happening to me. And suddenly I can't wait to find out what happens next.

Chapter 43

I'm a ball of nerves when Bertie and I walk into Beau's office this morning. When I woke up, I lay in bed reliving yesterday's whole day together. Of course, the majority of the time was spent rehashing our kiss.

Beau greets us with a warm smile and asks, "How was your dinner, Bertie?"

"Delicious," he replies. "One of these days I'll have to make you the meal I'm famous for."

"Reservations?" I wonder.

"No, no, no, your mom and I have recently tried something new. We take all the leftovers in the refrigerator and add them to two cans of chicken broth. It's a little something we like to call garbage soup. But I can't make it until I get enough leftovers."

"As appealing as that sounds," Beau politely manages, "why don't you leave the meals to us?"

Unsure whether he is serious or joking, I grimace at the thought of what those dinners must have tasted like and ask, "Is it ever edible?"

"Sometimes," my dad laughs. "Mostly, we do it for laughs

and wind up ordering in something new."

Beau collects some papers before leading the way down to his car. As my dad gets in the back-passenger side, Beau opens the door for me.

He leans in and whispers into my ear, "I had a wonderful time yesterday, thank you."

His hot breath sends shivers through my nervous system like the sure slow crawl of hot lava. It's a good thing I'm leaning against his car or I'd surely puddle to the ground. I realize I might be starting to embrace colorful southernisms. "Puddle to the ground" sounds like something Emmie's mom might say.

"I had a very nice time too, thank you," I reply. I don't say anything else as I climb in and try to calm my racing heart.

My dad fills the ride to my new house with excited chatter. When we arrive, there are already several cars parked in front of the house. "Who's here?" I ask. But before Beau can answer, most of his family converges on us. His mom, Emmie and Zach, Gracie, Davis, and Amelia. The only people missing are Jed and Jesse.

I get out and ask, "What are you all doing here?"

Emmie is the first to speak. "We're here to welcome you home. Beau told us everything over breakfast this morning, and we're so excited we can hardly stand it." She throws herself into my arms to punctuate her enthusiasm.

Lee tackles me next, and says, "This is the most excitin' thing that's ever happened in our family!"

Davis offers, "We're here for whatever you need."

"You let us know what that is and we're on it. I love to paint walls, so you can sign me up for that," Amelia says.

Gracie claps her hands together and exclaims, "Can I do the kitchen?"

I'm so overwhelmed by their eagerness I could cry. I have an extended family in Creek Water that I've never had before. It's a wonderful feeling.

When the building inspector pulls up, he's a bit taken aback by the number of people waiting on him. Beau says, "Homer, push us out of the way if we're a bother." Then he jokes, "But good luck with that."

Homer, an older man wearing blue jeans and a flannel shirt, responds, "As long as all y'all aren't in the same room with me at the same time, we're good."

We head toward the front door like a crowd of Christmas carolers. I don't care what problems the inspector finds, I'm buying this house. I walk through the front door and fancy that a host of long-lost relatives are welcoming me home.

Beau's family splits up and starts taking stock of the work that interests them, leaving me and Beau in the entryway by ourselves. He says, "You're going to have to rein them in at some point or they'll take over."

"I like that they're this excited," I tell him.

He suggests, "We need to get Myrah over here. I bet she'll be a lot of help knowing where to put the furniture."

"We have to close on the house before I can even think about bringing the furniture over. But I agree. I can't wait for Myrah and Clovis to visit."

Beau reaches over and takes my hand in his. I quickly pull away and say, "Beau, about last night …"

But he doesn't let me finish. He says, "We need to do that again soon."

"Don't you think we should talk about …"

He doesn't let me finish. Instead he leans in and kisses me. And sure enough, I let him. Sensational fireworks explode through me, shooting down my extremities and beyond. Kissing this man feels as right as buying this house. I finally push him away long after I should have, and say, "We shouldn't."

He smiles with a glint in his eye and says, "You're wrong. We should do that all the time."

Before I have a chance to respond, there's a knock on the door. Who in the world could that be?

Chapter 44

"Mom?" I ask. "What are you doing here?"

My mother is standing on my new doorstep looking mad, determined, and a little something else that I can't quite define. "What do you think I'm doing here? I've come to ascertain whether or not your father has lost his mind."

I step back to indicate that she should come in. "How did you know where we were?

"I installed an app on Bertie's phone that lets me track him," she answers. "The older he gets the more I worry about him." *That's actually a really good idea.* My mom looks around and demands, "Whose house is this?" then, stating the obvious, says, "It's empty."

Beau interrupts, "I'm Emmie's cousin, Beau Frothingham." He extends his hand and adds, "I'm *very* pleased to make your acquaintance." He's turning on the charm.

My mom came here in a snit, and I'm pretty sure no display of Southern manners is going to change that. If anything, it'll annoy her more by reminding her that she's not in New York. I'm guessing she'll cling to her mood until she completes her mission, which is most likely to rip my dad a new one.

Beau says, "This amazing home is one of the first used in the Underground Railroad. I'm the listing agent."

My mom is momentarily at a loss for words. While I'm sure she'd be interested in knowing more about the house, her desire to see my father is too strong to be sidetracked. She takes Beau's hand, gives it a perfunctory shake and says, "Nice to meet you, Beau." Then to me she asks, "Where's Bertie?"

Catching my eye, Beau suggests, "Why don't you take your mama for a walk around the grounds. That way you can talk privately."

"Great idea." I march out the door, pulling Regina with me.

She demands, "Alexis, what's going on here?"

"I've been trying to call you to explain all kinds of things, but you didn't answer. Mom, this house is one of the things I've wanted to talk to you about."

Looking confused, she asks, "What about it?"

I might as well get it over with. "I bought it."

"You what?" she demands. "What do you mean you bought it?"

"I mean that in a couple weeks, I'm moving in. I already have my financing in order, and I'm going to apply for some grants to help me renovate, then I'm going to turn the place into a bed and breakfast."

"I thought you were moving to Atlanta," she says, her voice heavy with confusion.

I shake my head. "Not anymore. Once I saw this house, I knew that I needed to live here. There's something about it, Mom." *Now to tell her the unusual story of its history.*

She stares at me in shock for a minute and then turns away

and looks at the property like I told her I was going to relocate to Saturn to open a massage parlor. When she finally turns around, she asks, "When were you going to tell me this?"

"When you returned my phone call."

Ignoring that her ignorance is actually her own fault, she asks, "What does Bertie think?"

"He loves the idea as much as I do. He's excited that I'm moving here. He's inside seeing the house for the first time." While I'm sure I made things a load worse for my dad, it's better to get the whole truth out in one fell swoop.

My mom looks a little unsteady on her feet. "Where?" she demands while zig-zagging her finger at the windows of the house.

"Dunno. But Mom, I need to tell you the rest." I'd love to relay the story in pieces, but with all the Frothinghams inside, I have to tell her now. She cannot walk inside without knowing everything.

"What rest? What more could you possibly say than you're leaving home to move god knows where?"

"Well, we know where. I'm moving to Creek Water, Missouri. Which turns out to be the home of your ancestors," I say, lowering the boom.

"Alexis, what are you talking about? My family has never lived here. We're New Yorkers."

I spy a bench near the rose arbor and say, "Let's sit down, Mom."

Seated, I relay everything Myrah told me. I explain how our ancestor, Elsie, used to live in this house and that she even foretold my buying it one day. I describe the letter from Regina

Frothingham, the woman she was named after.

My mom declares, "I wasn't named after anyone. I've never heard of Regina Frothingham before now." She adds, "Mimi said she named me Regina because she wanted me to know that I was always queen of my own destiny."

"Are you sure that's all she said?" I ask.

"She might have mentioned that she went to see that crazy fortune-teller of hers when she was pregnant with me. The old coot told Mimi she thought it would be a fitting name."

Then I pull out the letter I've been carrying since Myrah gave it to me. I hand it to my mom and wait while she opens it up.

"What's this?" she demands.

"It's from Regina Frothingham."

My mom's eyes bug open and she takes the envelope. She pulls out the stationery, unfolds it, and begins to read. She doesn't look up until she's finished. "This can't be real," she says. It's the exact reaction I expected her to have.

I point to the date on the letter which clearly shows that it was written in 1864. She shakes her head and asks, "How? Why didn't we know about this before now? Why didn't my mother know?" She's as shocked as I was.

"I guess because Mimi's mother never told her."

My mom looks like she's digging through her memories before she answers, "All I know is that my great-grandmother moved to New York with her husband because the house they were working in was being sold and the family they worked for wouldn't need as many household staff in their new situation."

If this is so, then surely Myrah's family would have kept in touch with them. I'll have to make sure to ask her about this.

"Mimi's mother told her they'd heard all about New York City from someone and thought it was the perfect opportunity to see what life there was all about. They liked the idea of redefining themselves."

"And you never knew they moved from Missouri? Didn't you wonder about their accents?" I ask.

"They died while I was very young. I guess I never consciously realized they had one." Trying to process this information she reiterates, "You and Emmie became friends in New York City, and it was her family that saved ours all those years ago, right here in Missouri. I can't wrap my head around it."

"It's big, right?" Then I announce, "Mimi took me to her fortune-teller once."

"I'm not surprised. What did she tell you?" my mom asks.

"She told me that in my thirtieth year, a dog would jump over me, and my life would change in the most unexpected ways." I tell her about that afternoon in Central Park when Hanzie the German shepherd jumped over me, immediately followed by learning that my apartment was going condo, and that I was begin *promoted* to Atlanta. "If all of that isn't unexpected, I don't know what is. Then I found this house and learned the truth about our family history."

"I always thought that woman was nuts," she says, shaking her head like she's trying to get this information to fall into place.

"Did she ever tell you anything?" I ask.

Regina answers, "She told me all kinds of crazy stuff."

"Like what?" I ask.

"Like I'd get married under the tracks of change. I don't even know what that means. Obviously she was wrong, because as you know, I've never been married." Then she adds, "Currently, I don't even feel like I'm in a good relationship."

"Mom, how can you say that? You know what dad is like. Just because he didn't discuss his trip with you before leaving doesn't mean that he doesn't love you or that your relationship isn't good."

"That's your opinion. I say a good relationship doesn't involve packing up and leaving your partner without talking about it first. Now, while this," she waves Regina Frothingham's letter in the air, "is very interesting and I have many questions I'd like to have answered, I think it's time you take me to your father."

Poor Bertie. I was hoping to not only share my future with my mom, but perhaps derail a bit of anger she was feeling toward my dad. I don't think it worked.

Chapter 45

I lead my mom into my new home ostensibly to search for Bertie. While I know we'll eventually run into him, I take her to the bedroom at the top of the second-floor stairs, hoping to prolong that eventuality.

When I ask her to join me in the closet, she says, "Quit stalling, Alexis. I want to see your father."

"I'm not stalling," I say. "Come in here."

Unable to ignore her curiosity, she does so. She jumps like I did when I dislodge the clothes rack and cause the back wall to pop open. "What's this?" she demands as she follows me up the back stairs.

"Wait," I tell her.

When we reach the landing in front of the secret room in the attic, I explain, "This is one of the rooms the Frothinghams used in the Underground Railroad."

Regina can't help but be affected by this news. She walks in slowly before gently touching the walls. The dingy gray looks like it hasn't been painted in decades. She circles the full perimeter of the space quietly, before asking, "Are you feeling what I'm feeling?"

I answer, "I feel hope. What about you?" I'm excited to hear her response.

She looks up wild-eyed. "I feel fear and confusion, not to mention a good deal of panic."

"I'm sure there was a lot of that in here," I reply. How could there not be with people fleeing for their lives?

"Why do you want to live here?" my mom asks, truly confused.

"Because it's a part of history. I want schools, genealogy groups, history buffs, *whoever* comes up here, to shut the door for a couple of minutes. I want them to imagine what it was like for the slaves who came through here to be hidden away, afraid."

"Lexi, it was such a horrible time. How can you want to live with that every day?"

I'm completely surprised by my mom's reaction. I thought she would love the historic element of my new home.

"You need to visit Myrah," I tell her. "What happened in this house wasn't horrible. It was beautiful. People were helped and their lives changed forever."

She nods her head slowly. "I believe this history needs to be taught and never forgotten, but to live here … I'm not sure I understand your desire to do so."

"This house has been on and off the market for years and no one has ever bought it. It's a rare treasure. Someone has to be the bridge between the past and present. Why not me?"

"Are people down here going to welcome such a thing?" she asks.

"Mom, people have been nothing but kind and welcoming," —if you don't count Shelby's mother, that is— "You need to stay for a while so that you can see that for yourself."

"I have classes to teach, Alexis," she tells me. While that's true, she's also using that as an excuse to avoid learning more about my new life.

"You have a teaching assistant," I reply. "And, if I recall, you've taught via Skype in the past when you were sick and didn't feel up to going in to work. Why can't you do that from here?"

She gives me the side-eye; she's not at all happy I've come up with a reasonable-sounding plan that would allow her to stay. Then a brilliant thought comes to me. "Imagine doing a lecture series on the power of women from as far back as the Civil War. You could do that from this very house and give your class a tour as you speak. Sounds like the perfect women's studies topic to me."

"Don't try to manipulate me, Alexis," my mom snaps. But I can tell from her expression that I've successfully planted a seed that she's going to have a tough time ignoring. "Where's your father?" she demands.

I shrug. "Don't know, but I'm happy to show you through the rest of the house. We're bound to run into him." She probably doesn't pick up her phone and call him because she's relying on the element of surprise.

We wind up running into everyone but my dad. Lee and Gracie spot us in the second-floor hallway. I introduce, "Lee, Gracie, I'd like you to meet my mother, Regina."

My mom is in no way prepared for the storm of excitement that meets her. Gracie throws herself into my mom's arms and declares, "We're so thrilled to have you here!" She hugs my mom for a bit before dancing around a little more. Regina acts as nervous as if she were being attacked by band of roving leprechauns. She doesn't seem to know how to react, but you can tell she wants her space.

Lee joins in with, "Aren't Lexi's plans for this house exciting?" Then, in pure attention-deficit fashion, she changes the subject and says, "You have to come to dinner tonight."

Lee and Gracie start chattering like magpies about where we should eat. They finally decide that going back to the club would be the best option. My mom looks like she's about to spray mace on them to get them to calm down.

Regina finally says, "I'm not sure what I'll be doing for dinner, but thank you for your invitation."

Lee grabs her hand and acts like she doesn't understand the brush off. "Lexi, have your folks there at six. I'll make sure Chef Jarvis has something special prepared for us."

Then Gracie says, "If y'all are going to be here for a while, I'll run down to the Piggly Wiggly and get some pastries and coffee."

Lee says, "What a wonderful idea! You get those and I'll go over to the Delish Deli and pick up some sandwiches for lunch. We can have a picnic."

The Frothingham women become completely enraptured by the idea of a picnic lunch and run off to make good on their threat. As they go, Emmie and Amelia come out of one of the bedrooms.

Emmie gasps like a heroine in a medieval romance when she sees my mom. "Regina, what are you doin' here?"

My mom smiles at my friend before answering, "I'm looking for Bertie."

Emmie blanches. "Don't be too mad at him," she says. "I mean, I know what a dumb fool thing that was to run off like he did, but I think he's really gonna to make some magic down here."

My mom listens even though she doesn't seem too pleased that her feud with my dad is common knowledge. She opts not to respond to her though, and looks at Amelia. She says, "I'm Regina."

Amelia, who's all dolled-up in some kind of sixties throwback style, smiles brightly at my mom. "I'm Emmie's cousin, Amelia. Welcome to Creek Water."

I can tell my mom had not been expecting to be treated like an honored guest. It's kind of throwing her off her game. So, instead of looking for a way to break free, she allows Emmie and Amelia to show her around.

I sneak off to look for my dad, hoping to give him warning that Hurricane Regina has arrived.

Chapter 46

I find Bertie in the basement. It's dark, dank, and thoroughly creepy down here. I'm pretty sure that aside from giving tours, I won't be spending any time within its depths. I finally locate my dad in one of the secret rooms, sitting on the dirt floor with his eyes closed. I say, "Dad, what are you doing down here?" but he doesn't answer.

So, I shake his shoulder. "DAD!" I try shouting, but he doesn't move. He must be meditating again, so I recite the lyrics from that Beatles song. Nothing.

After carefully weighing the pros and cons, I pull out my phone to ask my mom what to do. She answers right away with, "Where are you?"

"I'm in the basement. I found Dad, but I can't get him to wake up."

"Did you try the song?" she asks.

"Yeah, but he's not responding to it." I instruct, "I'll meet you at the bottom of the steps."

A few minutes later, my mom comes down the stairs. When she reaches the last one, she looks around for a minute. Then, stepping down, she kicks the dirt floor and says, "This is straight-up old-school."

The dim bulb hanging overhead doesn't allow for much light, but there's enough that you can see the ancient furnace in the corner. "I don't suppose they used this area for more than storage." Then I shudder and add, "You know, unless they had a body they needed to bury or something."

My mom releases a bark of laughter. "Lexi, are you afraid?"

"Aren't you?" I demand.

She shakes her head. "No. This space feels honest to me. It's not trying to hide what it is."

"You're wrong. I'll show you what it's hiding." I take her through one large doorway before pointing to a much smaller one that's no higher than three feet. I'm guessing the original owners put flour sacks or something against it when it was closed to hide its existence from curious eyes.

I indicate that she should crawl through the doorway and she declares, "I'll get dirty."

All I need to say is, "Dad's in there," before she's on the ground moving. I tell her, "I left my flashlight app on. He's in the corner." The secret rooms don't have any light switches that I've been able to find, not that I've looked too hard. The only reason I knew Bertie was in this room was because the hidden door was open.

I don't hear anything as I'm sure the brick walls absorb a lot of the sound. "Mom, what's going on in there?" I shout.

She peeks her head out of the doorway. "I'm not sure what to do to get him to wake up. Let's get him out of here while I think about it."

"How?" I demand but she doesn't answer. Instead she goes back in. Within moments I see my dad's feet pop out of the doorway. Regina instructs, "Pull him out."

I pull while my mom pushes, and we eventually succeed in our task. Regina crawls out next and brushes the dirt off her pants as she stands up. Staring down at my dad, she says, "I tried the Beatles, and I tried a couple other things he's used over the years, but nothing's working."

"Do you think he's had a stroke or something?" I ask, genuinely fearful.

"I don't think so," she says. "He looks like he always does when he's meditating." She kneels down to take his pulse. "It's slow but it's there."

I punch Beau's number into my phone. When he answers, I demand, "Come to the basement right away." I'm not sure what he can do, but we'll need some muscle if we decide to carry Bertie anywhere.

I turn to my mom. "I don't remember Dad being unresponsive when meditating before. What's going on?"

"He started taking this self-hypnosis class so that he could tap into his inner creativity. It turns out he has a real knack for it. So much so that he's had to program safe words so someone else could bring him out." She points to her head and says, "He gets kind of lost up there."

"Dad told me about that," I reply. "But it sounds like it could be dangerous."

"That's why we have trigger words to bring him back."

"He's obviously programmed one no one knows about," I say.

Regina shrugs. "Your father isn't like everyone else, honey." She says that almost admiringly, which makes me realize that her love for him still outweighs her anger.

Beau comes running down the stairs and asks, "What's going on?"

I point to my dad. "We think he's meditating, but we don't know how to get him to snap out of it."

"Why stop him? Why not wait until he comes to on his own?" Beau asks.

"You mean leave him down here?" That doesn't sound very safe.

"What could happen?" he asks. "We're all upstairs and from what I understand, we will be at least through lunch." He suggests, "I have a blanket in my trunk. I can go out and get it in case you're worried he'll be too cold."

My mom answers, "Let him get cold." Then she steps over him and starts up the stairs.

Beau looks at me and states the obvious, "She's pretty mad, huh?"

"You could say that. I've never seen her this upset with Bertie before and I don't know what to do to fix it."

"Why do you need to fix it?" he asks.

"Because if I hadn't sent my dad those pictures, he would have never come, and he and my mom wouldn't be fighting."

Beau answers, "You didn't force him to come. In fact, the way I see it, you've given him his creativity back. Didn't you say he'd been in a slump?"

"Yeah, but I don't want to cause any trouble between him and my mom."

"Lexi, if there's trouble, it was there before he came here. It's not your doin' and you can't fix it for them. They're grownups. Let them deal with it."

I suppose Beau might be on to something, but I still feel obligated to do something. Although as long as my dad is unconscious, I can't imagine what that is.

Chapter 47

Gracie and Lee come back with all manner of food. There are sandwiches and cookies, macaroni salad and chips. They set up a buffet on the kitchen counter.

As we gather around our lunch, Amelia announces that she has to go back to work. She takes a moment to tell my mom how happy she is that we're all having dinner together tonight. After she leaves Regina leans in and whispers, "Why are they so determined that I join them for dinner?"

I smack her arm and say, "Mother, they're my friends and they're being nice. Why don't you try it? I'm pretty sure it won't kill you."

She shoots me the hairy eyeball. The one I always get when she thinks I'm being impertinent. Then she picks up a paper plate and examines her choices.

While we're sitting on the floor in the breakfast nook, Davis comes in.

He walks right over to my mom. "You must be Regina. I'm Beau's brother Davis."

My mom nods her head once like the queen she is and replies, "Nice to meet you."

Without further ado, he reports to me, "I've been with Homer. It looks like most of the big repairs are cosmetic, with the exception of the electric. I was surprised to discover that the Benters replaced the plumbing with copper several years ago, so you're all set there."

"That's great news. Isn't it?" I ask him for reassurance.

"Great news."

Apparently, that's all I need to know because Davis plops down on the floor next to my mom and says, "I'm mighty pleased to meet you, ma'am. We think the world of your daughter down here."

"Why?"

"Why what? Why am I pleased to meet you or why do we think so highly of Lexi?"

"Both," she answers.

Davis doesn't seem the least bit afraid of my mom, which is the reaction her outrageous behavior is intended to elicit. "Lexi is a friend of my cousins, and Emmie's always had very good taste in folks. Not only is your daughter a lovely woman in her own right, but from what we've just discovered, our families go way back. We have a long-standing built-in bond between us. That has to mean somethin'."

Regina finally pries her manners open and says, "I'm pleased to meet you too, Davis. Are you planning on helping Lexi fix up the place?"

"Yes, ma'am. We all are. We consider it a family project."

I sneak a peek at my mom and can tell she isn't sure what to make of this. She doesn't know Emmie's family from Adam, but they're so warm and welcoming, they're making it hard for her to be standoffish. Although, I'm sure she's still distrustful.

Davis sits with us through the rest of our meal and doesn't get up until Homer comes into the room. The building inspector says, "Everything looks to be in pretty decent order."

"What about the roof?" I ask. I remember Beau warning me that it probably only had a couple years of life left and that a new one would cost a small fortune.

Homer says, "It was replaced ten years ago. You probably got another fifteen years or so on it." So, that was just another thing Beau was making up to turn me off the idea of buying this house. If he hadn't so recently changed his tune, I'd call him out on it.

Homer adds, "Tell Beau I'll email him the whole report by the end of business today."

As Homer walks out of the kitchen, who should come strolling through but my dad. He looks dazed and confused. I cannot believe that all the commotion didn't bring him out of his trance earlier.

"Dad," I say. "Mom's here."

Bertie looks down and sees my mom; a myriad of emotions cross his face, the predominant one being joy. Oblivious to his audience, he drops down next to her and pulls her in for a full-body hug. You can tell Regina wants to yell at him, but he doesn't give her the opportunity. Instead he kisses her quickly and in a voice thick with emotion admits, "I'm so glad you're here. Honey, something miraculous is happening, and it wouldn't be right for it to happen without you."

My mom finally pushes him off of her and admonishes, "Lambertos, what are you rambling about? I'm not here for anything miraculous. I'm here to find out what in the world is going on with you. How dare you pick up and leave without discussing it with me first?"

My dad doesn't respond to her anger. Instead, he says, "I know what my series is going to be about and it's going to be the most important thing I've ever done."

"What?" she demands.

"You know I can't talk about it until the first painting is done. You have to trust me."

"I'm mad at you, Bertie. I don't feel like trusting you," she says.

Instead of apologizing to her again, he very uncharacteristically stands up for himself, and tells her, "I'm mad at you too, Regina."

"What? Why?" she demands. "You're the one who ran away from me. I didn't leave you."

He shakes his head. "You've kept me at arm's length during our entire relationship."

"What in the world are you talking about?" she demands.

He replies, "I've asked you to marry me thirty-four times. You've said no the same number of times."

My mom scoffs. "I never said yes because I don't believe in marriage."

"But I do," he replies. "It's my understanding that relationships are about give and take. The way I see it, we've lived the last thirty-five years honoring your beliefs. I think it's time for you to bend and spend the next thirty-five honoring mine."

"Dammit, Bertie!" my mom yells. "I don't need a piece of paper from the state of New York to tell me how much you mean to me."

"That's not what it's about," he says. "It's about standing

before God and man and pledging ourselves forever. *That* means something to me."

My mom shakes her head. "You run out on me and then have the nerve to demand that I do something I don't believe in? That takes balls, Bertie."

"No," he answers her. "I told you why I'm here. I'm here to create the most important work of my career. If you can't understand that, then you don't think very highly of what I do. If you can't compromise your ideals to do something that matters to me, like I've done for you, then clearly our partnership is not an equal one. I'm tired of being the one to make the concessions."

"What are you saying?" my mom demands.

"I'm saying that I love you, Regina Cohen. We've created a family together and it means more to me than anything in this world. I'm saying that if you don't want to marry me, then I'm going to take that as a sign that you don't love me as much as I love you and I'm going to walk away."

My mom looks like she's been punched in the gut. "Where did this come from?" she demands. "You've never spoken to me like this."

Bertie leans in and gently kisses my mother on the lips. She doesn't move an inch. He pulls back and says, "Before you decide, you'd better know that I'm through keeping my feelings to myself. I'm going to tell you exactly what's on my mind from here on out."

Regina snaps, "You're not selling your case very well."

He shakes his head. "It's all of me or nothing, Regina. You'd better think about that." Then he walks out of the room, leaving both Mom and me more than a bit shell-shocked. Something is very definitely going on with Bertie, and as far as I can see, those changes are for the better. Now we have to sit back and see how my mom is going to handle it. I don't doubt that she loves my dad. I know she does. I'm just not sure she has what it takes to compromise to the degree he's asking of her.

Chapter 48

My mother sits on the floor completely mute. I'm sure she never thought my dad would talk to her like that. That hasn't been their dynamic. Normally, she's the one telling everyone how it's going to be, and we've let her.

I look up and see that Beau walked in at some point during Bertie's speech. From the look on his face, I'm guessing he caught most of it.

I suggest, "Mom, why don't we go find a nice hotel for you?" I'm guessing hell will freeze over before she goes over to my dad's apartment now. I turn to Beau and ask, "Can you recommend one?"

He strides over to my mom and reaches his hand down to her. "I don't think your mama needs a hotel," he says.

"What do you think she needs? A park bench and a blanket?" I ask more than a little sarcastically.

"She needs family," he announces, ignoring my tone. My mom silently stares at him, so he continues, "Come with me, ma'am. I'm gonna to take you over to meet Myrah and Clovis." I scramble to my feet to join them, but Beau says, "I think your mama needs to go on her own. I'll pick you up after I drop her off."

I expect Regina to tear into Beau for being so presumptuous, and quite honestly I'm looking forward to the fireworks. I don't appreciate his coming in here and trying to run the show when it's not his show to run. But much to my surprise, my mom lets him help her up and even says, "I think that might be the ticket."

I watch in shock as Beau and Regina leave the house together. What just happened?

I follow them out onto the front porch and see Bertie sitting on the front steps. My mom walks right past him without saying a word.

I sit down next to him. "Wow, that was quite a scene."

"Damn straight," he answers. "Don't follow in my footsteps, Lexi. When you find the person you want to spend your life with, make sure you let them know up front what matters to you. And if those things change, don't stay quiet about it. You can't grow together unless you communicate your feelings."

"Did you really mean it when you said you'd walk away from Mom if she didn't agree to marry you? That seems a bit drastic, don't you think?"

"I love your mother enough to live with her forever the way things stand now. But I'm getting a little insecure in my old age, and I want a grand gesture. Marriage is the gesture I'm looking for."

I'm glad my dad is standing up for what he wants, but I worry what will happen to him when my mom doesn't give in to his demands. "What do you want to do now?" I ask.

"I'm going to walk back to the loft and get started painting," he says.

"I'll bring dinner." I ask, "You in the mood for any particular textures?"

He thinks for a minute before saying, "Gooey. But not hot gooey, like melted cheese."

"What would that be then?" I wonder out loud.

He shrugs. "I don't know, but I don't want it to be sticky, just gooey." Then he stands up and announces, "Tell your mom that I've started and that I don't want her interrupting my flow unless she's ready to concede to my wishes."

"Dad," I caution, "you know this probably isn't the best way to deal with her." Especially as he's never acted this way before, so she's totally unprepared.

"Tough. Maybe it's time she learns that this isn't the best way to deal with me." Then he speeds off down the sidewalk like he's a magnet being pulled home.

Holy crap, talk about unexpected events. I'm not sure how everything is going to work out or even if it is. My parents are both in town and not speaking to each other, I'm buying a house and starting a new business, and I'm falling for a guy who may or may not be in a relationship with another woman.

I'm not sure what to do next. So, I decide to go back inside and spend some time visualizing myself in my new home. I should pick out what bedroom I want and which to renovate for guests. Instead, I pull a small pad of paper out of my purse and begin a list.

- Fill out grant applications.
- Call an electrician.
- Look into ways to hypnotize my mother into doing my dad's bidding.

Chapter 49

I'm still annoyed with Beau when he gets back from dropping my mom off at Myrah and Clovis's. I demand, "Well, how did it go? Were they surprised to see her?" Before he can answer, I add, "You know, I would have liked to have witnessed their meeting for myself."

Beau puts both hands out in front of him with his fingers spread like he's getting ready to catch a basketball. "I know. I'm sorry about that, but I felt like your mama needed a break from people who know her. You know what I mean?"

"No. She came here for us, why would she need a break?" I demand.

"She seemed overwhelmed, Lexi, especially after your daddy's little speech." He explains, "I didn't take her right out to the farm. I drove her around town for a bit to help her get her bearings."

"You did?" I ask. "Where did you go?"

"We went to the factory first, so she could see where your dad has been staying. I wanted her to see what drew him here. I thought it might help her understand his odd behavior a little better."

To say I'm surprised would be a massive understatement. So far, my impression of Beau is that he's a ruggedly great-looking alpha-male type, not necessarily Mr. Sensitive. Showing her Dad's place must have really helped Regina get her balance. There are a lot of unknowns and surprises for her here, what with never having set foot in Missouri before, let alone in a small town like Creek Water. "What did she think of it?" I ask.

"She didn't say a lot. She walked around, looked out the windows, and got a feel for the space. Then she spent several minutes staring at the blank canvases your dad has lined up against the wall. She thanked me for taking her there. I think she understood Bertie's decision a little more."

"Thank you." I don't know what else to say. It turns out Beau is quite intuitive and that makes him a hundred times more appealing.

"Did you take her out to the farm after that?" I ask.

He shakes his head. "No. I drove her down by the river first. I've always thought there was somethin' about the Mississippi River that helps a person think."

"What did she say?" I ask.

"Nothing. We sat there and stared for about twenty minutes. When I finally broke the silence, I asked her if she was ready to go to the farm."

As touched as I am about the care Beau took with my mom, I wish I had been there so I could have seen how she reacted to meeting her long-lost family. "How did it go? Was she excited? What did they say?" I demand.

He shrugs his shoulders. "I don't know. She didn't want me to come in with her. She just got out of the car and walked in by herself."

"What about the dogs?" I remember Beau warning me to stay put until Clovis assured them I was okay.

"They ran up to her and she yelled 'sit' and those two beasts hit the dirt. They laid down like their mistress had arrived." I laugh at the surprise written across his face. "You must have grown up with dogs," he says.

"Nope. Bertie couldn't run the risk of them knocking into canvases or getting in his way when he was creating something."

"Then how in the world did she control them so well?" he wonders.

"Regina is the queen of control," I tell him. "Once, she and I were about to get mugged in the subway. I kid you not, two burly creeps were coming right at us. It was late at night and no one else was around, so shouting for help wouldn't have helped."

"What happened?" he asks.

"My mom pushed me behind her and shoved her hand in her purse. She walked straight at them, pulled out her NYU employee badge and stuck it right in the first guy's face. Not only was he completely taken off guard by the fact that my mom approached him, but he couldn't read the ID that close up."

Beau demands, "What happened next?"

"She leaned in and said, 'I'm with a black-ops branch of the CIA and you assholes are about to ruin three years of hard work. The shadows are crawling with my people, so you'd better turn around and get the hell out of here before I signal them to shoot you between the eyes.'"

"How old were you?" he asks.

"Eighteen. And, believe me, I didn't look capable of shooting anyone. It was all I could do not to pee my pants."

"Did they run?" he asks.

I say, "Yeah, but not before my mom mugged *them*."

"What?" he asks. He's clearly as astonished as I was at the time.

"She told them to hand over their wallets. Then she took out their IDs before giving them back. She told them that if they ever tried to steal from anyone again, she'd have them taken out."

Beau bursts out laughing. "She did that all without a weapon? Were they idiots?"

"I'm guessing they were meaner than they were smart, but that goes to show you how intense Regina can be. I have no doubt that had they tried to actually hurt us, she would have sprayed them with mace and thrown them in front of an oncoming train before they could have gotten anything from us."

Beau shakes his head. "I don't know what to say. I guess I can see how she'd had enough of feeling vulnerable today and wanted to meet her family without witnesses."

I say, "Your mom wants my family to join them at the club for dinner tonight. I think that might be a bit much for Regina."

He pulls out his phone and makes a call. "Myrah," he asks, "how surprised were you?"

I don't know what she's saying, but I hear a lot of joyous sounds on the other end of the line. He continues, "Y'all up to meeting us at the club for dinner tonight at six?" He listens closely for several moments before saying, "I sure do love you, too. See you then."

Then he tells me, "Your mom is going to stay with them while she's in Creek Water. They'll meet us for dinner."

Will wonders never cease? The anger I've been feeling toward

Beau evaporates like steam in a cold breeze. "This day is not turning out like I expected. But I'm glad my mom is here. It's the only way for my parents to resolve the feelings going on between them."

Beau says, "Relationships aren't always easy. You've got to be willing to put up with a lot, and trust that the rewards will far outweigh the frustrations."

I can't help but wonder if he's talking from personal experience. "Beau, what's going on between you and Shelby?" I finally ask.

A look of sadness crosses his face. "I'm not at liberty to say," he tells me before adding, "but I can tell you this: I like you, Lexi, a whole lot. Not only are you a breath of fresh air around here, but I love spending time with you. I'm glad you're moving to Creek Water."

I'm more confused than ever. Beau drives me back to my dad's loft in silence. My thoughts run along the lines of wondering why he's trying to romance me before he's prepared to say that he and Shelby are through.

I suppose I could pretend the last twenty-four hours never happened and go back to thinking of him as nothing more than Emmie's cousin but, to tell the truth, I don't want to do that. I want something real to happen between us, but I have no idea how that can happen if he's not going to be honest with me.

Chapter 50

Beau pulls up in front of the old sewing machine factory, and I am pulled out of my thoughts when he says, "I have a couple of errands to run. I'll pick you and Bertie up at five thirty, okay?"

"No, thanks," I tell him. "I'll drive us." I figure it's best to have a little distance between me and Beau. Also, this way, if someone—like me—needs to make a getaway, I'll be able to do so without relying on anyone else. Dinner with my parents and the Frothinghams could be delightful or it could be a complete nightmare for multiple reasons.

My parents are not country club types, so I imagine they might not feel very comfortable there. At least Bertie has gotten to know Emmie and Beau's family a bit, so I'm pretty sure he won't be up in arms about going, but I can't say the same for Regina. Also, there's no telling how my folks are going to get along with each other after their confrontation this afternoon.

I get out of the car without even thanking Beau for the day. My mind is so focused on what's going on between us, that I've lost all interest in small talk.

Bertie is in full painting mode when I get upstairs. He's got some Native American flute music playing and he's finally applied paint to a canvas. "Hi, Dad; I'm back." He doesn't even know that I'm there.

I decide to take a shower and spend the next couple of hours on my laptop working on grant applications. I figure with the documented history of the house, I should be a shoo-in. Once I've filled out three different forms, along with one to get the house on the National Historic Registry, I jump into the shower.

There's nothing like hot water beating down on your head to bring clarity. During my extended twenty-minute cleansing, I decide that first and foremost I'm going to take care of me. My parents are adults with a long history. They'll either get through this bump in the road or not. But whatever happens, it's on them.

Then I conclude that Beau needs to take care of his own house before he can get involved with me. I can't be worried about what he and Shelby are to each other. When he's ready to talk to me honestly, I'll listen; but until then, I'm determined that no more romantic moments, especially kissing, will take place between us.

I put on a pair of slacks and a sweater, no dressing up tonight. Although, I do take extra care with my hair and makeup. I don't allow myself to analyze why. Once I'm ready, I go back into the main living space to say goodbye to my dad, who I know isn't going anywhere now that he's started painting.

Bertie is so engrossed in what he's doing I could probably bring in a troop of fire-eating belly dancers and he wouldn't notice. I say, "Dad, I know you probably can't hear me, but I'm going out to dinner. I shouldn't be late."

His only response is to change his music to Led Zeppelin, a

sure sign he's heading into an all-nighter. I make a mental note to stop by the store to buy some earplugs, so the music doesn't keep me awake.

While driving through the streets of Creek Water, I'm flooded by a feeling of continuity. My ancestors walked these streets. They built lives here. I have no idea what living here was like for them, but I'm guessing they liked it well enough. I mean, Myrah and Clovis are still here. That's got to be an endorsement.

I don't know how to find the club on my own yet, so I rely on GPS to keep me on track. The long, tree-lined drive makes me feel like I'm driving back in time. I can almost imagine what it was like to make this trip in a horse-drawn carriage, which is both enchanting and unnerving.

Had I lived here at a time before cars, I would most certainly not be coming here to dine. I'd probably be washing dishes in the back. It's not a sensation I've ever experienced in New York. My grandmother was a well-known jazz singer and as such, she was treated with great respect in both the African-American community as well as the white community, even though she was once accused of shoplifting by a white store owner in Manhattan.

The owner called the police and demanded that Mimi be taken to jail. The Irish cop who took the call recognized Mimi and told the man he was full of it. Thelma—Mimi's real name—Cohen didn't need to steal. After showing the store owner the inside of her purse, something he wouldn't let her do before calling the police, Mimi told the cop that she hoped he'd come by the club where she sang, so she could repay his kindness. Paddy Dickenson became a regular, often bringing along fellow officers. Mimi had herself quite a fan base in the NYPD.

My mother's colleagues have always treated her with respect. While there are still way more white professors than black ones, there are also Asian and Middle-Eastern faculty as well. Times are not what they once were and I'm very aware of how fortunate I am to live in the time I do.

I appreciate, in a way I haven't before, that it was the work of other generations that have made my life possible. The lesson my mom was always keen for me to learn is really hitting home here in Creek Water.

I park my rental car out under a large tree in in the parking area and walk toward the club's entrance. I can't imagine I'll ever think it's worth the money to join a place like this, but it is nice not to feel uncomfortable being here.

Then I see Shelby walking up ahead with her parents. While I'd like to say hello to her, I don't look forward to seeing her mother again. I come to a stop. What if Cootie says something to my mother? Oh, lord …

Chapter 51

Emmie is already inside with her mom, aunt, and uncles when I arrive. "Where are Zach and Faye?" I ask.

My friend answers, "We're trying to get the baby on a better sleep schedule. Zach read this book about how sleep breeds sleep and that if we put Faye to bed by six o'clock at night, she's supposed to pass out for a minimum of twelve hours before waking up."

"That seems counterintuitive," I reply. "But there must be something to it."

"I hope so," she says. "I'm ready to have an uninterrupted night already."

Before I greet the rest of her family, I say, "It's nice that your mom and Uncle Jesse are dating. Have they been a couple for long?"

Emmie looks at me like I've asked how many warthogs she's planning on eating for dinner. "What are you talking about? They're not a couple."

"Really? Whenever I see them, they're together, always talking to each other and sitting by each other. I just assumed."

Emmie turns to look at them before saying. "Jesse's my

daddy's brother. Plus, he's nine years younger than Mama." Turning back to me, she adds, "They're family."

"If you say so." It's plain as the nose on my face that there's something more going on there, but maybe they're not ready to make it public yet.

When the hostess takes us into the dining room, Emmie asks, "Uncle Jesse, would you mind if I sat next to Mama?" It's obvious my comment is filling her head and she's hoping to get some answers.

Jesse moves away from his usual place by Gracie's side and answers, "Sure thing, honey." That's how he comes to sit next to me. We're still expecting my mom, Myrah, and Clovis, so we order a drink while we wait.

After asking for a glass of wine, I lean over to Jesse and ask, "So how long have you and Gracie been seeing each other?"

"About a year," he says. "But don't tell her, she doesn't know it yet."

"What do you mean she doesn't know?" I release a bubble of laughter at the thought that they're dating but Emmie's mom doesn't realize it.

He answers, "Gracie thinks of me as Reed's little brother. I'm trying to get her to see me as a man in my own right."

"How's that going?" I ask. I mean, the whole thing is too absurd for words.

He tilts his head to the side as though really considering his answer. "I don't really know. Sometimes, I think she realizes how much fun she has with me and wishes it was more, but then she inevitably says something like, 'We need to find you a nice young lady, Jesse.' She says it like I'm eighteen and she's ninety."

I ask, "Have you ever considered trying to make her jealous?"

"That's a fine idea, but I don't want to mislead anyone else."

Before we can plot any further, Clovis and Myrah come in with Regina. There's a radiance about my older family members that makes me want to bask in their presence. My mom looks genuinely happy to be here, although I think that's more to do with being reunited with her new family than seeing me and Dad. Both of us are clearly on her *list*.

Myrah stops to greet each Frothingham. She hugs them and exchanges loving words before she gets to me. I wrap my arms around her and say, "I'm so happy you're getting a chance to know my mom."

"Child, this here is like a decade full of Christmas mornings for me. Regina is an amazin' woman. I already feel like she's one of my own."

Clovis touches his wife's cheek affectionately and says, "The gals in this family are a wonder, that's for sure."

Myrah replies, "Don't you ever doubt it."

Then they find their seats. My mom is across the table from me so I don't have a chance to ask her anything, but I can tell she's turned her day around from the last time I saw her, when she was getting told off by my dad.

Regina orders a beverage and then looks at me. "Where's your father, Alexis?" She asks in such a way you'd think she was inquiring after a particularly virulent fungal infection. She continues to use my full name as parents do when you're in trouble. Which I've apparently been since she arrived in town.

"He started painting," I tell her. She nods her head once, knowing as well as I do that Bertie painting is essentially the same thing as him falling off the edge of the earth: neither of us know when we'll hear from him again.

Beau is the last to arrive. He seems a little flustered as he sits down. He apologizes, "I hope I didn't hold y'all up."

His mother assures him that he did and demands, "Why are you late?"

"I got caught on a call."

He smiles at me and asks, "Where's your daddy?"

I take that opportunity to make Bertie's apologies to everyone and explain, "My dad has started a new series of paintings. I don't think he'll be around much until he's done."

"I think that's such an excitin' profession," Emmie's mom gushes. She smiles at my mom and adds, "And you being a professor, Regina, that blows me away. I'd love to know more about your work."

Before my mom can regale her audience with tales of female suffering and injustice, the waiter comes to take our order. Once we're all done, I shift the conversation to Clovis's most recent hobby of beekeeping. Mom will have plenty of opportunity to share her opinions. "Tell us about your bees, Clovis."

He says, "I spun honey for the first time ever last month and got thirty-three pounds! Lee, Gracie, I brought you some, but I left it in the truck. Donchoo be leavin' without gettin' it."

They thank him profusely and just when I start to think this is going to be a perfectly delightful meal after all, Shelby comes over. She greets everyone before leaning into Beau and whispering something in his ear.

He appears highly uncomfortable as he clears his throat and announces, "If y'all will excuse me, I've been invited to join

Shelby's family for dinner." Then he shoots me an apologetic look as he stands up.

You can tell Lee is chomping at the bit, wanting to tell her son not to be rude and to sit down, but she apparently doesn't want to hurt Shelby's feelings, either.

As they walk away, I feel irritated and as I'm about to think some decidedly foul thoughts, I get the most wonderful idea, and I lean over and share it with Jesse. After all, he could benefit from it as much I could.

Chapter 52

Jesse listens to me with great interest before putting his hand on top of mine and offering a conspiratorial squeeze. "That's brilliant. Count me in."

"Here goes nothing," I whisper back. Then I let loose with a flirtatious giggle that sounds utterly foreign to my ears—I'm not a giggler—and say, "Oh, Jesse, you *are* a charmer, aren't you?"

I might as well have thrown a bucket of ice water on Emmie's mom. Gracie looks at us like she's had the most horrible thought. The very thought we want her to be having. She unsuccessfully tries to smile while suggesting, "Lee, I think that we should introduce Lexi to that nice Sherman boy."

Lee, who was obviously hoping something would transpire between me and Beau, unenthusiastically replies, "I s'pose."

Jesse says, "I don't think y'all should try too hard to find Lexi a suitor until you let present company have a chance at charmin' her." Gracie and Lee look horrified.

Lee's husband Jed announces, "Jesse, you rascal. You've dated half the women in this town, I don't think you need another notch in your belt."

I giggle playfully, while I sneak a peek at Beau who just sat down two tables over with Shelby's family. He's staring right at me and he's obviously not pleased. I reach out and touch his uncle's arm and say, "Clearly, Jesse's been looking for the right woman. It's my good fortune he hasn't found her, yet."

Emmie stares alternately between the spectacle Jesse and I are making and the shocked face of her mother. She seems to be realizing that her mom has feelings for her uncle after all. She tests the waters by saying, "Personally, I'd love to have Lexi for an aunt."

My mom raises her eyebrow as if she's witnessing some particularly bad theater. She knows me too well to buy what I'm selling.

Lee called ahead and ordered a pork loin with several side dishes to be served family-style. When our food arrives, she changes the subject and says, "I would have had y'all over to the house, but I was too busy dreamin' about what the old family home is gonna look like after it's all fixed up."

Myrah responds, "Honey, any meal I don't have to prepare myself is a real pleasure. This looks delicious."

Lee tells my mom, "Regina, you're in for a real treat staying with Myrah. This here lady can cook like nobody's business. The only reason I know how to make biscuits and gravy as well as I do is because Myrah taught me. She's got the touch of an angel."

"Don't leave me outta this," Clovis says. "I make a mean stew an' y'all know it."

Jed says, "That's the truth. Clovis goes huntin' with us every year. He brings his stew along to keep us motivated."

Jesse laughs, "Motivated enough to nap. Remember the last two years how we built us a fire and fell asleep after lunch?"

"Then you came home empty-handed," Lee says.

Gracie adds, "Y'all ought to call it your annual eating and napping trip."

Everyone enjoys a laugh at the men's expense.

Dinner is delicious and conversation organically diminishes as we enjoy our meal. When our plates are cleared, Lee announces, "I ordered a soufflé for dessert, but they don't put it in the oven until our dinner plates are cleared. Why don't we get some coffee and after-dinner drinks while we wait?"

Jesse announces, "I ate so much, I could sure use a little fresh air to perk me up." Then he offers me his hand and says, "Would you care to join me for a walk around the grounds, Lexi?"

I bound to my feet like an eager puppy. "What a wonderful idea."

Clovis pulls out his car keys and hands them over to Jesse. "Son, would you mind gettin' the honey out of the truck fer me? It's in a shoppin' bag in the front seat."

"My pleasure, Clovis," he tells the older man before offering me his arm. "Ma'am."

I try not to cast a look over at Beau but darned if I don't feel his eyes boring holes through me. Jesse and I walk out of the dining room thoroughly satisfied that we've created a source of gossip to keep everyone occupied until we get back.

Once we exit the room, Jesse bursts out a with snort of laughter. "Did you see their faces? I haven't had this much fun in ages."

"I'm not sure whether Gracie is ever going to talk to you again," I tell him.

"Oh, she will. She'll probably start with telling me that you're too young for me and then list all the reasons I should find an appropriate woman to date."

"How old are you?" I ask. I know he's a good deal younger than Jed, I just don't know how much.

"Forty-one," he answers.

"You're only eleven years older than me. That's an age gap you see all the time."

"Yes, ma'am, it is. And I'll make sure to tell her that. Then I'll follow it up with letting her know that a nine-year difference might be more appropriate. Maybe she'll take the hint."

We walk out the front door of the club onto the porch. Jesse takes my arm and leads me around back. "I'm gonna stop right in front of the windows outside the dining room. So, play along."

"You're devious," I tell him. I love that we have each other to help us figure out our romantic situations.

When Jesse finally stops walking, he leans on a large white column. I stand next to him and ask, "Have you ever hinted to Gracie about how you feel?"

"Never. I don't want to wig her out. I was only ten when she married my brother, so it's gonna take some work on my part to prove to her that I'm mate material."

"Put your arm around me," I tell him. "The only way she's going to see you that way is to feel real jealousy."

Jesse slides his arm around my waist. "You're tryin' to make Beau jealous, aren't you?"

"You bet I am," I reply. "He flirts up a storm with me, takes me out to dinner, and even kisses me, then he runs off and has dinner with Shelby. That's not going to wash with me, and he better learn that fast."

"For what it's worth," he says, "I don't think there's anything goin' on with him and Shelby anymore."

"Then why is he eating with her?"

Jesse shakes his head, "I don't know." He pulls me closer to his side, "But I say we give them both something to think about."

After a few minutes, Jesse takes my hand and we walk out to the parking lot. When we're out of sight of the restaurant, he drops it and says, "I surely appreciate your helping me out. It's nice to have you in the family, Lexi."

I know he's talking about having me in Creek Water and in their family home, but a chill of excitement runs straight up my spine and sends tingles of optimism throughout my brain. If Beau comes to his senses in time that I'm not mad at him forever, it's possible that some day we might be a real family.

Chapter 53

Jesse and I retrieve the honey from Clovis's truck. We've probably been gone a good twenty minutes by the time we get back to the club house. Wouldn't you know it, Gracie is standing on the porch peering out into the darkness when we get there.

Jesse grabs my hand quickly and says, "Look at that. I think our little ruse might be workin."

When Gracie spots us, she says, "I was coming after you two. Dessert is being served." Then she looks down at our hands.

I love Emmie's mom and hate to be party to upsetting her, which she obviously is by the slack-jawed look she's giving us, but we're doing this for her own good, as well as for ourselves.

I pull my hand away from Jesse's, like I'm trying to hide what we're doing. "That sounds wonderful." I walk by her, fully aware that she's staring daggers at her brother-in-law.

He says, "The club's soufflé isn't nearly as good as the one Gracie makes. You ever gonna make me that chocolate orange soufflé again, Grace?"

She makes a non-committal sound. Then she says, "I'm not feelin' so good. I think maybe I'll head home and go to bed early." She asks, "Jesse, can I take your car, and you catch a ride with Jed and Lee?"

"No, ma'am," he says, taking her elbow like she's frail. "I drove you here and I'll take you home. Let's get you inside to get your coat and purse." I'm pretty sure she was hoping he would insist on driving her.

She smacks his hand, "Quit treating me like I'm your granny, Jesse. I can walk on my own."

I shoot him a conspiratorial grin as we enter the dining room. Things are looking up for Jesse already. It takes all my will power not to look over at Beau as I get back to the table. I sit down and announce, "It's a beautiful night."

Gracie picks up her purse. "I have a bit of a headache. I'm gonna say good night to y'all now and head home."

Jesse stands behind her. "I'm gonna drive her."

That's when Emmie bounds to her feet. "Nonsense. I should be getting back to check on Faye. I'll take her." Then to her uncle, she adds, "You stay and enjoy your night."

My friend is clearly onboard with helping her mother discover her true feelings for her uncle and has decided the best way to do that is to prolong her jealousy. So, I gush, "Thanks, Emmie." Then to Gracie I say, "I hope you're feeling better soon."

Gracie suddenly looks like she doesn't want to go anywhere and says, "Maybe I'll stay for a bite or two."

But Emmie shakes her head. "No, Mama, I think we should get you home to rest. It's been a long day for you."

If smoke could really pour out of someone's ears, Gracie would have a hard time seeing through the haze. She demands,

"Will you stop treating me like I'm decrepit? I can stay if I want."

Emmie sits back. "Okay, Mama, but I don't want you to overdo it."

This whole scene is too funny. I can only hope Beau is as annoyed as Gracie.

I dig into the soufflé sitting in front me and not two bites in, Beau returns. He sits down in the chair he vacated before we started dinner and announces, "I'm back."

Jesse takes that as his cue to ratchet things up and he leans in close to me. He whispers in my ear quietly enough not to be overheard, "I'm having so much fun I can hardly stand it."

I channel every romantic comedy heroine I've ever seen and release a trill of laughter in response. Then I say loudly, "We should *definitely* do this again."

Beau's face is unnaturally flushed.

My mom is watching everything like she's at an amateur dinner theater. I can tell she's amused and has figured out what's going on. Regina is nobody's fool. She says, "I feel a lot better with you living here, Lexi, knowing that you have such a nice family to keep an eye on you."

"Oh, we'll keep an eye on her," Jesse replies.

Between Gracie and Beau, the tension level is rising faster than a pressure cooker. Beau declares, "Looks like there have been some new developments since I left."

His uncle replies, "Nothing more than me expressing my admiration for Lexi here. It's nice when a beautiful lady moves to town, don't you think, Beau?"

Gracie stands up so quickly, her chair nearly topples. "I'm ready to go after all," she declares.

Jesse says, "I'll take you, Grace."

"No, thank you," she nearly spits. "Emmie will see me home." Then she turns and storms out of the room without seeing if her daughter is following her.

Emmie gets up next. "Uncle Jed, Auntie Lee, thank you for dinner." Then she stops to hug Myrah and Clovis. She asks Myrah, "Can I come by sometime this week? I want to get your gingerbread recipe."

"Sure thing, honey," my newly discovered relation responds. "Bring your mama along. I don't see near enough of you gals."

Emmie leaves after assuring Myrah she will, then she says goodbye to the rest of us. Our table feels like the fallout after a bomb is dropped.

Jesse says, "Beau, why don't you ask Shelby to join us?"

"She's fine where she is," he grumbles.

Lee, who's obviously still mad at Beau for deserting us, tells her son, "I hope you enjoyed your meal." Her tone clearly suggesting that she hopes he choked on it. I'm guessing she's crediting his departure for the upsets that have occurred at our table, namely me and Jesse.

Before things can settle down, Shelby comes over with her mother. "I wanted to thank y'all for letting Beau join us." Lee rolls her eyes but doesn't say anything.

I take the opportunity to say, "Shelby, Mrs. Wilcox, I'd like you to meet my mother, Regina. Mom, Shelby is Beau's girlfriend." Emphasis on the last word.

Shelby says, "I'm very pleased to make your acquaintance." Then she walks over to take my mom's hand.

My mother nods her head regally while arching an eyebrow,

indicating she'll have questions for me later. "I'm pleased to meet you both," she offers.

Shelby's mom announces, "You're a lot darker than your daughter. I couldn't tell what she was right off."

Oh, boy! It's on now. Regina purposefully misunderstands and asks, "You couldn't tell she was a person?"

"I couldn't tell she was black," Cootie snaps.

"Yes, well," my mother says, "ignorance is often a lot easier to recognize than skin color."

"Are you callin' me ignorant?" Cootie demands.

Before my mom can respond, Jed says, "She's just speaking the truth, Cootie. The minute you open your mouth, you sound like a horse's ass."

Cootie gasps and looks at Beau. "Are you goin' to let your daddy talk to me like that?"

"Yes, ma'am," he answers. "My daddy knows a horse's ass when he sees one."

Shelby giggles and Cootie demands, "What are you laughin' at, girl?"

"Oh, Mama," she answers. "You need to get off your high horse and quit actin' like you're better than other folks. You're terrible. You're a racist."

Cootie squints her eyes like she's trying to activate a death laser. "You better watch yourself, young lady."

"Or what? You gonna disown me?"

Cootie says, "Girl, you can go anytime you want. You can start by findin' your own way home." Then she storms off.

Regina smiles at Shelby and offers, "Why don't you join us for dessert?"

Shelby sits in Gracie's vacated chair next to my mom and apologizes. "I'm sorry my mama isn't nicer. I swear, I don't know what's wrong with her."

Myrah says, "Honey, some folks is so unhappy they've got to share it with others. Don't be too hard on her."

"How can you say that, Myrah? Mama's never been nice to you or Clovis."

"Child, when you get to be my age, you learn to pity folks like your mama. It's up to each one of us to find our own happiness and Cootie doesn't know where to look. She's searchin' outside herself, but that's not where it is. She needs to look inside, and I think she's afraid of what she'll find if she does that."

I'm pretty sure Myrah's words hit home for us all. At least I know they do for me and my mom. We both have a lot on our plates right now. Regina has to decide what she's going to do with my dad, and I need to find my own happiness regardless of whether or not Beau is in my life.

Shelby smiles at Myrah. "You should teach a class, you know that? I think folks need to hear what you said. I know I did."

"It's plain common sense," Myrah says. "When you realize your happiness is your own to claim, you start to make the decisions that will lead you to it."

Once the evening has wound down, we all get up to leave. Beau walks next to me like he wants to say something, but he can't with Shelby and the rest of his family so close by. I ignore him entirely and speed up to walk next to my mom.

Regina quietly announces, "I'm going to want a full report on what's going on here."

"Sure thing. I'll come by sometime tomorrow," I tell her.

"Whenever," she says. "I'm not in a rush." At my questioning look, she explains, "I've decided to stay through Thanksgiving. I have a week off school then, anyway. I'll teach my classes remotely until then."

"Does this mean you've made a decision about Dad?"

"Not even close," she says. "It means nothing more than I want to get to know Myrah and Clovis and see my daughter safely moved into her new home."

I'll take it. As far as my mom goes, she's making great strides just by staying.

Our group breaks apart as we find our cars. Beau catches up to me and says, "We need to talk."

I try to look innocent and ask, "What about?"

"I think you know the answer to that."

I tell him, "All I know is that until you're ready to answer my questions, I'm not going to answer yours."

Let him think about that. I stop at my car and shout out to Shelby who's several steps ahead, "Good to see you again, Shelby. You have a nice night."

"Thanks, Lexi, you too."

Beau glares at me like I'm at the top of his hit list. That's okay by me, because he's at the top of mine.

Chapter 54

My dad is still going strong when I get back to his apartment. He's frantically moving around the canvas like he's trying to paint a hurricane or something. "Hey, Dad," I say. I throw him a chocolate-covered caramel candy bar I picked up at the gas station on my way home from dinner. I explain, "I brought you gooey without being hot, cheese, or sticky."

He picks at my offering and tears the wrapper off. Before biting into it, he says, "Thanks, honey" and nothing more. I'm actually surprised I got that much out of him.

On my way up the stairs, I say, "I'm going to take your bed. You can have my air mattress down here so you can be close to your painting." Although I'm pretty sure he won't sleep tonight.

I put on my nightgown before crawling into bed. Once I get there I give over to all the thoughts swirling in my head. Today feels like it's lasted a week. My mom showed up out of nowhere; Beau seems to be remembering that he's Shelby's boyfriend, all the while trying to stake a claim on me; but my parents' relationship is a big question mark.

I have no idea how this is all going to work out. I finally fall asleep only to dream about the day Mimi took me to see her fortune-teller. Everything seems to happen in real time, like I'm ten again. My hair is hanging down my back in corkscrew curls and my grandmother is running her hands through it.

She tells me, "Honey, life is a miracle."

"Why do say that, Mimi?"

"Because it is. We are so blessed to live on this beautiful planet in this wonderful city. We have each other and we have hope. There's nothing but joy for us."

I shake my head. "I don't know about that. Melissa Fellows at school is being a real snot and I don't feel too joyous about that."

"Come with me, I'm going to take you to meet a lady I know." She reaches out her hand for me to grab. I love Mimi's hands. They're small, but they're strong like a vise. When my hand is in hers, I know I'm safe.

We walk down 112th Street past a bodega and a discount clothing store. She stops at an old brick building where four teenagers are drinking out of a bottle hidden in a paper bag. Before going inside, Mimi holds out her hand to the boys and says, "Give it over."

The oldest tries to look tough and says, "We're not giving you shit, old lady."

She clucks her tongue and says, "You'd better, Clarence, or your mama's gonna you give you something worse when I tell her what you're up to."

The youngest-looking one says, "Man, Thelma, you ruin all our fun. Why don't you mind your own business?"

She smacks him on the back of the head and says, "You are my business, boy, and don't you forget it. We look out after our own here."

The oldest says, "If we give you the bag, will you still tell on us?"

"Damn straight," she says. "But I'll also say that you gave it over easily and that should count for something."

He reluctantly hands over the goods but not before taking another big swig. Mimi turns the bottle over right in front of them and pours it out onto the sidewalk, then she throws it in the garbage. "Just a bunch of wannabe hoodlums, those boys. They need a good kick in the britches, if you ask me."

"I'd be more afraid that they were going to kick you, Mimi. Be careful with them."

She shakes her head. "They'd need an army to take me on." Then she pulls me along into the building. There's no lobby, only a long hallway with doors on either side and a staircase straight ahead. We stop and knock at the second door on the right.

I hear a voice shout out, "Come in."

The lady inside has Rastafarian braids hanging down her back and she's wearing a colorful dress. "Thelma!" she greets my grandmother with a hug. "Who you bring me today?"

Mimi says, "Jaqweshia, this here's my granddaughter, Lexi."

She takes my hand in hers and asks, "Do you know what my name means?" I shake my head, so she explains, "It means half a queen. Your mama's name is Regina, which means full queen."

"What does my name mean?" I ask.

"You're Alexis, defender of man."

"I like that," I tell her. Then I say, "It smells like a skunk died in here."

"That's jus' my special herbs, honey. I burn them to clear the cobwebs in the air." I don't know about that because she winks at Mimi which suggests there's another reason altogether.

Jaqweshia asks, "How would you like me to tell you your fortune?"

"Like a gypsy or something?" I wonder.

"The gypsies have their way. I have mine." She leads me over to a card table in the middle of her living room and tells me to sit down. Then she hands me a cup like the kind we use at home when we play Yahtzee. She puts several small chicken bones in front of me and instructs, "Hold the bones so they can read your energy. Then when you're ready, put them in the cup and throw them down on the table."

I do what she says, all the while wondering how in the world she's going to be able to read my future by looking at a bunch of bones.

Once they're lying on the table in front of her, she claims, "You have an interesting future ahead of you, young lady."

"What do you see?" I ask.

"In your thirtieth year, when the dog jumps over you, your life is going to change in the most unexpected ways."

I laugh like she just told me a really good knock-knock joke. "That's silly," I tell her.

She shrugs her shoulders. "Remember that things aren't always what they seem. You need to make your desires heard and not be afraid to say what you want."

I ask, "How will I know when I'm supposed to say something?"

"Always speak your piece, but for the sake of this reading, you'll know it's time when your family is reunited."

Mimi and I leave a short time later. We walk down the street and I confess, "I don't know what any of that meant."

"You will someday," she tells me. "But for now, all you need to know is that you're my girl and I love you more than all the stars in the heavens."

"I love you too, Mimi," I tell her. And in that moment in my dream, I feel her with me as sure as if she never left.

When I wake up I remember everything like it was yesterday. I realize that I'd forgotten part of the fortune, to speak my desires. I know what I have to do.

Chapter 55

As soon as my eyes open, I hop out of bed and get into the shower. I take extra pains to look nice while getting ready for the day. Once I'm convinced I can't look any better, I leave the apartment and take the elevator down to the second floor. I walk right into Frothingham Realty.

The receptionist smiles and asks, "Are you here to see Beau?"

"I am," I tell her.

I wait while she calls him to let him know I'm here. He doesn't answer her. Instead, he charges down the hall like a bull in Pamplona. He stops right in front of me, takes my elbow, and pulls me back down the hall into his office.

"Good morning," I greet. "Looks like someone got up on the wrong side of the bed."

"What was that all about last night?"

"Dinner?" I ask innocently.

"Not dinner. What was going on with you and my uncle?"

"Oh, that," I answer. "We were just enjoying our time together."

"What does that mean, Lexi? Why were you flirtin' with him like you were interested in him?"

271

"Who says I'm not?" I demand.

"What about us? I thought we were starting something.'"

"I might have thought so too, but I'm not interested in competing with Shelby for your affections. You're either with her or you're not. Which is it?"

He shakes his head and picks up his phone. He ignores my questioning look while he places a call. He says, "I need to tell someone else what's going on. It's important."

He listens for a moment before saying, "Yeah, Lexi. Yes, I do. Okay, I'll tell her. Thank you." Then he puts his phone down. "Shelby and I are not seeing each other."

"Why should I believe you?" I ask.

He looks shocked. "Why wouldn't you believe me? When have I ever lied to you?"

"I saw you at my house the day my offer was accepted," I tell him. He looks confused so I clarify, "Out front, hugging each other."

"Oh, for Pete's sake. What you saw was Shelby setting me free. She told me that she would always be fond of me but that there was no way we should be together. She said that we were just too different. Then she asked me if I'd pretend we were still a couple for a while."

"Why?" I want to know.

He says, "She wanted to keep Cootie off her back while she tries to decide what to do with her life. She figured if her mama didn't know we weren't together then she'd never guess what she really wanted to do until it was too late."

"What does Shelby want to do?" I ask.

"She wants out of Creek Water. She wants to try life in a big city but doesn't know how to go about making that happen." I file that information away for future use.

"She was planning on leaving without telling her parents?"

He shakes his head. "No, but she was hoping to make a plan and be ready to set it into motion before she told them. Cootie can be pretty persuasive."

A smile creeps to my lips as I finally absorb the news that Beau is free. Instead of saying anything to him though, I close the gap between us and kiss him like I'm staking my claim. He doesn't let me get carried away. Instead, he pushes me back a few inches and demands, "What about Jesse?"

I laugh, "Jesse is in love with your Aunt Gracie and we were trying to make her jealous, so she'd realize that she feels the same way."

"What? When did that happen?" he demands.

"Jesse says that he's been courting her for a year, but she doesn't know it. He says she thinks of him like a little brother."

He pulls me back into his arms and says, "If Aunt Gracie was half as mad as I was, I'm willing to bet she'll realize how she feels pretty darn quick." Then he asks, "You're sure you're not interested in him?"

I confess, "I may have been trying to force you to realize your feelings as well."

"You didn't need to force me, Lexi. I already knew what I felt." Then he lowers his lips to mine before declaring, "Let me show you."

Chapter 56

Beau and I go over to see my mom at Myrah and Clovis's. I'd promised to fill her in on what was going on last night and figure she might enjoy seeing Beau and me together when I deliver the news that we're officially an item.

Clovis opens the door when we get there, and jokes, "I see the dogs didn't eat ya. Now that they know ya, you'll be fine with them."

"That's what Beau said," I say before giving him a hug. Then I ask, "Where're my mom and Myrah?"

"Lawd, those women are jawin' away in the kitchen. I swear there hasn't been a moment of quiet all mornin'."

Beau knocks Clovis in the shoulder. "It's a nice sound, isn't it?"

Clovis smiles ear to ear. "Sweeter than honey," he says. Then he leads the way to the other room.

Myrah jumps up and declares, "Good thing I made extra breakfast this mornin'."

I look down and see that the table is set for five. "Are we interrupting? It looks like you were expecting somebody."

"We was," she answers. "We was expectin' you."

"How?" I ask.

My mom answers, "Myrah has the sight." My mom doesn't believe in that stuff any more than I do. Or should I say, *did?* If nothing else, the last couple of days have certainly taught me that things occur in our world far beyond my understanding.

Regina says, "The first thing she said when she saw me this morning was that you and Beau were joining us for breakfast."

Beau kisses Myrah on the cheek before sitting down and saying, "I'm starved. I hope you made your sticky buns."

She turns around and opens the oven door and pulls out a pan. "Course I did." Then she puts them on the table.

I'm afraid living in Creek Water is going to have a dramatic effect on my waistline. I don't ever recall eating as much as I have here. Over breakfast I answer all of Regina's questions.

I finish the story by telling her, "Shelby wants to live in a big city for a while but doesn't know how to go about doing that."

My mom asks me, "Do you like Shelby?"

"I do," I tell her. "The only thing I didn't like was thinking that she and Beau were together."

My mom nods her head. "I can see that." She asks, "Beau, why don't you see if you can get me and Shelby in the same room sometime? I'd like to talk to her."

Beau looks surprised. "What about?"

I answer for Regina. "My mom is going to offer to help her in New York City."

Myrah teases, "Look who has the sight now."

"No, ma'am," I shake my head, realizing I'm starting to sound a bit Southern myself. "You don't have to be psychic to know that Regina is going to help out another woman if it's in her power to do so."

"Plus," my mom interjects, "who knows how long Bertie is going to be down here painting? I have the space. This way, Shelby can see what it's like to live in a city without having to incur all of the expenses of renting an apartment. She can also explore different neighborhoods to get a feel for what area feels like home to her."

I love these moments when I see my mom outside of our dynamic as mother and child. She's strong, opinionated, and often frightening, but she's also kind, caring, and selfless. I ask, "Do you think you can ship my boxes down to me when you get home?"

"I can do that," she says.

"What about Dad?" I ask.

"What about him?"

"What are you going to do regarding his ultimatum?" I'm sure she'd rather not discuss this in a room full of people, but I really want to know.

"I'll let you know when I decide," she tells me.

After an hour or so, Beau and I take our leave. We promise to see everyone soon before driving over to my new house.

When we get there, Beau asks, "How would you like to see your neighbor's house?"

"Depends on which neighbor," I say.

"I know for a fact that the guy in the brick colonial wants to invite you over."

"Well, then," I answer, "in that case, I accept."

Beau's house suits him. It's big and masculine like he is. He has a real thing for large, heavy furniture and leather. It's positively gorgeous. He sits me down on the living room couch and says, "Stay here. I'll be right back."

He runs up the stairs and can't be gone for two minutes before he's back. He hands me a slip of paper.

I open it while asking, "What's this?"

"It's something Myrah gave me years ago after she read my tea leaves for the first time."

I look down and read the following:

"The dog will jump before she moves. She'll be your neighbor, she'll be your family, she is your future."

"You're kidding?" I demand. Then I tell him about the fortune-teller from Harlem. He leans in close to me and offers the sweetest kiss. It's says more than words ever could and I know in that moment that I'm exactly where I belong.

Epilogue

I convince everyone to have Thanksgiving dinner at my new house. We haven't started any restoration projects yet, but we've moved all the furniture from Myrah and Clovis's hay loft over here, so there are enough chairs to seat everyone.

Lee is bringing the turkey, stuffing, and mashed potatoes; Myrah is supplying rolls and pies; and Gracie is taking care of everything else. The only thing I'm responsible for are the drinks.

After Beau builds a fire in the fireplace, he leaves to pick up my dad. Meanwhile, I run around lighting candles and putting the finishing touches on the table. As the house starts filling up with guests, the air crackles like something magical is occurring. The past and future are colliding in a way that was forecasted generations ago. The feeling of celebration is heady, to say the least.

Emmie, Zach, and Faye sit together on the couch looking like the perfect little family. Gracie and Jesse are very definitely on good terms, and if their constant touching is any indication, they've finally changed the definition of their relationship. Davis and Amelia are there as are Myrah, Clovis, and my mom. We're just waiting on Beau to bring my dad.

Bertie and Regina have not seen each other since that day when my mom showed up unexpectedly right here at my house. For most people that might seem like a bad sign, but with Dad's painting schedule, I don't find it too upsetting. Although I am a bit nervous to see how today goes. It's obvious Regina is a little more dressed-up than normal.

When the doorbell rings, I get up to answer it. Beau and Bertie are carrying a large present between them. My dad says, "I brought you a housewarming gift." They bring it into the living room, and everyone assembles to watch me open it.

My dad says, "It's a sketch I made for one of the pieces in my new series."

I excitedly tear the paper off it and when I see what it is, my eyes fill with tears. My dad has replicated the photograph of Regina Frothingham and my ancestor Elsie. The two women are standing with an arm around each other, their eyes filled with determination, hope, and love.

Everyone is as touched as I am. "I know the perfect place for it. Beau, Dad, can you put it on the mantle above the fireplace?"

After my dad's art is situated, my mom says, "I have a bit of an announcement to make myself."

All eyes turn to her. My dad seems especially interested to hear what she has to say. She clears her throat before offering, "Clovis was kind enough to go online and get himself ordained by the Church of the Loving God."

I can't say that I saw that coming. She continues, "Bertie, you didn't say what church I had to marry you in, so I'm hoping you won't mind doing the deed right here in our daughter's home."

My dad is overwhelmed by emotion as she continues, "I would like to pledge myself to you before God and family today, if you're game."

Bertie walks over to my mom and takes her in his arms. "Thank you, Regina. This means the world to me."

She embraces him meaningfully, and announces, "I'm not taking your name. But you can take mine if you want."

He shakes his head. "I'm good."

We gather in a circle around them, and right there in my living room, facing each other, while holding hands, standing under the image of our ancestors and before God and family, my parents get married. It's a beautiful ceremony full of so much joy I feel like I'm going to burst out of my skin.

My life has changed so much in the last few weeks I can't even begin to process it. But I do know one thing for certain. I'm home.

Thank you all for taking the time to read Lexi's story! If you enjoyed it, please take a moment to leave a review. Reviews are the best way to show your support.

If you aren't already signed up for my newsletter, please do so! This way I can keep you apprised of new releases, promotions, etc.

https://whitneydineen.com/newsletter/

Preorder The Plan (Book 3 in The Creek Water Series) – Coming in March of 2020!

Bead shop owner Amelia Frothingham has been keeping a secret from everyone she knows.

She pretends to be the ultimate care-free bohemian chick, but the truth is, she's the world's biggest control freak. Much to the delight of her Southern family, Amelia's life appears to be smooth sailing. That is until bad boy rockstar Huck Wiley mysteriously blows into town like a spring tornado.

Like every other woman under eighty with a pulse, Amelia's intrigued. So when Huck starts showing up at her shop with flirtation in mind, she finds herself getting sucked into the rock god vortex. But her previous attempts at long-distance love have always ended on a sour note, so Amelia has vowed never to repeat the experience.

What Amelia doesn't know is that Huck has a secret of his own, and he has no intention of returning to Los Angeles before he's good and ready.

Will Huck stay in town, scattering the beads Amelia has finally gotten sorted? Or will he head back to his glamorous life and take her last chance at spontaneity and love along with him?

Find out in this deliciously funny romcom about love and life in Creek Water, Missouri!

About the Author

Whitney Dineen is an award-winning author of romantic comedies, non-fiction humor, thrillers, and middle reader fiction. She lives in the beautiful Pacific Northwest with her husband and two daughters. When not weaving stories, Whitney can be found gardening, wrangling free-range chickens, or eating french fries. Not always in that order. She loves to hear from her fans and can be reached through her website at https://whitneydineen.com/.

Join me!

Mailing List Sign Up
whitneydineen.com/newsletter/

BookBub
www.bookbub.com/authors/whitney-dineen

Facebook
www.facebook.com/Whitney-Dineen-11687019412/

Twitter
twitter.com/WhitneyDineen

Email
WhitneyDineenAuthor@gmail.com

Goodreads
www.goodreads.com/author/show/8145525.Whitney_Dineen

Blog
whitneydineen.com/blog/

Please write a review on Amazon, Goodreads, or BookBub. Reviews are the best way you can support a story you love!

While you're waiting for The Plan, check out Whitney's multi-award-winning, The Reinvention of Mimi Finnegan!

Chapter 1

"A BUNION?" I shriek.

"It would appear so," answers Dr. Foster, the podiatrist referred by my HMO.

"Aren't bunions something that old people get?"

"Yes," he replies. "That's normally the case, but not always. Bunions grow after years of walking incorrectly, or in some instances, not wearing the proper shoes."

Still perplexed, I ask, "What am I doing with one then? I'm only thirty-four."

He says that by the atypical location of my bunion, he can deduce that I have the tendency to walk on the outsides of my feet. He explains that while some people walk on the insides of their feet, giving them a knock-kneed appearance, others, like myself, rotate their feet outward, causing a waddle, if you will. I have a look of horror on my face when he says the word "waddle." I have never been accused of such a disgusting thing in my life. But before I can form a coherent response, he continues, "The extra . . . weight (and I'm sure he pauses to emphasize the word) that the outside of the foot is forced to endure by walking that way eventually causes it to grow extra padding to help support the . . . load." Am I wrong or does he pause again when he says that word?

Playing dumb, I ask, "And I'm getting one so young, why?"

Clearing his throat, Dr. Foster answers, "Well, a lot of it has to do with genetics and the structure of your foot." Then adds, "And a lot of it has to do with the extra weight (pause and meaningful look) you're placing on it."

I am so aghast by this whole conversation that I finally confess, "I have just lost forty pounds." Which is a total lie by the way. In actuality I have just gained two. But I simply can't bear the humiliation of him calling me fat, or what I perceive as him calling me fat.

The doctor smiles and declares my previous poundage did not help the inflammation at all and announces it may have contributed to my bunion. He checks his chart and declares, "I see you're a hundred and seventy pounds. At one hundred and fifty, you should be feeling a lot better."

"But I'm five-eleven," I explain.

"Yes?"

"I'm big boned!"

He looks at me closely and says, "Actually, you're not." Picking up my wrist, he concludes, "I would say medium, which means one hundred and fifty pounds would be ideal." Of course the photo of the emaciated woman on his desk should have tipped me off as to what this guy considers ideal. She is wearing a swimsuit with no boobs or butt to fill it out and painfully sharp collar bones. She bears a striking resemblance to a death camp survivor.

All I can think is that I haven't been one-hundred-and fifty-pounds since high school. There is simply no way I can lose twenty pounds. I want to tell him he has no idea how much I deprive myself to weigh one seventy. In order to actually lose weight, I'd only be able to ingest rice cakes and Metamucil. But I don't say this because he'd think I'm weak and unmotivated and he'd be right, too. Plus, I just bragged that I lost a record forty pounds, so he already assumes I am capable of losing weight, which of course would be the truth if it weren't such an out-and-out lie.

The doctor writes a prescription for a special shoe insert that will help tip my foot into the correct walking position and then leaves, giving me privacy to cover my naked, misshapen appendage. As I put my sock back on I decide I am not going to go on a diet. I'm happy or happyish with the way I look and that's all there is to it. When I leave the room, Dr. Foster tells me to come back in two months so he can recheck my bunion. In my head I respond, "Yeah right, buddy. Take a good look, this is the last time you're ever going to see me or my growth." I plan on wearing my shoe insert and never again speaking of my hideous deformity.

The true cruelty of this whole bunion fiasco is that I am the one in my family with pretty feet. I have three sisters and we are all a year apart. Tell me that doesn't make for a crazy upbringing. At any rate, the year we were all in high school at the same time, my sisters and I were sitting on my bed having a nice familial chat, which was a rare occurrence as I'm sure you know girls that age are abominable as a whole. But put them under the same roof fighting over bathroom time, make-up, and let's not forget the all-important telephone. It was an ungodly ordeal to say the least.

My sisters, to my undying disgust, are all gorgeous and talented. Renée, the oldest one of the group is the unparalleled beauty of the family. Lest you think I'm exaggerating and she's not really all that *and* a bag of chips, let me ask if the name Renée Finnegan means anything to you. Yes, that's right, "The" Renée Finnegan, the gorgeous Midwestern girl that won the coveted Cover Girl contract when she was only seventeen, fresh out of high school. Try surviving two whole years at Pipsy High with people asking, "You're Renée's sister? Really?" The tone of incredulity was more than I could bear.

Next is Ginger. She's the brain. But please, before you picture an unfortunate looking nerd with braces and braids, I should tell you that she is only marginally less gorgeous than Renée. She was also the recipient of a Rhodes scholarship, which funded her degree in the history of renaissance art, which she acquired at Oxford. Yes, Oxford, not the shoes, not the cloth, but the actual university in England.

The youngest of our quartet is Muffy, born Margaret Fay, but abbreviated to Muffy when at the tender age of two she couldn't pronounce Margaret Fay and began referring to herself as one might a forty-two-year-old socialite. Muffy is the jock. She plays tennis and even enjoyed a run on the pro-circuit before a knee injury forced her to retire. She did, however, play Wimbledon three years in a row and, while she never actually won, the experience allows her to start sentences with, "Yes, well, when I played Wimbledon …" And make pronouncements like, "There's nothing like the courts at Wimbledon in the fall." Muffy is now the tennis pro at The Langley Country Club. Her husband Tom is the men's tennis pro, ensuring they are the tannest, most fit couple on the entire planet. Their perfection is enough to make you barf.

I am the third child in my family, christened Miriam May Finnegan which against my express consent got shortened to Mimi. For years I demanded, "It's Miriam, call me Miriam!" No one listened, as is the way in my family.

While sitting on my white quilted bedspread from JCPenneys, my sisters, in a moment of domestic harmony, decided we were all quite extraordinary. Renée was deemed the beautiful one, Ginger, the smart one, and Muffy, the athletic one. With those proclamations made, they appeared to be ready to switch topics when I demanded to know, "What am I?"

It's not that my sisters don't love me. I don't think they thought I was troll-like or stupid, it's just compared to them, I didn't have any quality that outshone any one of theirs. So after much thoughtful consideration and examination, like a prized heifer at the state fair, Renée announced, "You have the prettiest feet." Ginger and Muffy readily agreed.

Listen, I know you're thinking "prettiest feet" isn't something I should brag about. But in my family, I would have been thrilled to have the prettiest anything, and I am. They could have just as easily said I had the most blackheads, or the worst split ends. But they didn't, they awarded me prettiest feet and I was proud of it. Until now. Now I have a bunion.

As I sit in front of my car in front of the Chesterton Medical Center, I become undone by the horror of having lost my identity in my family. "Who will I be now?" I wonder. Oh wait, I know, I'll be the spinster, or the one without naturally blonde hair, my true color hovering somewhere between bacon grease and baby poop. Hey wait, I know, I'll be the one who needs to lose twenty pounds!

I turn on the ignition in my Honda and hop on the freeway heading for the Mercer Street exit. Yet somehow, I miss my turnoff and I've hit Randolph before I know it. With a will of its own, my car takes the exit and drives itself to the Burger City a half mile down the road. I demand, "What did you do that for? This is no way to lose twenty pounds." Not that I had agreed to do any such thing. But, I wasn't looking to gain weight either.

Typically, my car doesn't answer back, a fact for which I am eternally grateful. It simply makes its wishes known by transporting me to destinations of its choosing: Burger City, The Yummy Freeze, Dairy Queen, Pizza Hut. I've actually thought about trading it in, in hopes of upgrading to a car that likes to go to the gym and health food stores. But, no, this is my car and as a faithful person by nature, I realize I should do what it's telling me.

As the window automatically lowers and the car accelerates to the take-out speaker, I hear the disembodied voice of a teenager say, "Welcome to Burger City. What can I get you today?"

Someone, who is surely not me, answers, "I'd like a double cheeseburger with grilled onions, two orders of fries and a root beer, large."

He asks, "Will that be all?"

Still not sure who's doing the answering, I hear someone sounding remarkably like me say, "I'd like an extra bun, too."

"What do you mean an extra bun?" He squeaks. "You mean with no burger on it or anything?"

"That's right." He informs me that he'll have to charge me for a whole other burger even though I just want the bun. I tell him that's no problem and agree to pay the dollar seventy-five for it. I'm not sure what causes me to order the extra bread but I think it boils down to my need for carbohydrates. I have either been on The South Beach Diet or Atkins for the better part of two years and I've become desperate for empty calorie, high glycemic index white bread.

You may be wondering how I could have been high protein dieting for two years and still need to lose twenty pounds. The truth is that I cheat, a lot. For two weeks I jump start the diet with the serious deprivation they encourage and then by week three when you're allowed to start slowly adding carbs back into your life, I become the wildebeest of cheaters. They suggest you start with an apple or a quarter of a baked sweet potato. I start with an apple pie and three orders of french fries. I have been losing and gaining the same thirteen pounds for the last twenty-four months.

As soon as my food arrives, I pull over on a side street and inhale the heavenly aroma of danger. The fries call to me, the double cheeseburger begs to be devoured in two bites, but the bun screams loudest, "I have no redeeming nutritional value at all!" So I start with it. And it's pure pleasure. Soft and white, clean and bright … it looks at me and sings, "You look happy to meet me." But wait, this isn't Edelweiss, this is a hamburger bun.

After the bun, I eat a bag of fries, then the burger, then the other bag of fries, all the while slurping down my non-diet root beer. My tummy is cheering me on, "You go, girl! That's right, keep it coming … mmm hmm … faster … more." From the floorboards I hear a small squeak, "Stop, you're killing me!" It's my bunion. I decide its voice isn't nearly as powerful as my stomach's. While I'm masticating away I start to think about the word bunion. It's kind of like bun and onion. B-U-N-I-O-N. That's when I notice I've just eaten a bun and a burger with onion. I start to feel nauseated. If you squish the words together, I've just eaten a bunion. Oh, no. I think that this may have possibly put me off Burger City forever.

I have a long history of going off my food for various and sundry reasons. For instance in high school, Robby Blinken had the worst case of acne I'd ever seen. It was so bad that his whole face looked like an open, inflamed sore. I felt really sorry for him too because he was shy and awkward to begin with. Having bad skin did nothing for his popularity. Then one day, Mike Pinker shouts across algebra to Robby, "Hey, pizza face, that's lots of pepperoni you've got!"

I cringed in disgust, looked over at poor Robby whose face turned an even brighter shade of red due to the public humiliation and bam, I was off pizza for a whole year. And pizza was one of my favorite foods too. It's just that every time I looked at it or smelled it, I thought about Robby's complexion and there was no going back.

Then there was the time I went off onions in college. A girl in my dorm was blind in one eye and there was this white kind of film covering her iris. Whenever I talked to her, I couldn't help but stare right into the blind eye. I was drawn to it by a strange magnetic pull. Then one day it hits me, Ellen's pupil looks like a small piece of onion. I went off onions for three years.

Now at thirty-four, years since I've had a food repulsion, I realize that after my first bun in months I may have gone off them. The onions aren't such a loss as I already have a history there, but buns? I love buns!

Around the second bag of fries, I unbutton my jeans to let my stomach pop out of its confines. Sitting in my red Honda with my belly hanging out, sick at the thought that I just ate a bunion, I do what any reasonable person would do. I drive to the strip mall where the Weight Watchers sign flashes encouraging subliminal cheers to the masses. "Be thin, we'll help!" "We love you!" "You can do it, you can do it …"

So like the little engine that could, I squeeze into a compact spot and walk through the front door before I can come out of my trance. Twelve dollars later, I've received an information package and a weigh-in book. Marge, my group leader, takes me in the back to weigh me. "One seventy-two," she declares. I want to tell her I was just one seventy at the doctor's office but then I remember the bunion I just ate. Marge continues, "You know, you are right inside the acceptable weight for your height. Are you sure you want to lose twenty pounds?"

I'm sure. After all, I'm single with a bunion. It feels like it's time for some drastic measures. As I have shown up in between meeting times, Marge gives me the basics of the Weight Watchers program and encourages me to come to at least one meeting a week. She also suggests I get weighed at the same time every week as the weight of the human body can vacillate up to six pounds during a twenty-four-hour period. "Consistency of weigh-in times," she claims, "is the answer." I briefly wonder if Doctor Foster would have told me to lose weight if I was only one hundred and sixty-four pounds.

Chapter 2

I am allowed to eat twenty-nine points a day. I keep telling myself this as I sit at my desk and wait for lunch. With my handy little points app I discover that my forage to Burger City the other day was worth thirty-two points. Thank goodness I ate that bunion. That'll be one less temptation for me while I attempt to lose this weight.

Three days ago after my trip to WWI (Weight Watchers, first attempt, not to be confused with the World War) I stopped by Rite Aid to pick up my shoe insert. I've been wearing it since and am having serious equilibrium issues. I can only wear it with loafers or tennis shoes as it's a foot-shaped silicone wedge and won't fit into heels. The whole contraption pushes me toward my proper posture but I swear it's dislocating my center of gravity at the same time. I have never been considered graceful but now I'm downright klutzy, as demonstrated by the five large bruises covering my legs. I seem to tip as easily as a sleeping cow and have not been landing in the softest of places either.

Eleven fifty-eight, eleven fifty-nine, come on noon. I want to eat. I had a bowl, and by that I mean one cup (which is really only half of a bowl), of raisin bran and half a cup of skim milk for breakfast. At ten, I gobbled up an apple and an ounce of part-skim mozzarella cheese. For lunch I'm having a turkey sandwich on the softest white bread on the planet. It's low-cal but has enough fiber to jumpstart a dead person's bowels, ergo giving it the Weight Watcher's seal of approval. I'm also having a salad with fat-free raspberry vinaigrette. When I packed my lunch this morning, I registered how beautiful the food looked, all orange and green and red. It really was a feast for the eyes even though the portions would leave a Lilliputian begging for more.

I'm trying to do what Marge told me and that is to appreciate my food on all levels. Enjoy the beauty of it, the smell of it and last but not least, the taste, which I am supposed to do while chewing the ever loving crap out of it before swallowing. This way it will take me longer to eat and I will start to fill up before overdoing it. It's all a load of hooey if you ask me. I'm so hungry by feeding time that I've inhaled my meal before I know it. Yesterday I was crawling around the base of my desk when my co-worker Elaine asked me what I was looking for.

"My lunch," I answered, "I think I dropped it."

Elaine looked slightly alarmed and declared, "Mimi, you just ate your lunch."

"Really?" I asked, more than a little surprised by this knowledge.

Elaine confirmed it was so, but that didn't stop me from picking up and eating a stray peanut I found on the floor from my South Beach days. Tick, tick, tick, NOON! Time to strap on the old feed bag.

I scurry into the break room and fill a glass with cold water. I know I'm blending diet tips here but South Beach recommends a glass of Metamucil before each meal to help fill you up. It works beautifully too, except that with all the fiber I get on Weight Watchers, I find I need to be close to a bathroom at all times. As I munch on my salad, my boss, Jonathan Becker, walks into the break room.

Jonathan embodies all that is right with the world. He is thirty-eight, smart, funny, remarkably good looking and talented. He is also married to my sister Ginger. How, you wonder, did that happen when I should have had first dibs on him? I haven't a clue, really. It must have been fate. I mean heaven knows I didn't introduce them. I am not in the habit of trying to help my perfect sisters show me up even more by introducing them to perfect men. That is not my way.

Ginger met Jonathan completely independently of me as she was showing a tour group through the Museum of Contemporary Art. She is the director of the museum, but still enjoys educating the masses by pitching in with docent duties every once in a while. At any rate, Jonathan's parents were in town and he was taking them to the requisite tourist spots when they stumbled into the museum. In front of one particularly abstract painting, Felicity Becker declared, "I suppose the medium here is human feces?"

Ginger smiled, and explained how the artist was trying to express the sepia tonality of his native Cuba; the tobacco and human waste were representative of a culture that repressed its own and refused to let it rise above menial servitude. I think she may have quoted Descartes and then conjugated several verbs in Latin for effect. Whatever she did, it was like a mating dance to Jonathan because he asked her out that afternoon and thereafter until they became man and wife a short year later.

When they first started dating, Ginger carried on and on about how smart and funny her boyfriend Jonathan was. Then the day came when she brought him to brunch to meet the family. I had just regained the thirteen pounds I lost on Phase I of South Beach and was not looking forward to meeting the Ken to my sister's Barbie. I remember pulling on my brown skirt with the elastic waist thinking, "Who am I trying to impress anyway? It's not like this guy is coming to see me."

When I drove up to my parents' house, I saw that Muffy and Tom were already there as well as Renée and her husband, Laurent, along with their two kids, Finn and Camille. I walked in and made all the appropriate rounds of kisses and hugs. But the truth was my heart just wasn't in it. Once Ginger introduced her new boyfriend, it would just be me, Mimi Finnegan, spinster.

Ginger and Jonathan walked in the front door as I was filling the water glasses on the dining room table. I heard them before I saw them. Ginger announced, "Hello everyone, we're here!" The whole family tore off towards the entry like a stampeding herd of cattle at the sound of her voice. Everyone that is, but me. I wanted to enjoy the last few moments of not being the only sister without a significant other. So I poured water and concentrated on breathing deeply.

They all came into the dining room moments later and I plastered a smile on my face, prepared to be all that is gracious to Ginger's new beau. When I first saw Jonathan, I was confused and mistakenly thought maybe my Jonathan from work had somehow shown up to be my date so I wouldn't be the family pariah. Then he saw me and I knew that wasn't the case. His face morphed somewhere between total and utter shock and open-mouthed bass. "Miriam, is that you?" Because before Jonathan learned my family nickname, I went by my real name at work. Now they all call me Mimi, too.

"Jonathan?" I squeaked.

He strode over and slapped me on the shoulder in a very platonic way and said, "Well, I'll be. I didn't know you and Ginger were sisters!"

I countered, "And I had no idea you two were dating." It occurred to me Ginger should have known Jonathan and I work for the same PR firm. You would think that when he revealed that he worked at Parliament, Ginger would have remembered that I work there, too. But the truth is, while brilliant, Ginger has never been wired for details. For instance, she knows the square root of one million, six hundred forty-two thousand and eight, but she can barely remember her own birthday. She's kind of like Rain Man that way.

The brunch was unbearable and lasted about twelve days. I must have gained three pounds, as the meal became show and tell for the Finnegan family (as I didn't have that much to show or tell, I ate). Jonathan had never met us as a whole, so we owed it to him to trot out the whole dog and pony show. With circus music running through my head I could see myself as the ringmaster. "If I could have your attention in the center ring, I'd like to introduce you to Renée! Yes, that's Renée "supermodel turned designer" Finnegan and her high profile fashion photographer husband, Laurent Bouvier. But please, before you leave center ring, notice their perfect and charming offspring,

Finn, who was recently featured in the Gap Kids ad, and little Camille, the Ivory Soap baby!"

I drank so many mimosas that day I was forced to stay over at my parents' house and sleep it off. In my drunken haze, I swear I heard my mother say, "Now if only Mimi could find someone to love her." There was laughter and then my dead Grandma Sissy started reciting dirty limericks.

Chapter 3

I weigh in right after lunch today. It's hard to believe that I've only been on this diet for seven days as I can't remember the last time I was actually full after eating a meal. Well, yes I can. That would have been last week right before I joined up, signed on, and volunteered to go to war for my bunion. It did have a sort of military feel to it. I'm kind of like *Private Benjamin* without being cute, tiny, and rich.

I'm discovering that the weekends are going to be a little tougher for me than the Monday through Friday stint. At least during the week, I'm required to actually work, thus limiting my constant obsession over the next morsel I'm allowed to put into my mouth. When I woke up this morning, I forgot I was on Weight Watchers at all and longed for the cheesy omelet and turkey bacon from my South Beach days. Of course that particular meal translated into six hundred and forty-two Weight Watchers points, so I tried to gear up for more raisin bran. Ugh. I pick up my little red tips booklet and search out a more appealing option. After all, it's the weekend, I don't have to rush. I can plan, execute, and enjoy more complicated fare today. I decide on french toast with fat free syrup. Here's a tip for you on

Weight Watchers approved french toast. The bread is so thin that you can't let it soak in the egg for more than an eighth of a second. If you don't heed this rule, the pathetic slice simply falls apart, disintegrating before your very eyes. There's just not enough substance to withstand a normal drenching.

After eight slices of bread and four eggs, I am finally able to salvage three somewhat questionable-looking pieces. I do as the book recommends and heat my one tablespoon of syrup so it spreads farther, consequently making it feel like more (though it isn't even enough for one piece) and dig in. The problem is I have finished my breakfast in forty-seven seconds. I feel as though I've just had my appetizer and now I'm salivating for the main course. I know! I'll drink another glass of water. That's always so satisfying.

Its seven forty-three a.m. and I don't get to eat again for another two hours and seventeen minutes. What to do … what to do … I could always wash my clothes, but that would involve going through the kitchen to get to the laundry room and I'm afraid I'm not strong enough for that yet. I could run errands, but my car can't be trusted not to take me to Pete's House of Pie against my will. So I decide to go through my closet and try on every garment that I own. This way I can have a full before and after appreciation of how everything fits. I start with the clothes I wear all the time, the size twelves.

Next I pull out the tens. I squeeze myself into the Ralph Lauren jeans, a process involving a coat hanger and lying on the floor (and Crisco if I had any). Once I inhale and fasten the top button, I roll over onto my stomach and attempt to bring myself to a kneeling position. It feels like I'm on the receiving end of a denim enema. By the time I'm in the praying position and leaning against my bed, I'm panting like I've just run a six minute mile. I'm sure if I don't remove the offending garment soon, I'll be on my way to a nasty yeast infection. Pushing up into a standing pose, I goose step over to the full length mirror and check out the final result. Do the words camel-toe mean anything to you?

The last item I try on is my all-time favorite black cocktail dress. Working in PR as I do, I'm often required to attend launch parties for books and products we've signed on to promote. So I need to have several dressy options in my closet. I bought this one at Marshalls of all places and while I know the dresses there are crap, this one was the pearl in the oyster. It's a Mui Mui, size eight (my dad calls this designer Mahi-Mahi) and it has tiny spaghetti straps to hold up the plunging neckline and flirty little skirt. The bargain basement price tag of one hundred and ninety-nine dollars is still hanging on it as I bought it too small and have yet to fit into it. I needed to lose ten pounds at the time of purchase. Now I need to lose twenty-three.

I can't wait for the day when I'm finally able to show this little number off at a launch party. For the last seven months I've felt like one of the ugly stepsisters lusting after Cinderella's glass slipper. I slide the dress over my head and the nice flowy little skirt is skin tight on me. But I'm not deterred. Inch-by-inch I scooch it down my body until it hits mid-thigh where it finally gives up the ghost. Then I zip the bodice up as far as I can (about an inch), then squinch my eyes so the whole effect won't throw me right into cardiac arrest. Very slowly, I open them, taking in my full reflection bit-by-bit. As I stare at myself, I wonder what

I was thinking when I bought this thing. It looks like a sausage casing. One guess who the sausage is.

I have one hour and twelve minutes until my snack. I briefly consider taking a nap to fritter away some time when the phone rings. It's my mom, Maureen O'Callaghan-Finnegan, not a non-Irish bone in her body. While my parents are both one hundred percent Irish, they are also one hundred percent American. It can be a very odd combination at times. While Mo, as her friends call her, has never declared, "Faith and begorrah my wee bairn, tell Father McMurphy all yur many sins." She has demanded that we eat every last bit of our potatoes in honor of the thousands upon thousands that died during the black rot, otherwise known as the Irish Potato Famine. She is also fully convinced fairies live in the backyard and are responsible for killing her begonias. She's taken to leaving them homemade soda bread in hopes of gaining their favor. I don't know about the fairies, but the squirrels love her.

My mom greets, "Happy Saturday, Meems." The only name I hate worse than my nickname is my nickname's nickname.

"Hiya, Ma, what's up?"

"Just checking to make sure that you didn't forget that tomorrow is Camille's second birthday. We're all meeting at Renée and Laurent's at one."

Shit, I had forgotten! The very last thing I needed was to be at a gathering with my perfect family and not be able to self-medicate by eating my way into a coma. So I bluff, "Of course I didn't forget. I'm picking up her present this afternoon."

Mom reminds me, "She's registered at Pottery Barn Kids."

Is it just me or has this registering thing gotten totally out of hand? It used to be something only brides and expectant mothers did as they could logically suppose that a shower in their honor would involve gift giving. But now, everyone does it, for every occasion imaginable, high school graduations, house warmings, bar mitzvahs, first communions, two-year-old birthday parties. Hello, my name is Wanda and I'm an alcoholic and I'm registered at Macy's. When did our society get so greedy we just assumed people should be buying us nonstop booty? Well, that's that, then. I have to leave the house. I throw an apple and cheese stick in my purse and gulp down a half glass of Fibercon and I'm off.

Camille is the most gorgeous, adorable, lovely, child in the world. Every time I look at her, I feel an egg drop. She is the poster baby for the kids I want some day, as well as being the Gymboree poster child. When I retrieve her list at Pottery Barn Kids, I discover she has impeccable taste for someone whose age, until tomorrow, is still measured in months. I can see the work of her mother here.

Renée has decided it's time Camille's room retires as the nursery and become a full-fledged little girl's room. This must be why she's registered for a complete bedroom set including duvet, drapes and lamps. I'm just guessing here, but I can't see Camille performing a clog dance in appreciation of these items, which is why I make the decision to boycott the registry altogether. I pick out the sweetest little white wicker rocking chair and a pretty in pink baby doll. Renée won't be thrilled but it's not her birthday, is it?

In the Pottery Barn Kids parking lot, I inhale my apple and cheese stick, realizing it's almost time for lunch. While I'm out,

I decide to drive by Weight Watchers and get my weigh-in over with. Checking my purse to make sure I have my loss/gain chart with me, I take off. Before you can sing "Danny Boy," I'm there, but not at Weight Watchers. Burger City, again. "What am I doing here?" I chastise my car and it replies with a rev of the engine.

"Absolutely not," I tell it. "I'm about to weigh in!" But before I can back out of the line, a minivan pulls up behind me, trapping me in the fast food queue at lunch time. Oh God, the smells are going to undo me. I now feel obligated to order something because I'm in line, but what? What on this whole menu is Weight Watchers approved? I start to drool, the smell of cheeseburgers is wafting through the breeze. My stomach growls like a rabid dog. "Feed me ... feed me ... feed me ..." I've got to get control of myself.

That's when I hear another voice call out, "Don't do it!" It's my bunion to the rescue! It reminds me I'm off Burger City because they serve bunions, delicious smelling, and mouth-watering, but bunions all the same. So when it's my turn, I order a large Diet Coke and keep it for after the weigh in.

Marge declares, "You've lost 3.7 pounds. Good for you!" And while I'm not one who fancies my weight being broadcast in anyway, ever, I find I'm okay with this. This is a loss, baby! Slurping down my large Diet Coke, I force my car to take me home so I can prepare a healthy lunch. A lunch that feels vastly more satisfying knowing it is going to help the scale go down even more. I'm so euphoric to be on a downward trend I put on my *Priscilla, Queen of the Desert* soundtrack and fast forward to Gloria Gaynor's "I Will Survive."

Standing on my couch, singing into the remote for my DVD player, I belt out, "Walk, walk out the door. Just turn around now, you're not welcome anymore." I'm not singing to an ex-lover that's done me wrong, either. I'm serenading my fat clothes and I can actually see them dancing down the steps before they leave the house, never to return.

I'm convinced only good things can happen from here on out …

Available Now!

Made in the USA
Middletown, DE
19 May 2020